Lieutenant Lamb

Lieutenant Lamb

Kenneth Maynard

Weidenfeld and Nicolson
London

Typeset by Deltatype, Ellesmere Port
Printed in Great Britain by
Butler & Tanner Ltd
Frome & London

Chapter 1

The wind, for so long in the west, had that day shifted to the east and flurries of snow had now appeared. The day was darkening rapidly under the loom of low-lying clouds the colour of chimney smoke, but the wherry, propelled by the brawny arms of the Deal boatmen, was now close enough for Lamb to discern the broad, black stripe running along the frigate's waterline and the yellow and red upperworks. As the boat rounded her stern he glanced up at the wide stern-windows; they showed no gleam of light – perhaps the captain was ashore?

The wherry hooked on to the chains by the ladder and Lamb fumbled in his pockets for some coins.

'Thankee, sir, thankee,' said the boatman, touching his hand to his forehead, and in a bellow to the rolling deck above: 'Send us a line down, mates.'

The officer of the watch, a stocky young man dressed in old working rig, greeted Lamb as he climbed aboard. As they exchanged names and shook hands the officer cast a knowing look at Lamb's uniform and raised an eyebrow very slightly. The newcomer caught the unspoken question and gave a dry laugh.

'Yes, you are right, it is quite unworn. Four months to the day since my ordeal at the Navy Office and my commission arrived yesterday.'

Lieutenant Tyler was polite enough not to show any relief.

'Well, that makes you junior to me but not by so many months. I'm the third, Kennedy is the second – a very decent sort – and Maxwell is the first. He is a bit of a martinet and he likes to keep a smart ship.'

Lamb glanced about him. The standing rigging was taut and well-tarred, the paintwork fresh, the deck uncluttered and there was not a judas rope in sight. If nothing else, he thought, the first lieutenant is an excellent housekeeper.

I

'The captain is ashore at the moment, dining with his wife at the Royal. She posted down from London today, apparently. In the meantime, if you would like to make yourself known to the gunroom, I'll have your chest taken below.'

'Thank you, sir.' Lamb touched his hat and headed aft.

Tyler looked at his retreating back with a slight smile on his face. The new fourth was very thin, almost cadaverous, and so tall that he had towered over the diminutive Tyler, who was now massaging his neck in the earnest hope that it was not permanently cricked. He wondered how often Lamb's head had collided with a deck beam; ships were not constructed to accommodate men of his height, or even of normal stature, come to that.

A voice, raised in some anger, grew louder and clearer as Lamb descended the companionway to the gunroom.

'– scientifically authenticated – yes, yes, don't snigger, sir – scientifically authenticated that such apparitions do indeed exist. I have been on ships where to walk past a certain spot at night was sufficient to make your hair stand on end – and that phenomenon is a very well-established proof of a haunting. So do not poppycock me, doctor!'

Lamb ducked his head and entered the gunroom. He had been accustomed to serving in larger ships, fourth-rates and above, where the officers were accommodated in the ward-room; but in a frigate, which had but one gun-deck and no poop, the captain's cabin took this space and the officers were relegated to the gunroom; the midshipmen and master's mates, in their turn, were turned out to make the best of it in the cockpit.

The light from the several lanterns and candles was dim but he was aware of several heads turning in his direction. He announced himself to the room at large.

'Matthew Lamb, the new fourth.'

'Welcome aboard, Mr Lamb,' said one of the men, rising to his feet and advancing with outstretched hand. 'My name is Maxwell and this is Kennedy, our second.'

Maxwell was a Scot, pale-eyed and blue-chinned, with a habit of blinking rapidly. He gave Lamb the impression of a man with a short fuse to his temper. The second lieutenant, a handsome man in his early twenties with keen, blue eyes and fair, curling hair, smiled warmly as he gripped Lamb's hand.

'You put us to shame, Mr Lamb,' he said, eyeing the newcomer's smart new uniform. 'Old rig is generally the order of the day here.' He nodded at the Marine lieutenant lounging at full stretch in the corner. 'For those of us who work, that is, not that gorgeous peacock there.'

The Marine, resplendent in scarlet, rose languidly to his feet, offered Lamb his fingertips and muttered: 'Potter. Charmed, m'dear fellow, quite charmed.'

The master, Doubleday, greeted Lamb with a perfunctory nod and the briefest of handshakes. Stout and white-haired, he had met too many green young lieutenants in his time to be at all enthusiastic over meeting one more. He subsided back into his chair, the flush of anger still evident on his face after his brush with the surgeon, a pale, unshaven individual in a dirty frock-coat who honoured Lamb by taking his nose out of his book long enough to give a slight nod.

There came an uncomfortable little silence. Lamb stood uneasily just inside the door, his hat beneath his arm and his head bowed awkwardly beneath the low deck beams. Six years in the uniform of a midshipman on a ship of the line had marked indelibly for him the wide gulf that existed between the young gentlemen and the wardroom officers. It was not an easy gap to bridge in one step. A more outward-going man might have tossed his hat on to the table, stretched his legs under it from the comfort of a chair and delved into easy conversation. As it was, Lamb stood dumbly clutching his hat and feeling like an interloper.

Maxwell broke the silence abruptly. 'You have the morning watch, Mr Lamb. I suggest you store your gear and change out of those clothes. With the wind as it is I've no doubt we'll be getting under way the moment the captain returns.'

He wrapped a muffler around his throat and reached up to the hook of the bulkhead for his hat.

'I shall go and check the moorings,' he said, glancing at Kennedy. 'With Tyler on watch, forever dreaming about women, we could be on Walmer Sands before we know it. I'm damned sure his brains swing from his belly!'

The door banged shut behind him. Kennedy clapped Lamb on the shoulder.

3

'Sit yourself down, Matthew. If you stand like that much longer you will end up a permanent question-mark. Now, a glass of wine or some hot coffee?'

'Coffee would be very welcome, sir,' said Lamb, damp and chilled from his boat journey.

Kennedy banged his fist on the hatch to the steward's pantry.

'Surbrown! Open up, you villain. Hot coffee in here, toot sweet. D'you hear me, you rogue?'

'Aye aye, sir,' came the muffled and surly reply. 'Hot coffee it is, sir.'

Kennedy grinned at Lamb. 'Quite a handle for a steward, Surbrown, ain't it? He won't answer to Brown, the sulky brute – insists on his full set of syllables.'

'Perhaps you could shorten it to Sur?' suggested Lamb with a smile.

Kennedy laughed. 'Yes, he'd love that – might cause a little confusion, though.'

He changed tack abruptly. 'The captain – John Cutler – have you come across him before?'

Lamb shook his head. 'No, sir.'

'We know he had the *Excelsior*, thirty-two, and that he recently returned from the American station but apart from that we know very little about him; a bit of a dark horse, I think. I know he is very keen on guns – he spent the whole of the forenoon watch with the gunner going over them, and he must have a very good friend at the Navy Yard because we have nearly twice the powder below that we are entitled to.'

'Do you know where we are bound, sir?' asked Lamb, who had spent the last two years of his life as a midshipman beating up and down the northern coast of France and was desperately anxious not to renew his acquaintance with that inhospitable stretch of water.

'Officially, no, but between you, me and the scuttlebutt, we are going to honour the Earl St Vincent – John Jervis, as was – with our presence and assistance off Cadiz. Have you been that way before?'

'No, sir. I never got further south than St Nazaire and I only saw that from the masthead.'

The coffee arrived, hot, strong and welcome.

4

'I was very pleased to see you come on board,' said Kennedy between sips. 'Otherwise Tyler and I would have been standing watch and watch. Our Lords of the Admiralty did not give you much notice, did they?'

'Indeed they did not, sir.' Nonetheless, short notice or not, he had been overjoyed to receive his commission and after reading it through fifteen or twenty times with particular concentration on the line of incredible beauty and harmony which read: 'To Lieutenant Matthew Lamb hereby appointed Lieutenant of His Majesty's Ship *Sturdy* –' and which read even more strikingly aloud, he had kissed his aged landlady several times on her whiskered cheek and so forgot himself as to give sixpence to her detested little grandson. The twenty-seventh day of February, 1798, was, and would ever be, he was convinced, the happiest and greatest day of his life.

A separate note had informed him that he was, by proceeding with all possible speed, to join his ship in the Downs, off Deal; she had already left her berth at Chatham and was now proceeding down river. An hour of frantic activity and the brutal rape of his small store of long-hoarded sovereigns saw him on his way, post-chaising through Kent with his commission crackling comfortably in the breast pocket of his handsome blue coat and he filling the air with the scent of mothballs. At the long halts, at Maidstone and Canterbury, he strolled about stretching his legs, deporting himself with the quiet and authoritative dignity that he imagined the general public expected of their naval officers; in the privacy of the carriage he hugged himself and gave frequent little chuckles of jubilation – Lieutenant Matthew Lamb, holder of the King's commission and earning eight guineas a month!

'Yes,' said Kennedy, 'Vernon's hard luck was your good fortune. An hour to go before we weighed and the clumsy bugger has to fall into the cable-tier. Broke both legs! We had to carry him ashore strapped to a plank, poor devil.'

'What damned bad luck,' said Lamb, who would have been more than happy for Vernon to have broken only one leg.

He had not finished his coffee when a small midshipman put his head round the door.

'Mr Tyler's compliments, sir, and the captain's gig is in sight.'

5

Lamb joined Tyler and the first lieutenant at the entry port. The boatswain licked his lips and began the pipe as the captain's hat, worn fore-and-aft in the new fashion, came level with the deck. The officers saluted, the Marine guard banked their feet and presented their muskets, the pipe shrilled and Lamb swallowed nervously. Captain Cutler stepped on to the deck, faced aft and saluted the quarterdeck. The officers lowered their hands, the guard lowered their muskets and the awful keening of the boatswain's whistle stopped abruptly. The ceremony over, the captain began to walk aft but stopped as he saw the tall figure of Lamb, standing resplendent in his uniform of white-faced blue coat, white waistcoat and white breeches.

Captain Cutler smelled strongly of brandy. 'Ah! You will be Vernon's replacement, no doubt?'

Lamb removed his hat. 'Yes, sir. My name is Lamb, sir.'

'Pleased to have you on board, Mr Lamb. We shall read you in later. Mr Maxwell! Are we in all respects ready to sail?'

The first lieutenant stepped forward and touched his hat.

'Yes, sir, although there is the small matter of the new cro'jack yard. You'll remember, sir –'

'Yes, yes, such details are your concern, Mr Maxwell. Prepare to get under way. We don't want to waste a moment of this wind.'

Maxwell sensibly forbore to mention that the captain had already squandered two hours of the precious easterly ensconced in the private rooms of the Royal Hotel.

'Aye aye, sir,' he said and cupped his hands to his mouth. 'All hands! All hands!'

The duty watch stirred themselves from the shelter of their little nooks and crannies of the deck and the off-duty watch tumbled up from below, encouraged to their stations by the persuasive shouts and rattans of the boatswain's mates. Men ran to the capstan, topmen scurried aloft and the new landsmen were pushed and cuffed into their places; some were so green that their hands had to be closed around the sheet or tack they were required to haul. Lamb went below to find his cabin; this was not his watch and it was time he stowed his gear and put away his precious uniform. It would soon be time for supper and he was ravenously hungry; then he must try to sleep if he was to take over his watch with any semblance of alertness at

6

four in the morning.

The *Sturdy* weathered Ushant in a blinding mixture of rain and hail, the wind blowing hard from the north-east and bringing green water over the starboard rail. The topsails were furled and the mainsail and foresail double-reefed and then reefed again. Visibility was little more than the width of the beam as the frigate thundered along under a bare mizzenmast with the torn remnants of the jib streaming away to leeward and three men at the wheel straining against the kicking rudder. The fattest French prize, had she been visible in the flying drift and the darkness, could have cocked a snook and passed by in perfect safety; with the *Sturdy*'s deck at the angle of a moderately sloping roof and her starboard gun-ports under water, Captain Cutler could have done no more than shake his fist in return. In the event, no French ships were seen. With their harbours heavily blockaded this was as it should be – only in the Mediterranean could they come and go as they pleased, and the exit and entrance to that sea was firmly under British eyes at Gibraltar.

The weather improved rapidly as the ship headed south and with the Bay of Biscay astern the temperature began to climb, the sky cleared and within the space of a watch or two the frigate was sailing blue seas under a warming sun. To larboard, just discernible as a smudge from the maintop, Spain met the northern border of Portugal. Shipping was sparse; apart from a few fishing boats and a homeward-bound sloop which had made her number abeam of Cape Finisterre, the *Sturdy* had seen nothing.

Cutler stepped on to his quarterdeck and raised his nose to the wind; he sniffed appreciatively and turned to Lamb who had moved discreetly to the other side of the deck.

'A fine morning, Mr Lamb. I take it you have not yet breakfasted?'

'No, sir, not yet.' Lamb had the watch and for the past ten minutes he had been itching for Tyler to relieve him for breakfast – the smell of coffee and bacon drifting up from the aft companionway had caused his juices to flow.

'Then perhaps I could have the pleasure of your company this morning – and that of Mr Blissenden here?'

He nodded in the direction of the duty midshipman who was

pretending to be deep in study of the signal flags book.

'Delighted, sir,' said Lamb.

'Thank you, sir,' squeaked the diminutive Blissenden, who was to food as Casanova de Seingalt was to women.

'As soon as you are relieved then,' said Cutler and returned below, from where a loud altercation with his steward immediately ensued. Lamb caught the odd word here and there – 'shaving water' came up quite distinctly.

Lamb turned to the midshipman. 'Get below and scrub yourself, Mr Blissenden. You are not fit to be seen in human company.'

'Aye aye, sir,' said Blissenden cheerfully, not at all put out by such insults, and scampered off to torment his colleagues in the cockpit with the news of his invitation.

The captain's servant, a roly-poly man with a monk's tonsure, provided bacon, chops, toast and coffee. Lamb was ravenous after his sojourn on deck but deemed it discourteous to pander to his appetite since Cutler did no more than nibble at toast. No such inhibitions troubled the midshipman; wolf-like, he crouched over his plate, which acted as the very briefest resting place between dish and stomach, and ate solidly and steadily as his superiors conversed.

The talk between the captain and his fourth lieutenant was easy and casual in one direction and formal and brief in the other. Was he related to Captain Lamb who was drowned off Quebec four or five years back? No, sir, he thought not. Was his family naval at all? No, sir, he came from a line of soldiers; his father was a major in the Buffs. Ah, the Buffs? It was a regiment with which Cutler had some slight acquaintance. A discourse followed on the Buffs. A little more coffee, Mr Lamb? That would be most welcome, sir.

Cutler poured the coffee. 'My servant has many faults but he does make excellent coffee – otherwise I might have got rid of him years ago. He has been with me since my wardroom days and is apt to be a little familiar at times. I really do not know why I suffer his rudeness.'

Lamb suspected that this little speech was a tactical move on Cutler's part, a manoeuvre in the running battle with his steward. That individual, engaged in removing dishes from the table, countered with a loud and significant sniff.

8

'We exchanged a few words this morning with reference to the temperature of my shaving water,' continued the captain, 'and now he will doubtless sulk for the rest of the day. You are sulking, are you not, Watson?'

'No, sir, I ain't,' growled Watson sulkily and removed himself and the dishes from the cabin.

Cutler grinned at Watson's retreating back and shook his head slightly. He fixed his eyes on Lamb. 'Gun drill this morning, Mr Lamb,' he said, his tone suddenly brisk. 'How are you with guns?'

'I have been in many a drill, of course, sir, but I have yet to hear a broadside fired in anger, I am afraid.'

The captain smiled. He held up his left hand; the little finger was missing.

'I lost that to a French sharpshooter on my very first voyage. I was a twelve-year-old middie – about the same age as Mr Blissenden here.' The midshipman gave a start on hearing his name and froze over his plate, his cheeks pouched. 'I didn't know it had gone for some little while – I was too busy removing the quartermaster's brains from my shoulder.'

He fell silent, an inward look on his face. Lamb felt that he and Blissenden had spent long enough at the captain's table; it would not do to outstay their welcome. He rose from his chair and thanked the captain for his hospitality, at the same time contriving to jab a tactful knuckle into the midshipman's spine. Blissenden removed himself hastily from his chair, his pockets somewhat distended by several pieces of greasy toast.

Cutler cast an anxious eye at Blissenden's stomach.

'Are you able to walk, Mr Blissenden?' he asked.

'Yes, thank you, sir,' replied the midshipman, looking disconsolately at a solitary piece of bacon which had somehow been overlooked.

'My compliments to Mr Maxwell, then, and I should be grateful for a few moments of his time.'

'Aye aye, sir,' piped the boy and dashed off with his spoils.

Cutler laughed. 'Little gannet! What it is to be young, eh, Mr Lamb?'

'Indeed, sir,' said Lamb gravely, with all the vast wisdom of his nineteen years.

'Now, be so good as to arm yourself with pen, paper and a

9

watch. This morning I intend to try the mettle of our guns and gun-crews. I shall be up directly.'

It was a fine day for exercising the guns. The wind was fresh but steady and the ship had no more than a slight heel to starboard. Lamb, armed as instructed, stood behind and to one side of the captain on the quarterdeck. Below, with the length of the gun-deck before him, was the first lieutenant, blue-chinned jaw jutting aggressively. Forward, Tyler and Kennedy hovered over their separate divisions of guns; their responsibilities were further divided among the quarter-gunners and then again to the individual gun-captains.

The *Sturdy* carried 215 men, not far short of her full complement. Many were prime seamen, experienced topmen, gunners and petty officers; she also carried a fair number of landmen, gaol-birds and men who were not far removed from idiots. The fittest of these were distributed as evenly as possible along the line of guns where they stood looking anxiously at their more experienced colleagues and the strange implements in their hands. The starboard guns were to fire first; the ship had insufficient men to work both lines of guns at once with full crews, and most of the men would cross the deck to man the larboard guns in their turn.

All was ready; the deck was sanded, the water-buckets filled and the coiled slow-matches were glowing in their tubs. The ports were hinged open and the guns ready to be run inboard for loading. Officers and men waited silently for Cutler to give the word; the only sounds were the rush of wind and water and the working of the ship's timbers and spars.

The captain called down to the first lieutenant, 'I shall be timing each gun individually, Mr Maxwell. Carry on.'

Maxwell touched his hat in acknowledgement and directed his grim gaze at the nearest gun.

'Stand by the starboard guns! Number one, load and fire!'

The gun-crew exploded into furious activity. Around them danced the stout figure of Mr Bryce, the warrant-officer gunner, exhorting and advising in his gentle, Welsh way.

'Clap hold of that train-tackle, Higgins, the gun won't move back on its bloody own – heave, you bastards – that's it, now the breeching – no, the breeching, not the fucking side-tackle! – take out the tampion first, you one-eyed cunt! Where's the bloody cartridge? – that's it, ram it down hard – harder yet, she ain't no bloody virgin! good, good, now the wad – right, boys, heave, heave, back she goes. Now stand clear – *stand clear, I say!* – fucking idiot farmer! stop your vent – swab out – Jesus bloody wept, what a fucking shambles!'

'Time, Mr Lamb?' asked Cutler as the gunsmoke billowed off to leeward.

'Two minutes and forty-two seconds, sir.'

The *Sturdy* was rated at thirty-six guns, each firing a twelve-pound ball. In fact, she carried more guns than this number, the others being the smaller but very powerful carronades and the little swivel-guns mounted in the tops. She was officially rated by the number of long-guns she carried on her maindeck and even if she had bristled with extra carronades from stem to stern, in the eyes of the Lords of the Admiralty she would obdurately remain a thirty-six-gun frigate.

The exercise – firing reduced charges without roundshot – continued along the starboard side, the reek of gunsmoke and burnt powder filling the deck and clouds of yellow-white smoke drifting off to leeward. The ship's timbers shook to the violent explosions and the abruptly-snubbed recoil of the gun-carriages upon her deck as they hurtled inboard to the limit of their restraining breechings. As each gun was fired, swabbed and secured to the ring-bolts in the side the men from its crew ran across the deck to the gun opposite. With the firing of the last starboard gun Maxwell continued the exercise without pause along the larboard side.

As the third of these guns was driven backwards by the forward propulsion of its exploding charge, a loud scream of agony shrilled out from one of its crew, a scream that continued as the gun was swabbed and heaved back to the side. A midshipman broke from the group of men at the gun and ran to where Maxwell stood impassively at the foot of the quarterdeck ladder.

'Mr Tyler sends his respects, sir, and may I please call the surgeon, sir.'

Maxwell nodded at the aft companionway. 'You are too late, Mr Cowan; he is here already.'

Cowan hurried across to where the surgeon stood blinking in the strong sunlight and as he did so the screaming abruptly stopped. The group of men bent over the thrashing figure on the deck straightened and backed away as Cowan and the surgeon approached.

'Make way there, you men. Make way for the surgeon,' ordered the midshipman importantly, the roar of the next gun giving an impressive stamp to his order.

One of the men remained crouching over the injured seaman, a massive, tar-stained hand clamped over the man's mouth. Blood was pumping from the crushed and mangled foot.

'It's Joe Demeza, sir,' said the attending seaman as the surgeon knelt beside him. 'I thought it best to put a stop to his noise, case he damaged his lungs, like. He's hurt his foot,' he added helpfully.

'Remove your hand, you fool,' said Meadows. 'Do you want to stifle him? In any case, the man has fainted. Now stand away.'

He removed the unconscious man's belt, buckled it tightly around the injured leg and beckoned to a couple of the gun-crew.

'You two, carry him to the sick-bay.'

The limp figure was carted off to the forecastle, leaving bright, scarlet splashes on the scrubbed deckboards. The next gun in line crashed out and recoiled.

'Three minutes exactly, sir,' said Lamb.

The captain faced his assembled officers across his table; gone was the easy-mannered breakfast host of the morning. In his place was a stern-faced man with a brisk, authoritative manner. He brandished a sheet of paper.

'I have here the individual times for each gun. They range from two minutes ten seconds to three minutes twelve. The average – supposing Mr Lamb's arithmetic to be correct – is two minutes forty seconds. That cannot be described as fast, gentlemen. In addition, one man was crippled – Doctor Meadows removed his foot a short while ago – and one rammer was fired off, somewhat optimistically, I thought, in the direction of Portugal.

'There is no need to look quite so glum, gentlemen! I overheard one officer describe the exercise as a shambles; I disagree. To be frank, I expected much worse. We must remember that half the men out there were pulling turnips or somesuch not too many days ago, and we must make due allowance. But not for long, gentlemen, not for long!

'Mr Lamb. From now on, when not on watch, you will spend your daylight hours working with Mr Bryce and the gun-crews. The weak and the useless will be removed. Consult Mr Maxwell and replace and exchange men as you and he think fit. Work up each gun-crew individually and keep a log of their progress for Mr Maxwell's daily inspection.

'Right! Tomorrow morning we will have another exercise and the day after, weather permitting, we will give the men some targets to aim at – double tots for the winning crew! Any questions, Mr Maxwell? Mr Lamb? Very good. Thank you, gentlemen.'

Lamb found in Mr Bryce an enthusiastic supporter of the captain's orders. A voluble, grey-haired man with the lilt of the Welsh valleys still in his voice after forty years at sea, he loved his guns and in spite of his girth and years could bound about the deck like a midshipman.

'Guns is what ships is for, when all's said and done, Mr Lamb,' he said, sliding his hand lasciviously along the flank of one of his black monsters. 'Without guns, where would we be? We'd have to come alongside the froggies and exchange swear-words, he! he! he! Mind you, sir, I have known captains who cared too much for their deckboards to have the guns run in and out – permanent fixtures to the sides, they was and never the smell of the smallest pinch of powder. This captain, now, he's a different man entirely, a man after my own heart when it comes to guns, sir.'

Together, they worked the guns one crew at a time. Lamb listened attentively to the advice of the quarter-gunners and the gun-captains and any man whom they considered to be less than useful was removed to other duties. The gun-crews were already stiffened with a fair distribution of Marines and Lamb found himself wishing that there were more he could use. They came on board already trained and fit and they were much more amenable to discipline than the average seaman, who would not think it amiss to scratch his private parts while being addressed by an officer.

The weather stayed fair and became warmer. The winds became listless and often contrary. Lamb, who was accustomed to ships being worked hard to take advantage of every breath of wind, was surprised by the captain's apparent indifference to their laggardly pace, and said as much to Kennedy.

'Well, with a ship so full of green landmen a slow passage can only be to his advantage,' said the second lieutenant. 'It will give him a little more time to work them up. I daresay he has no wish to report to Lord St Vincent with a ship full of men that couldn't tell a block from the hole in their arse.'

Exercising of the guns continued daily; morning and afternoon found the men sweating and straining at the black brutes. The average time to load and fire was brought down to less than two minutes and a number of floating barrels, illegally written off by the captain as damaged beyond repair, were demolished during target practice, although a greater number were left bobbing unscathed in the ship's wake. One memorable afternoon, to the gunners' great delight, the captain judged he could spare enough powder for a broadside of three rounds to each gun and for eleven glorious minutes the ship rocked to the ear-numbing thunder of first one line of guns and then the other firing almost in unison. As the last of the enormous roars faded, Lamb caught sight of Cutler on the quarterdeck; his head was nodding in approval and a wide smile was fixed on his face.

The following day was Sunday, the day given over to the captain's inspection of men and ship and a reading of the Articles of War or perhaps a sermon from the quarterdeck. Lamb stood in front of his division, lined up just abaft of the foremast and facing aft. With the advantage of his height he could see Cutler and the first lieutenant moving along the lines of Kennedy's division, the captain glancing from faces gleaming from their second shave of the week, down past clean shirts and ducks to horny toes lined up along the deck seams. Lamb's eye wandered a little, falling on faces that had become familiar to him during his work with the gun-crews. Restricted by the discipline and habit of the service to brief and respectful responses to their officers, the seamen contrived, nevertheless, to stamp their characters firmly on Lamb's mind. He picked out Ayers, quarter-gunner, a square-faced man who, after the very shortest of formal acquaintance, Lamb knew would be rock-like in the most trying of circumstances. And young Kennett, recently a potboy at a Chatham inn, whose earthy wit had manifested itself during a recent gun exercise when a clumsily wielded rammer had winded one of his mates with a blow to the stomach.

'He's all right, sir,' Kennett had assured Lamb. 'Six inches lower, though, and the rammer would have met its match!'

Beside Kennett stood Aspinall, a picture of dejection with his downcast head and his ill-fitting purser's slops. A schoolmaster from Maidstone, he had been foolish enough to walk into the hands of the press-gang at Chatham. Unlike Kennett, he had not the resolution or strength of mind to accept his present situation calmly or to put aside agonized thoughts of his family. Lamb, to his intense embarrassment, had come across the man noisily weeping on watch one evening. Uncertain of how to deal with him, he had thought it best to leave the man alone and had walked quickly away. Now he was not so certain that he had acted wisely; a curt word and a warning might have been sufficient to put some stiffening into the man's backbone. He was a healthy, well-built man of more intelligence than most and once he had got the self-pity out of his system he should be a useful asset to the ship's company.

The captain walked along the rear of Tyler's division and began to inspect Lamb's men, nodding to the lieutenant as he passed him. Maxwell followed behind with his slate, ready to take the names of those men who had not been sufficiently careful with their turnout, but Lamb was fairly sure that none of his men would be put on the list. He had carried out his own inspection earlier and was confident that Cutler would find little to criticize. As he stood in the bright sunshine, clothed in his new uniform and enveloped in the pride of his new-won, long-yearned-for status, Lamb felt a bubble of happiness swell and rise within him. The long years as a midshipman with an uncertain future and the hunger and discomfort of the orlop-deck were now behind him; he, Lieutenant Lamb, a member of the wardroom, now walked the quarterdeck as a duty and a right. The gap between cockpit and wardroom was wide, certainly, but surely only different in degree from that between wardroom and captain's cabin; he had bridged the first and it would only be a question of time before he bridged the second.

The captain was making his way to the quarterdeck; his weekly inspection of the ship was over and from the grim expression on Maxwell's face Lamb concluded that he had gathered a long list of miscreants and their associated crimes. He doubted if there was any very serious offence on the list – perhaps less than brilliant copper pans in the galley or damp canvas in the sail locker at worst – but as first lieutenant Maxwell would bear the brunt of the captain's displeasure. Lamb gave a wry smile; even after so short an acquaintance he knew that Maxwell would pass on his own displeasure in turn, with interest.

The hands were dismissed from their divisions and made their way aft to squat between the mainmast and the quarterdeck. Lamb caught up with Tyler and Kennedy and the three lieutenants made their way through the press of men and mounted the quarterdeck to take their places behind the captain.

The ship was fortunate, so far as most of the men and officers were concerned, in that she did not carry a chaplain. Cutler, in common with many of his peers, had little time for men of the cloth on board ship; he considered their presence there to be as useful as a plough. His officers, too, were happy not to be sharing their quarters with a sky-pilot; his company would have cruelly restricted their conversation, both in adjectives and content.

Cutler opened his Bible at random, saw that his thumb rested on Psalm 101, scanned quickly through it to make sure it contained no references to sexual parts and lifted his head, waiting for silence. He began to read in a strong, clear voice. The men listened attentively; the solemn words stirred nothing in their souls – indeed the captain might have read from the purser's slops list and received the same close attention – but they dearly loved the familiar ritual of the occasion. For those men new to the sea the old words they had heard as children forged a link between their strange surroundings and the homes they had so recently left, humble as they undoubtedly were. To the more experienced hands the weekly reading, be it from the Bible or the Articles, demonstrated that the world was turning evenly on its axis and the navy's routine was settled comfortingly in its familiar grooves. The British seaman was nothing if

16

not conservative.

Lamb, musing, suddenly realized from the captain's cadences that he was nearing the end of the reading and hastily brought back to his face the solemn look appropriate to the occasion. Cutler clapped shut his Bible and stood for a moment with his head bowed. It was, for Lamb, a moment of rare and moving beauty; the silent crew, the bowed head of the captain and the hushed ship beneath the blue bowl of the sky invoked in him a sense of awe at the quiet majesty of the scene and a feeling of deep gratitude that he was a part of it.

Dinner in the gunroom was a light-hearted affair; today was an undemanding one so far as duties were concerned and the seamen were free to make-and-mend immediately after their beef and figgy-dowdy. Even the master, without doubt the most heavily burdened man in the ship in the way of duties, succumbed to the holiday atmosphere sufficiently to relate yet again the story of how he, as a midshipman, had hidden himself beneath the sofa of a popular, accommodating woman while his captain crouched before it on one knee and proposed marriage to her.

'Laugh? I had to stuff my sleeve into my mouth to prevent myself from being heard. And of course, the lady in question, knowing that I was, for once, ha, ha, ha, beneath her and listening to every word, could do no more than burst into shrieks of laughter in reply. The captain was mortified. He jumped to his feet, stamped and swore and stormed out in a rage, slamming the door so hard that the plaster cracked. God knows what would have happened had he found me – skewered me on the spot where I lay, I imagine.'

Lamb, with the warming influence of several glasses of wine inside him, found the tale vastly amusing; he threw back his head and roared with laughter. His table companions, who had heard the story no more than seven or eight times, dutifully smiled and nodded.

Kennedy threw a sly glance at Doubleday's well-covered frame and remarked: 'You would find it a little difficult to hide beneath a sofa nowadays, I think.'

'A chance would be a fine thing!' retorted the master and laughed hugely, his stomach shaking and his large, round face turning a deep purple. The laughter rapidly became a cough, a cough so persistent that the professional interests of the surgeon were aroused sufficiently for him to lay aside his book and apply his training to succouring Doubleday by means of several violent slaps to the small of his back. The master, recovered, expressed his gratitude for this skilled attention by means of a savage glare.

'There was no need to fracture my spine, damn it,' he said, somewhat hoarsely.

Meadows merely shrugged and returned his sharp nose to his book. He was in his middle twenties, with speech and deportment some fifteen years older. Not long released on to a grateful navy after satisfying the Transport Board that the Surgeon's Hall had not granted a licence to a nincompoop, he was already jaundiced from close observation of humanity at its weakest and worst. Much given to moralizing, he was not popular in the wardroom; a state of open warfare existed between him and the master, not the least reason for which was the master's casual regard for personal cleanliness.

Kennedy conversed quietly with Lamb, touching on the possibility of a visit to Gibraltar, which was, as he put it, 'just around the corner from Cadiz'.

'You have called there before?' asked Lamb.

'Just the once but it is an amazing place and I should be happy to show you some of the sights. It has massive fortifications and miles of tunnels cut through the rock. An enormous amount of work has been done there in the past few years and the place fairly bristles with heavy guns and soldiers, although I have heard whispers that the place has not been given the attention it deserves, of late, considering that it is the gateway to the Med.'

Of the other three lieutenants, Kennedy was the one with whom Lamb felt the easiest. He had insisted on first-name terms from the outset when not on duty and the two had struck up a relationship that was friendly and warming. Kennedy's good looks and pleasant, open manner sat naturally with him and, unlike Maxwell, he never underlined his rank in the wardroom. Of similar age to Lamb, he saw in the lanky officer an intellect and ambition that he readily recognized as exceeding his own, but such was his nature that he cheerfully accepted both the talents and the shortcomings of most men in the same equable manner.

'And yet again,' he went on, lowering his voice, 'there are other interesting places we might visit. I know of one or two little establishments where personable young officers with a shilling or two in their pockets are made extremely welcome.'

The surgeon's ears were as sharp as his nose. He caught the last remark and tut-tutted loudly.

'Shame on you, Mr Kennedy, for attempting to lead young and unworldly officers astray. I would be gravely disappointed if either of you was to return from a trip ashore with self-inflicted wounds. My small supply of mercury is fast vanishing with the complaint of Venus amongst the lustful riff-raff for'ard, without the wardroom inflicting a further drain on it.'

Doubleday seized on the chance of delivering a broadside at his enemy.

'Riff-raff? Riff-raff?' he snorted. 'You should not speak so badly about the men on such short acquaintance, sir, with your Transport Board ticket not yet dry. Lustful they may be and good luck to that, but the British seaman is the salt of the earth, sir, the salt of the earth.'

The master's statement was hypocritical in the extreme. His view of the average seaman coincided closely with the opinion of the surgeon and he had frequently and forcefully expressed it in far less charitable terms. Meadows was well aware of this but refused to be drawn.

'Your opinion is noted, Mr Doubleday,' he contented himself with saying, and returning to his book he put up his draw-bridge.

Lamb went to his cabin. He was shortly to relieve Tyler on watch and he wished to add a page or two to the letter to his father he had started writing some days ago. If he finished it today it might be lucky enough to catch a homeward-bound packet when they reached Cadiz.

Light rain had been falling on and off since noon but with the setting of the sun the skies had cleared and now, as Lamb paced the quarterdeck in the last dog-watch, the towering canvas and rigging had ceased to drip upon his head and the ship was bathed in the soft, white light of the moon at full. Half an hour earlier the frigate had come about at the southernmost limit of her line of patrol and was now heading north. To starboard lay the northernmost tip of the African continent and many miles to the north was Cape Trafalgar, the other end of her line. The ship was very quiet; the sound of Lamb's footsteps on the boards of the quarterdeck was overlaid only by the hiss of water along the sides and the creak and rattle of the spars and blocks.

The *Sturdy* had been patrolling the same area of sea for the past two weeks, beating up and down across the western approaches to the Straits of Gibraltar like a watchman guarding the open gates of a vast prison, the prisoners in this instance being the ships of the French and Spanish fleets, busily engaged, it was rumoured, in preparing for massed action against the British. The frigate was a watchdog, the eyes of the distant fleet, ready to speed off and raise the alarm if the noses of the prisoners should poke through the gates of the Straits.

The patrol had grown wearisome; the weather had not been kind and the hands had been kept busy with the frequent and exhausting sail-handling as the frigate had struggled to maintain her station in the face of heavy weather and adverse winds. Little had been seen in the way of sail; the British were maintaining a close blockade of the Atlantic and Channel ports and the only vessels the *Sturdy* had glimpsed had been the occasional sloop or brig scurrying between Lord St Vincent's fleet off Cadiz and the garrison of Gibraltar. Bad weather had not been allowed to interrupt the daily exercising of the guns and while their crews had grown more efficient at their tasks, the heavy and dangerous work of handling guns on a steeply rolling deck had provided the surgeon with a growing number of sprains, strains, ruptures and the occasional more serious injury.

Lamb paced to and fro, deep in thought. He felt he had settled in well into the ship's company in general and the gunroom in particular. He was easier now in his new status as a commissioned officer and he no longer experienced the nervous doubts that had earlier plagued him when he performed his duties in the presence of the captain and under the cold eye of the first lieutenant. His fellow occupants of the gunroom, met with such shyness and trepidation when he first joined the ship, were now familiar figures with whom he felt at ease and whose very different personalities meshed reasonably comfortably with his own. He chuckled quietly to himself as the recollection of the most recent clash between the surgeon and the master came to mind.

Flatulence was a constant problem on board His Majesty's ships with the officers and hands alike, a condition associated with the heavily leguminous diet which was common to both. The master, to his delight, had discovered that the surgeon was prissily averse to both the sound and the lingering after-effects of eased internal pressures and had seized upon the knowledge to irritate the surgeon whenever the opportunity presented itself.

'Fire as you bear!' he would cry as he eased a massive haunch and his body would shake with suppressed merriment as a look of deep disgust crossed his enemy's face. Last night, however, had seen Doubleday's undoing; Lamb had caught sight of the master's face as he rolled his body to one side in preparation for the expected explosion and was amused to see his countenance go red with strain as his gun refused to fire. The master was nothing if not resolute, however, and he maintained the pressure with all the force that clenched lips and concentration could muster. His expression suddenly gave way to one of doubt, then just as swiftly to one of horror and rising from his chair he made for the door, keeping his backside to the bulkhead as he went. Lamb erupted into peals of laughter and it was some time before he could control his streaming eyes and his breath sufficiently to share with his colleagues the reason for his mirth. The memory of that joyous moment caused Lamb to laugh aloud as he walked the boards of the quarterdeck, raising the eyebrows of the quartermaster and helmsmen as the sound of his solitary laughter reached their ears.

Beneath Lamb's pacing feet, in the dimly lit solitude of his cabin, Captain Cutler sat at his table under the swaying lantern and thoughtfully tapped his fingers as he stared at the bottle before him. Cutler had been fighting a battle for many years, a battle within himself and one which he knew, ultimately, would get the better of him. His affliction had very nearly cost him his last ship and had gained him an official rebuke from his admiral – a rebuke which that gentleman had put in writing as a permanent debit on Cutler's record. He had been fortunate to be given the *Sturdy*, he knew, and one more such condemnation would mean the end of his seagoing activities. Cutler was addicted to alcohol as other men were given to breathing; it loomed larger in his life than money, women or food. He was an honest man in most things, even to himself, and he was fully cognizant of his weakness and its attendant risks. His craving, however, was such that although from time to time he made very real efforts to suppress it, in the end, inevitably, he would reach for his bottle as a drowning man would snatch at a breath of air. His craving was now so deep-seated that he regarded it as an integral part of his being, but by rigid control and the assistance of his long-serving steward he kept the thing almost quiescent with a strictly rationed intake which enabled him to perform his duties without any great impairment of his faculties. Occasionally, however, the beast within him would stretch and flex its muscles and he would embark on a marathon from which he would emerge several hours or even days later wretchedly ill and feeling close to death. Fortunately, such lapses were rare but he was sombrely aware that the intervals between them were growing shorter.

He eyed the bottle on his table with something akin to disgust, and poured himself a carefully judged half glass. Downing it in one swallow he banged the cork firmly back into the neck and rising from his chair, reached for his hat and made his way up to the damp moonlit deck.

Chapter 2

Lord St Vincent's fleet lay at anchor in deep water west of Cadiz. His inshore squadron had been recalled and now the ships of both squadrons were dispersed in a huge circular formation, snubbing at their anchors and rolling heavily in the long, deep swell. In the centre of the ring of vessels were anchored a group of ships and the eyes of the fleet were fixed on one in particular, the *Marlborough*.

The *Marlborough*, with several other ships, had recently arrived from England and with some of them had come the seeds which had been sown at Spithead and the Nore. St Vincent was characteristically quick to act. Determined to stamp out the flames of mutiny before they took firm hold, he had ordered the leader of the muttering troublemakers to be brought to the flagship in irons, where he had convened an immediate court martial.

The *Sturdy* had arrived in response to her recall in the dark hours and Cutler had been summoned to the flagship, the *Ville de Paris*, at first light. He was absent from his gig for a bare ten minutes and when he returned to the frigate his face was grim. As soon as he was on board he ordered Maxwell to call all hands aft and waited silently on the quarterdeck while the wondering seamen gathered in the waist and his officers, no less curious, ranged themselves behind him.

Cutler was terse and direct. 'Men, you are about to witness a hanging. You are doubtless aware of what happened at Spithead and the Nore – for all I know, some of you might have been present at one place or the other. Well, mutiny has raised its ugly head again – on those ships you see anchored there.'

He pointed with outflung arm to where the *Marlborough* lay, together with the *Princess Royal*, the *Lion* and the *Centaur*. Two hundred heads turned in the direction of his hand and duly swivelled back to the quarterdeck again.

Cutler paused and ran his eyes over the silent, upturned faces

23

of the men crowded below him. Not a man stirred; their gaze was fixed unblinkingly on the captain's face.

'Thankfully, I have seen no sign of such unrest on this ship nor has any been reported to me. Furthermore, I have just assured the Commander-in-Chief that I have every confidence that I can depend on your continuing loyalty and obedience to me, the service and the King.'

He pulled his watch from his waistcoat pocket and opened it.

'The execution will take place in four minutes. It is Lord St Vincent's express order that every man in the fleet shall witness it. You will all now turn and look out to starboard. Fix your eyes on the *Marlborough* – she flies the yellow flag.'

Officers and men turned and stared over the water to where the *Marlborough* lay, some two cables distant. Lamb followed Kennedy's example and reached for one of the ship's telescopes from the rack. The scene on the larboard side of the *Marlborough*'s maindeck sprang to his eye. The glass travelled along a line of men facing forward, each clutching a rope over his right shoulder with both hands. The rope was fed through a block on the deck and went up to the yardarm of the mainmast and vertically down again, where it ended in a noose held in the hands of a petty officer standing to the rear of a figure whose head was covered by a hood. Lamb's glass picked out a line of armed redcoats facing aft from below the quarterdeck and above them the motionless figures of the captain and his officers. He noticed that the captain was missing an arm; one empty sleeve was pinned to his shoulder.

It seemed a very long four minutes. Suddenly, a single gun fired. The line of men trotted forward and the hooded man rose quickly through the bright, morning air, up, up, plunging and kicking. A huge, collective sigh came from the assembled men in the waist of the *Sturdy*. The tiny figure continued to twist and jerk for what to Lamb seemed an age. Quite suddenly it was still, its head slumped forward, slowly rotating beneath the yardarm.

'Dismiss the men to their duties, Mr Maxwell,' Cutler ordered in a harsh voice, and went down to his quarters.

The men dispersed quietly, their faces sombre. Lamb saw one man stroke his throat and make a grimace to his mate. Yes, you are right, Lamb silently agreed; to strangle slowly, fighting for breath through a crushed windpipe, must be an ugly death.

Conversation in the wardroom was sober. Lamb sipped his coffee and listened to Maxwell loudly expounding on the necessity of justice being seen to be done, from trial to execution.

'Witnessing a sight like that from time to time can only be good for the service. There is nothing like a hanging to pull a man up sharp from mutinous thoughts. There are too many would-be revolutionists about, spreading their bloody Frenchified notions of equality. What say you, Mr Lamb?'

'I am not sure. A man can be a mutineer without being a revolutionist, surely? The one is simply trying to better his conditions and the other to change everyone's way of life.'

'Huh!' snorted Maxwell. 'They are all tarred with the same brush. Traitors, all of 'em.'

Meadows lifted his head from his book. 'That condemnation is a little sweeping, I think. If you remember, even those mutineers at Spithead swore their loyalty to King and country and stated they would not let their demands prevent their ships from sailing against the French, if the need arose.'

'Don't tell me you sympathized with them?' said Maxwell, frowning.

'In many respects, yes, as any right-minded man would have done. We all know the navy is not perfect. How can a man be content with such low rates of pay, less than a soldier's and often scandalously in arrears? How can a man happily serve in a ship when he knows that his wife and children are hungry and, like as not, he will get no leave to see them when his ship returns to England? How can the Admiralty be so indifferent to the petitions of its seamen when it would take so little to improve their lot? If our Lords of the Admiralty were not so blind and mule-headed then we would have no mutineers, sir, and such a scene as we saw this morning would never have been necessary.'

An awkward silence followed the surgeon's impassioned speech. Lamb looked thoughtfully into his cup. Privately he agreed with much of what Meadows had said but to state it so openly seemed to him to smack of near sedition. The surgeon, somewhat red of face, returned his nose to his book and turned a page with a trembling hand, muttering that he might as well

25

have talked to a brick wall. His sulk did not last for long, however, and when Tyler, talking to the purser, observed that a man about to be hanged should at least be allowed to go to his Maker with his eyes uncovered Meadows looked up and smiled thinly.

'The hood is put on for a very good reason. It is to protect the sensitive minds of the watching public. Do you know what an ugly sight a hanged man is? Face blue, eyes bolting and bleeding, tongue bitten through and lolling out. It is not a pretty sight, as I can testify. And the bowels evacuate, of course – though the hood is not much use in that respect, ha, ha, ha!'

Later that morning, after he had met with the captain, Maxwell informed the wardroom that more courts martial were planned and that no doubt the entertainment of this morning would be repeated. In his opinion, they were likely to be here for several more days. In the event, he was soon proved to be wrong. The course of the war had to be pursued, domestic problems notwithstanding, and shortly before noon Cutler was summoned again to the flagship. The instructions he received there were evidently less unpleasant than he had been given on his earlier visit for he was smiling slightly as he climbed back on board the frigate. Within moments the *Sturdy* was under way and within the hour only the masts of the fleet were visible from her deck as she made her way south-east to the Straits of Gibraltar.

There was little shipping in Gibraltar Bay and only a solitary sloop at the mole as the *Sturdy* was warped alongside. Cutler gave instructions to Maxwell that no shore leave was to be granted and an armed Marine was to guard the gangway.

'I am off to pay my respects to the port admiral. We may be here only a few hours, so you had better make the most of it. We need water and powder, of course – make those your first concern. So far as our other requirements are concerned – well, you can try your luck at the Navy Yard but I would not be too optimistic.'

Water was obtained without much difficulty and powder, too, eventually arrived after a little obsequious representation from the first lieutenant to the superintendent of the arsenal, although Mr Bryce shook his head sadly at its quality as he supervised its stowage, wearing his felt slippers. Tyler, despatched to the Navy Yard with six trusty hands – under the suspicious eye of the coxswain for whom no such animal existed – returned in a foul temper.

'The man was drunk – I had to wake him! – and the place was in shit order. Not a spar to be had and the mast-pond bone dry. He gave me plenty of excuses but precious little else. A few blocks, a fathom or two of rope and a little paint – I could have carried the lot back in my pocket!'

A messenger arrived, despatched from the port admiral's office, requesting six armed Marines and a sergeant to attend the office forthwith. Within the hour they were on their way back accompanied by the captain, two of the Marines carrying between them a small wooden chest secured by a brass lock the size of a dinner plate. Once on board, with the chest safely ensconced in his cabin behind the sentry at the door, Cutler ordered Maxwell to get the ship under way and paced up and down the quarterdeck as the frigate painfully picked her way among the fitful airs of the bay. Rounding Cabrita Point, the ship collected a moderate wind from the north-east and headed, close-hauled, westward into the Atlantic. Cutler, calling for the first lieutenant to join him, disappeared into his cabin, leaving the quarterdeck to Kennedy.

Lamb was dozing in his bunk when the canvas screen that served as a door was pulled to one side. He opened his eyes to see Maxwell standing there.

'Do you speak any French?' he asked brusquely.

Lamb scrambled to his feet. 'A very little, sir.'

'Well, little or none, the captain has a task for you,' said Maxwell cryptically. 'Dress yourself correctly and report to him straight away, if you please.'

Lamb stepped past the wooden-faced sentry and gave a smart tap at the captain's door.

'Enter!' called Cutler.

A chart was spread over his table, held down with a ship's book at each corner.

'Pull up a chair, Mr Lamb, and cast your eye on this chart,' said Cutler. His finger rested on a point on the chart a little north of the 40° line, where the Portuguese coastal plain west of the highlands of Serra da Estrala met the Atlantic Ocean. His voice was brisk.

'You will take a boat ashore here. You will leave the crew with the boat and make your way to the village of Cartosa which lies about a mile due east of the beach. Select two strong and reliable petty officers to carry the chest.'

He gestured at the padlocked box which sat on the deck beneath the wide stern-windows.

'Just before you come to the village you will find a bridge across a stream. Here, I am reliably informed, you will be met by two men, both Portuguese. Between them, apparently, they speak a little English and French. Passwords will be exchanged. Yours is – yours is – damn!'

He scrabbled among the papers on his table and selecting one, held it long-sightedly at arm's length.

'Yours is "Jervis" and the response is "Victory". Repeat those, please.'

' "Jervis" and "Victory", sir.'

'Very good.' Cutler glanced across at Lamb with a slight smile on his face. 'Take care not to forget them!'

'I shall not forget them, sir.'

'Good. When you have received the correct response you will hand over the chest to the two men. You may or may not be given a packet of papers in exchange. Your mission will then be complete. Return to the boat and rejoin the ship. Simple enough, is it not? Any questions?'

'What if I do not get the correct response, sir?'

Cutler shot him a cold look. 'Then you do not hand over the chest, Mr Lamb. I thought I made that quite clear. What action you take then I leave to you, but in any case the chest will be brought back tc this ship. Clear?'

'Yes, sir.'

'Now the two men are going to wait for two hours from midnight, starting tomorrow night. They will wait in vain then, of course, but with luck we should arrive for you to meet them on the next night, providing this wind holds.'

A perfunctory knock was followed by the opening of the door, around which showed the shining head of the captain's steward. He held forward a tray on which rested a coffee-pot and a single cup.

'Coffee time, sir,' he said briskly. 'Shall I bring it in or would you rather wait 'til Mr Lamb's gone – course, it'll be cold by

28

then but I can always make another pot, if you don't mind the waste.'

Cutler sucked his teeth in annoyance. 'Get another cup and bring it in,' he said testily. The head vanished.

'Some background information for you, Mr Lamb,' Cutler continued. 'As you probably know, there are certain factions in Portugal who do not take at all kindly to the French occupation of their country and it is in our interests to encourage those factions to arm and organize themselves – hence the gold.'

He paused while Watson bustled into the cabin and poured the coffee.

'Yes, Mr Lamb,' he went on as the door shut behind the steward, 'it is gold that you will be taking ashore, as perhaps you have guessed.'

Lamb had seen the chest and its armed escort come aboard and he had thought then that the authority responsible might just as well have painted the word GOLD on each of its six sides.

'I had an inkling the box might contain something of value, sir,' he said solemnly.

Cutler gave him a sharp glance. 'Yes, well, it will not do your peace of mind any good to know exactly what that chest is worth – sufficient for you to know that if you lose it on the way ashore you would be well advised not to report back!'

'In that case I shall guard it with my life, sir.'

'That goes without saying, Mr Lamb. A word of caution. Bear in mind that Boney's men are swarming all over the country and you might well come across some of them when you are ashore. If you see any, give them a wide berth. I want no heroics from you, do you understand?'

'Yes, sir.'

'I have debated whether to send a large party along but on balance I believe a small party will be able to move more quickly and quietly and conceal themselves, if the need should arise. Arm yourselves with pistols and cutlasses – you, too; a cutlass is handier at close quarters than a sword.'

'Yes, sir. May I take your cox'n with me, sir?'

'Stone? Yes, of course. You could not have picked a better man. Who else have you in mind?'

'I thought Ayers, sir, the gun-captain, starboard side.'

'Ayers? Oh yes, the big man. He should be useful in a tight

29

corner. But do not approach either of them just yet – the fewer people who know about your trip, the better. And whatever you do, don't mention what is in that chest – there is no point in taking needless risks.'

'No, sir,' said Lamb, thinking that there could not be a man on board who had not made a shrewd guess as to the contents of the box.

Cutler pushed his coffee away untasted. 'That is all, Mr Lamb.'

A half-moon showed intermittently behind ragged, slow-moving clouds as Lamb settled himself in the stern of the cutter. He reached forward, found the chest with his hand and patted it to give himself physical reassurance of its presence. The boat moved sharply away from the ship's side in response to Stone's low growl. 'Shove off. Out oars. Give way together.'

The men bent their backs and dug in their oars. As the cutter moved away Lamb glanced up and behind him. The side of the frigate was lined with dark, featureless heads and several figures were clinging to the ratlines. For a moment he felt as he had as a child, when he had been taken from his home for a reason now forgotten – a sense of loss of things safe and familiar. The feeling passed as swiftly as it came, leaving behind it a faint sense of unease.

The shoreline was quite invisible but the master had assured him that the frigate lay-to no more than a mile from the beach and indeed, after five minutes of hard pulling, he could hear the indistinct growl of distant rollers. Somewhere in the boat a foot slipped and an oar missed its stroke.

'Fuck!' said a low voice.

'Shut your bloody mouth, Hodges,' said the coxswain quietly, 'less you want my fist in it.'

The sound of rollers on the beach was suddenly louder and closer. Half rising to peer above the heads of the men, Lamb caught a glimpse of white water ahead as the boat rose to a swell.

'Steady, sir,' growled Stone, his years of experience as a coxswain allowing him to edge his voice with precisely enough irritation to keep it a whisker's breadth from insolence.

Lamb carefully seated himself again, his ears warm from the

implied rebuke. He had discovered, during his weeks on the *Sturdy*, that when faced by the solid, down-to-earth maturity of experienced petty officers such as the coxswain and the boatswain, the self-confidence that his recently-won commission and uniform carried would frequently evaporate to reveal the callow midshipman who was still not so far below the surface.

The cutter was beginning to rock fore and aft with increasing violence and the sound of the waves crashing on to the shore was now a thunderous roar.

'Pull! Pull!' shouted Stone as he struggled to hold the boat stern-on to the curling, white-topped waves, and then: 'In oars!' and the cutter was grating its keel on the bottom and slewing sideways-on to the beach. The men jumped into the water – now knee-deep, then waist-high – and heaving madly, dragged the boat clear of the tumbling surf. Lamb found that he was crouching over the chest, gripping it tightly with both hands. He straightened and making his way forward, stepped dry-shod on to the shingle.

'Well done, cox'n,' he said to Stone in passing. He gave a long look left and right along the moonlit beach. It was clear. He watched as the cutter was hauled well above the line of wrack and weed and left in the lee of a bank of shingle.

Ayers heaved the chest from the boat by its rope handles and dumped it heavily at Lamb's feet.

'Ah, that's bloody heavy, sir,' he grunted. 'Have we got to carry it far, like?'

'Not far,' said Lamb. 'Stay with it for a moment while I see to the men.'

The crew of the cutter was squatting beside the boat, having squirmed their backsides into the bank of shingle to make comfortable seats. Lamb beckoned to one of the older hands.

'I shall leave you in charge here, Smith. Post a lookout on top of the bank there. Keep the men absolutely quiet – there may well be French soldiers in the vicinity. If you see any horsemen or soldiers approaching you will immediately return to the ship without us. Understood?'

'Aye, sir, understood.'

Lamb had deliberately pitched his voice loud enough for all the men to hear. It would serve to add his stamp to Smith's authority over the men during his absence.

'Good,' he said. 'All being well, we should be back long before then.'

He plodded back through the loose shingle to where Stone and Ayers stood by the chest.

'Right, gentlemen, let us be on our way.'

The two men hoisted the chest between them and followed Lamb as he scrambled his way up the shingle bank. He turned as he reached the top and looked out to sea. The frigate was just visible as a dark patch way out on the darker water; then, as the moon found a gap in the clouds, he saw her clearly, a pattern of black and white on the silver-streaked sea. He turned again and headed inland, keeping the moon over his right shoulder.

The going grew firmer once they were clear of the beach, the low, coarse grass feeling strange under his feet after so long away from the land. The moon, skipping in and out of the clouds, gave occasional glimpses of the countryside around them. The grass and scrub extended out of sight to left and right and before them was the black outline of a small copse, populated with stunted trees leaning away from the Atlantic winds. Lamb called a halt as soon as they reached the shelter of the trees; he was warm beneath his heavy coat and more than a trifle out of breath. Ayers and Stone lowered the chest to the ground and flexed their carrying arms to and fro. Lamb calculated that they had walked some four hundred yards or so – they should be nearly half-way to the village. A cloud passed over the moon and the copse was suddenly very dark. He felt for the pistol in his belt – it was primed and loaded and needed but a single movement of his thumb to cock it. He considered this briefly but decided against it. A cocked pistol was too unstable a weapon with which to stumble over dark and unknown country. Better, he thought, to transfer his cutlass to his left hand and leave his right free, ready to snatch the pistol from his belt if the need should arise.

'Stay here,' he murmured to the two barely visible men beside him. 'I'm going to see what is on the other side of the trees.'

Holding his arm outstretched before him to guard his eyes, Lamb picked his way through the trees. Wiry branches snagged at his coat and a rotten log nearly brought him to his knees. Providentially, the moon reasserted itself as he reached the edge of the copse and the countryside before him was revealed bathed in harsh, white light almost as clear as day. A narrow, rutted path left the copse a few yards to his left and ran down a moderate slope to a line of trees and scrub, beyond which he could see the gleam of water. The land rose again steeply on the far side of the stream, pausing at a narrow plateau before continuing its upward slope. On the plateau was a jumble of low, angular shapes, huddled together in untidy proximity. Lamb felt a warm glow of triumph. They had found the stream and the village – all they had to do now was find the bridge. That, he thought, would almost certainly be found by following the track down to the stream. Keeping in the shadow of the trees, he made a careful search of the land around him. There was no sign of life, not even a browsing goat. The air was quite still – the wind had died and Lamb's breathing seemed unnaturally loud. He turned and fumbled his way back through the dark trees to Stone and Ayers, almost passing them without knowing. Only a quiet 'All right, sir?' from the coxswain revealed their presence.

Lamb passed his information in a whisper. The two made no comment and together they made their way to the edge of the copse. Lamb waited until the moon briefly showed itself and then pointed out the path, the stream and the distant, sleeping village.

'Fix the track in your minds,' he said softly. 'The moment the moon goes in again we will follow it down to the trees by the stream.'

The moon's illumination lasted for only a few more seconds and with the dark the men scurried for the path. It was easy to follow – the white chalk of its hard-trodden surface showed clearly against the blackness of the surrounding turf. Lamb, leading the way, slowed as they reached the bottom of the little valley and neared the line of low trees and bushes which edged the tiny river. He eased his pistol from his belt and cocked it; the metallic click as the hammer moved past its hold was very loud in the quiet air. Should he order the two men behind him to cock their pistols? No, he decided, after a moment's thought. The notion of two loaded and cocked guns close to his back was not a comforting one. He moved on into the trees.

33

Dark as it was, he could see the bridge distinctly – its straight lines and angles showed clearly against the disorder of the overhanging branches of the trees beside it. The sulky murmur of slow-running water came to his ears. He turned and put his mouth close to the ear of one of the petty officers almost invisible behind him – he guessed it was Ayers from his bulk.

'Wait here,' he breathed.

His heart beat loud and fast as he moved on towards the bridge and he felt more than a shade nauseous, a cold, churning motion in the pit of his stomach. He edged off the track and into the long grass beside it, his eyes fixed on the bridge. A hand clamped on to his outstretched forearm, gripping like a vice. His blood froze and the shock, so awful in its suddenness, very nearly brought forth an involuntary yell of fright. The hand pulled him closer to its owner, a short, heavy-set dark bulk standing in the shadow of the trees. The stench of stale garlic hit Lamb with almost physical force as the man spoke in a hoarse, urgent whisper.

'Victoree? Victoree?'

For a second Lamb was nonplussed. The bloody fool had given the response first! Was that acceptable? Or was his own word the response and not the challenge? Come to that, did it matter? He eased back the hammer of his pistol.

'Jervis,' he muttered.

'*Bien, bien,*' the other replied. He hissed a name into the darkness and a second dark shape appeared.

'*Où se trouve l'or?*' asked the first man.

His rapid speech and accent were almost too much for Lamb's limited knowledge of the language but he caught the last word.

'*Oui. Un moment,*' he said, hoping the man would understand him. He turned and called in a low voice. 'Bring the chest up, cox'n.'

The two men trotted up and set down the chest at Lamb's feet.

'Everything all right, sir?' enquired Stone in a cheerful, matter-of-fact voice, as if meeting strange foreigners on a black night whilst carrying a fortune in gold was quite an everyday occurrence.

'I believe so, cox'n,' said Lamb. He gave the chest a slight kick.

'*C'est dans la boite, ici,*' he said haltingly.

'*Bien!*' said the short man. He knelt and fumbled at the lock.

Lamb realized suddenly that he had not been given a key and cursed inwardly at his stupidity in overlooking the fact.

'*Avez-vous la clef?*' asked the man, turning his pale face up to Lamb.

'*Je regret, non.*'

'*Oh, ça ne fait rien,*' said the man, apparently unconcerned, rising from his knees. He reached out, found Lamb's hand in the darkness and passed him a small package.

'*Pour vous, monsieur.*'

'*Merci,*' said Lamb and stuffed the packet into his coat pocket. '*C'est tout?*'

The man broke into a swift rush of French. Lamb missed much of it but the gist was clear enough. The two men had many friends in the mountains and soon they would have many guns. One day, God willing, all the accursed Frenchmen would be driven out of their country. Lamb must take care. French dragoons were at the village this morning. There were many soldiers with horses everywhere. Long live King George!

He found Lamb's hand again and shook it warmly. The taller man, who had not said a word so far, stepped close to Lamb and peered, grinning widely, into his face.

'Good morning!' he said brightly.

Lamb grinned back in return. This must be the English-speaking half of the pair.

'Good morning to you!' he said.

The man beamed even wider and threw an arm around Lamb's shoulder in a bear-like hug, almost choking him in the stench of garlic.

'Good morning! Good morning!' he repeated, delighted that his little store of English had been understood.

The short man muttered something sharply in his own language and to his vast relief, Lamb found himself released. The two men picked up the chest and hefted its weight.

'*Bonne chance!*' said the short man and within seconds the pair had trotted over the bridge and vanished into the darkness beyond.

For a moment the three Englishmen stood staring after them.

Lamb puffed his cheeks and blew a long, slow breath. So that was it, mission completed! For all his fears and fancies, it had been a simple and straightforward operation. Sweat trickled down his forehead and into his eyes. He hastily brushed his sleeve across his face.

'Right, you two, let us get back to the boat,' he said, turning his back on the bridge. They began to make their way along the chalk path. The cloud was more broken now and glimpses of the moon were more frequent. Lamb paused to give a quick glance left and right along the grassy valley as they left the shelter of the trees. He could see nothing untoward. His eye followed the narrow track up the sloping ground to where it ran into the blackness of the copse; all was clear.

He motioned the men to move on and as they left the darkness of the little fringe of trees the moon gave up its game of hide and seek with the clouds and moved into a large patch of clear sky.

They had crossed the narrow valley floor and were about to ascend the steep rise when a very sudden and very loud drumming noise came from behind them. Lamb whirled round. What the devil was that? Ayers gave the answer even as he realized it himself.

'Horses, sir – crossing the bridge.'

'Run like the devil!' snapped Lamb and began to race uphill to the shelter of the copse. He cast a glance over his shoulder just in time to see the cavalrymen burst from the trees beside the stream, perhaps seventy yards behind them. There were three of them, bent low over the necks of their mounts. Their sabres flashed silver in the moonlight. A yell from one of them told Lamb they had been seen and he knew, with sickening certainty, that they would be outrun long before they could reach the copse.

'Stop! Stop!' he panted, breathless. 'Make a stand. Pistols first, then your blades.'

They turned and faced the oncoming horsemen, their pistols cocked and outstretched. Lamb, panting hard from his uphill run, tried desperately to keep his arm steady. Best to let them get as close as possible, he thought, or I shall be certain to miss.

'Don't fire till I give the word,' he shouted over the thunder of the approaching hoofbeats.

The horsemen, riding abreast, split their formation as they came within thirty yards. The outside riders veered left and right to circle the trio; the other man rode straight at them, standing high in his stirrups with his sabre outstretched before him.

Lamb fired. The pistol gave a deafening report and kicked his arm upwards. His numbed ears rang again to the simultaneous explosions of the pistols of his two men an instant later as they took his action in place of his order. He ducked and fell to his knees as the enormous bulk of the horse and rider loomed over him and felt the wind off the sabre's downward slash as he threw himself desperately to one side. Then horse and rider were past and he was struggling to his feet, his pistol discarded and his cutlass in his right hand. Ayers was on the ground, his arms wide-spread and his face to the sky. Stone stood wide-legged over him, his pistol smoking in his hand and his eyes fixed on the flanking horsemen as they pulled their mounts round to renew the attack. The centre cavalryman was slumped in his saddle, his horse shying away from the slope. As Lamb watched, the man fell to one side and was dragged along the ground by his stirrups.

'I got him, by God!' Lamb shouted exultantly.

The two remaining riders hesitated, pulling at the reins, the horses rearing. One of them flung out an arm towards the fleeing horse and the man bumping along on his back beside it. His companion wheeled his mount, dug in his spurs and set off in pursuit; the other set his horse at the Englishmen, whirling his sabre high in the air and giving a loud, unintelligible shout.

Stone, standing fast over the prone body of Ayers, shifted his cutlass into his right hand and called urgently to Lamb.

'The horse, sir – go for the horse!'

Man and beast were towering over them, the rider striking down with his sabre at Stone on his right. Lamb took one quick step forward and struck hard at the horse's throat, using both hands. He felt the blade bite deep before the weapon was torn from his hand as the animal shied away, rearing in shock and pain. Blood, black in the moonlight, burst from its throat as it plunged and screamed, its rider sawing frantically at the reins. Suddenly the horse was down, its life-blood spurting, a high-pitched bubbling coming from between its drawn-back lips.

The Frenchman was also down, his leg trapped beneath the body of the horse. Before Lamb could speak or act, Stone was standing over the man, his cutlass flashing down hard at his neck. The man jerked once and fell back, his sabre falling across the neck of his dying horse.

Lamb peered along the narrow valley. Some two hundred yards away he could make out the shapes of two horses standing side by side with a smaller, indistinct shape beside them, bending over something on the ground. Well, that is two of the bastards done for, he thought – and if the last one comes back we'll do for him too, he added, his blood up.

Stone was kneeling beside Ayers and Lamb stooped to examine the gunner. His fur cap was wet with blood; removing it, Lamb's finger felt a deep gash several inches long on the left side of his head. If he was still alive, it was his thick fur cap that had saved him. A strange noise came to Lamb's ears and lowering his head nearer to the man's face, he listened closely. He looked up at Stone with a smile on his face.

'Well, he's alive, all right. He's snoring!'

Stone grunted. 'I'm not surprised, sir. He always was one for his sleep – could sleep on a bowline, that one!'

Working quickly, Lamb removed the neckcloth from around the unconscious man's throat, bound it tightly over the wound and replaced the fur cap over it.

Now, how to carry him? Thoughts of a makeshift stretcher flashed through his mind – perhaps with some timber from the copse above them? Stone neatly solved the problem. He levered Ayers to his feet, ducked and caught him across his shoulder. Straightening, he turned to Lamb and murmured: 'When you're ready, sir.'

The sound of drumming hooves stopped them before they had gone a dozen yards. The last surviving Frenchman was returning at a gallop. He reined in sharply at the bodies of horse and man and gave them a long look. His gaze came up and fixed on Lamb and Stone, standing motionless further up the slope. Frenchman and Englishmen stared at each other for several long seconds and then Stone, with Ayers draped over his shoulder, took two quick paces forward and raised his cutlass.

'Fuck off, froggy!' he said firmly.

The horseman muttered something between his teeth,

whirled his horse around and set off down the hill in the direction of the bridge.

'Well done, cox'n,' said Lamb. Had he not said the same words earlier as he stepped out of the boat? He fumbled his watch out of his waistcoat pocket and opened its cover. For a moment he thought it had stopped and he held it to his ear. It ticked reassuringly. To his astonishment, less than sixty minutes had passed since he set off from the beach.

Lamb was panting hard when they reached the copse and Stone, he thought, must be exhausted with the dead weight of Ayers across his shoulder.

'Let me spell you for a while, cox'n,' he suggested.

Stone gave a short glance at Lamb's thin frame and smiled grimly.

'Not to worry, sir, I can manage. I'll just put him over my other shoulder – a change is as good as a rest, they say, sir.'

Ayers suddenly spoke as Stone heaved his limp body across to his other shoulder.

'Apples, is it?' he said loudly. 'Yes, I'll give her bloody apples!' His voice tailed off into a mumble and then into a loud snore.

Stone chuckled. 'Sounds like he's having a fair old dream, sir.'

Once clear of the copse and on to the firm, downward slope to the beach, the going became much easier. As they neared the shingle bank a shout came up from the watching lookout and the men scrambled up and ran to meet them. Ayers was passed into the hands of two of them and the party crunched their way down the shingle to the boat. Smith made his way to Lamb's side and spoke to him as he watched Ayers being placed on the bottom boards of the cutter.

'We 'eard a shot, sir, maybe two. We didn't know whether or not you needed an 'and, sir. In two minds, we was, about stayin' 'ere or goin' to look for you, sir.'

Lamb inwardly shuddered. The thought of the men dispersed about the dark countryside, getting lost, blundering into armed troops, was enough to bring on a cold sweat.

'You had your orders,' he said curtly.

The tide was on the ebb but even so the trip back to the ship was hazardous. The cutter was rolled on to its side and swamped at the first attempt to launch it and Ayers' unconscious body had to be scrabbled for as it rolled to and fro in the hissing surf.

Bruised, exhausted and dripping water, Lamb was met at the side by Tyler as he dragged himself on board. The little lieutenant grinned as he surveyed Lamb's saturated clothing.

'Enjoy your run ashore?' he enquired brightly.

Dawn found the *Sturdy* sailing south by south-west, close-hauled under a strong westerly growing stronger by the hour. After reporting to the captain and handing over the packet, Lamb had spent a fitful couple of hours in his cot and was now on watch, his eyes gritty from lack of sleep and his stomach cramped for want of food.

Cutler appeared briefly on deck at first light and after surveying the grey, lumpy sea and the distant thickening of the horizon that was Portugal, had ordered the topsails to be double-reefed and the helm put over two points to starboard.

'The glass is falling, Mr Lamb,' he observed. 'We may well need a little sea-room.'

By the time Lamb was relieved for his breakfast the wind had increased noticeably and the frigate was rolling heavily and plunging fore and aft, burying her nose in the sea as the waves lifted her stern. Low, dirty clouds covered the sky, giving the water an ugly, metallic colour. When Lamb returned to the quarterdeck Cutler was standing by the weather rail. He saw that the courses had been furled, another reef taken in the topsails, and the topgallantsails, normally set after the hands had finished their breakfast, were still tightly rolled to the yard. He touched his hat to the captain and joined Tyler at the lee side.

'You took your time,' said Tyler, who had relieved Lamb for his breakfast. 'Did you have to wait while they killed and cured the pig?'

Cutler's voice stopped Lamb's indignant retort. 'Mr Tyler, before you go below be so good as to take the bo'sun and ensure that all is secure on deck. Pay particular heed to the boats.'

'Aye aye, sir,' said Tyler and sprang down the ladder to the maindeck, bawling for the boatswain.

'Mr Moriarty! Mr Moriarty!'

Lamb smiled to himself. Moriarty would undoubtedly be enjoying his leisurely breakfast at this time, ensconced in his snug little berth adjoining the cockpit, and would not take kindly to being rudely parted from his vittles. A law unto himself below decks, he was a man of considerable years and vast experience and was well-known for his irascibility before breakfast. Even lieutenants took care to treat him with rather more respect than his rank deserved. The hands, of course, shunned him as they would a madman with an axe. The cold eye of the boatswain was enough to make a man spring from his sick-bed and run up the shrouds like a young monkey, even if he was at death's door.

Lamb was aware of the captain standing beside him.

'The surgeon had a word a few minutes ago, Mr Lamb. You will be pleased to hear that Ayers is now conscious and apart from a monumental headache, seems to be no worse for his ordeal.'

'I am glad to hear it, sir,' said Lamb with sincerity, his mind's eye seeing again the coxswain standing wide-legged over Ayers with his cutlass upraised at the charging horseman. 'He and Stone are both very good men.'

'Yes, would that I had a hundred more like them. Their sort are the very backbone of the service, Mr Lamb, and it has long been my opinion that it is they, not the officers nor their captains, who make the navy what it is. Look at the French – excellent commanders, brave and resourceful men – but their seamen are something else entirely.'

'And long may they remain so, sir,' said Lamb.

Cutler laughed. 'Yes indeed, Mr Lamb.'

On the maindeck Lamb could see the first lieutenant, accompanied by the gunner and several hands, checking the lashings and wedges of the guns, and in the waist the boatswain and his mates were double-lashing the ship's boats nestling one inside the other. They were having difficulty in keeping their feet on the steeply rolling deck and a few minutes later Moriarty was supervising the rigging of lifelines between the forecastle and the quarterdeck. The day was becoming darker by the minute and as Lamb called to the duty midshipman to fetch him his tarpaulins from his cabin, the rain began to fall, huge, stinging drops sheeting across the deck and soaking him in

41

seconds. Unbidden, Watson appeared on deck with the captain's wet-weather gear and stood by with a helping hand, the rain bouncing from his bald head, as Cutler struggled into it.

Lamb pulled his sou'wester low down over his forehead. The rain was coming low across the deck hard with the wind, streaming off the naked backs of the hands as they doubled the breechings of the guns. The waves – driven by the wind with the full expanse of the North Atlantic behind it and little to check its progress other than the Azores – were now much steeper and the distance from crest to crest had grown considerably greater in the past hour. Lamb and Cutler, each to his own side of the quarterdeck, clung to the mizzen shrouds as the ship's roll increased, the heel of the deck showing a decided preference for the starboard side.

'Call the hands, Mr Lamb,' shouted Cutler. 'We are making too much leeway. Quartermaster, I want her as near the wind as she will go.'

The frigate did not give of her best when sailing close-hauled. In point of fact, with the wind in any quarter forward of her beam, her performance fell off considerably. Tyler, whose previous ship had been a frigate built by the French and who had been subsequently spoiled for British-built ships – 'cut off by the yard' he described them – had likened the *Sturdy*'s sailing qualities to those of a lead bucket, but he had taken care that Maxwell was not in earshot when he made the remark. Now, with the yards hauled round sharp, the frigate was within about six points of the wind. Cutler eyed the shivering maintopgallant mast and laid his hand on the quivering backstay.

'Ease her a trifle,' he called to the helmsmen. The wheel turned, the bow came away from the wind half a point and the trembling of the maintopgallant mast lessened. Satisfied, Cutler nodded to the quartermaster.

'Keep her so!' he shouted and stood watching the long, green, foam-streaked waves advancing on the starboard quarter.

Wind and weather worsened as the day wore on and when Lamb relieved Kennedy in the early evening he had to fight his way up a viciously dancing ladder to reach the quarterdeck, his body bent forward against the driving, horizontal rain.

Kennedy was delighted to see him. Rainwater streamed from their sou'westers as Lamb lowered his head a foot or so in order to bring his ear close to Kennedy's mouth. Normal handing-over of the watch went by the board as Kennedy bawled into Lamb's ear over the devilish noise of wind, rain, whistling rigging and crashing sea. No compass course, keep her close to the wind as she is – check guns and boats every two bells – the helmsmen are to be relieved every hour – keep one eye on Goodchild, he is almost certainly drunk – enjoy your watch!

Kennedy made his grateful way below and, left to himself, Lamb tightened his grip on the shrouds and lowered his head against the rain. The captain was a motionless, dark figure across the deck, huddled broodingly beneath the mizzen shrouds with one arm hooked through the ratlines. Lamb wondered whether he had been there all day. Three men were at the wheel and beside them stood Goodchild, the quarter-master, his knees flexing easily with the roll of the deck and his face turned forward, squinting against the rain. He did not appear to be the worse for drink, but then, Lamb reflected, he had been astonished before now at seamen's capacity for liquor and their amazing ability to conceal its effects in the face of authority. Drunk or not, Goodchild was a competent, reliable petty officer and provided that he managed to keep upright throughout his watch Lamb was not concerned, even if he was awash with rum. It was very often better for authority to see with one eye closed, he had long learned.

As it grew darker Maxwell came up on deck and joined Lamb on the lee of the quarterdeck, saying nothing by way of greeting and maintaining his silence throughout his stay. Lamb was not surprised; the first lieutenant had never shown any liking for small talk and would often sit through an entire meal in the gunroom without uttering a word.

Shortly after two bells, as Lamb was making his way back to the quarterdeck after checking on the security of the boats and guns, the foretopmast staysail blew into tatters and wrapped its sodden remnants around the bowsprit. Cutler ordered Max-well to leave it as it was – to have sent men to clear it would have been akin to murder in that weather. The parting of one of the mainmast mainstays, however, called for immediate action and Maxwell hurtled from the quarterdeck, bawling for the duty watch to rouse themselves and yelling for the boatswain. The mainstay, which ran from the maintop down to the bowsprit and served to discourage the mainmast from falling back into the arms of the mizzenmast, was a vital part of the standing rigging and even if the wind had been twice as strong and the waves twice as high, Cutler would not have hesitated to send men up to the top and into the plunging bows to replace it. It was a perilous business on this black, foul night and a very wet affair in the bow, but Maxwell was a very determined officer and the boatswain was a superb seaman, and in the end it was done, with little more injury than the odd fingernail lost and one or two distressed hernias.

During the last hour of the last dog-watch the wind eased and the rain finally ceased altogether. Cutler sent young Blissenden down with a message for his steward and presently Watson appeared on the quarterdeck with a mug of steaming coffee and a plate of ship's bread and cheese. Chewing busily, the captain wandered over to the wheel and peered in at the binnacle, then stood and frowned into the darkness, sipping at his coffee. Lamb could almost hear his thoughts: the number of hours on this heading since their last known position, their estimated rate of progress, a calculated guess at the leeway. It was a straightforward-enough little problem and as Tyler came up the ladder to relieve Lamb at the end of his watch, Cutler ordered the helm to be shifted two points to larboard.

The next morning, midway through his watch, Lamb saw the rising sun peep redly through the tail-end of the storm clouds to the east. The sea was much diminished from the afternoon before, although lumpy and sullen-looking, as if still sulking from its brief fit of bad temper. Forward, he could hear the boatswain's mates screaming in histrionic rage as they roused the men from their hammocks at the start of another day. Presently the deck was awash with water from the pump and busy with men kneeling behind their holystones under the watchful eyes of the boatswain's mates and the sleepy eyes of the duty midshipman.

Lamb paced slowly back and forth along the lee of the quarterdeck from the forward rail to the taffrail, turning on his heel at each end of his little walk, his hands behind his back and his head bowed as if deep in thought, occasionally raising it to

44

make sure that all was well with his watch. In truth, his thoughts went no deeper than those concerned with coffee and breakfast and the chances of finding clean linen when he went below, today being Tuesday and thus, according to his strict laundry schedule, the day for a clean shirt.

At seven bells the decks resounded to the noise of hundreds of feet as the men's hammocks, each neatly rolled and lashed and showing its number, were brought up on deck to be stowed in their nettings along the sides. The captain emerged from his quarters, nodded to his sentry, turned his face to the sky, sniffed the air, glanced at the sea and returned to his cabin. Lamb's stomach, anticipating breakfast within the half-hour, clamoured anew, while its owner, striving to ignore its insistent demands, took a deep breath, determined to drive all thoughts of hot coffee and bacon and fried biscuit from his mind and concentrate on thoughts of greater import. What should he ponder over? Sex? a voice murmured from a corner of his mind. He firmly rejected the suggestion; heavens, those thoughts were troublesome enough in the privacy of his cot! Their destination, perhaps? That would appear to be a subject that he could muse over without involving his gross, bodily urges. The captain had given no hint of where they were bound – Cadiz again, possibly, Lamb thought, or even Gibraltar. Let us say Gibraltar, then, and let us suppose that shore leave is granted. Hmm. What was it Kennedy had said about certain establishments in Gibraltar? At this point his mental defences crumpled under a sudden onslaught of gross thoughts, not at all connected with food. He stamped his foot on the deck in vexation at the weakness of mind over body and turned to see the smiling face of Tyler before him, eyebrows raised quizzically.

'Practising the quadrille, are we – or killing a few ants?' he enquired.

'Neither,' said Lamb loftily. 'If you must know, I was thinking of Gibraltar and its importance in terms of naval strategy.'

'Naval strategy, my arse!' retorted Tyler with a knowing grin. 'If you had said you were dreaming of cunt, I might have believed you.'

'How coarse you are, Tyler,' said Lamb with enormous dignity and went below for his breakfast.

45

Gibraltar it was and after Cutler's return from the Navy Office, shore leave was granted, watch and watch. The admiral, Cutler informed Lamb, was gratified to receive the packet of papers from Portugal and had no doubt but that its contents would prove of inestimable worth to the military intelligence service.

'How he divined this I do not know, seeing as the papers were penned in very small foreign script and the admiral is not only extremely near-sighted but also boasts of not speaking a word of anything but the King's English. Still, being nearer to God than we lesser mortals, he may have certain talents denied us. He asked particularly that his best wishes be given to you for a task well done. Moreover, he invites the officers of the *Sturdy* to a grand supper tonight, in honour of his birthday, an invitation which I have gratefully accepted on behalf of you all.'

Bathed, shaved to a tender pink and turned out in their best uniforms, the officers and midshipmen of the *Sturdy* stood stiffly in a small group of other naval officers in one corner of the admiral's large drawing room and sipped dry sherry from exceedingly small glasses. The admiral had never been very lucky in the way of prize money as a seagoing officer but he had married well – if money be the sole consideration. Lamb studied the admiral's lady as she giggled and simpered among a handful of senior military officers at the far side of the room. To be fat, mused Lamb, is unfortunate for a woman; to be ugly is a decided drawback; to suffer a combination of both qualities in such high degree suggests downright divine cruelty.

There were perhaps thirty officers from both arms of the services and half as many ladies in the room. The plain blue and white of the navy contrasted soberly with the bright scarlet and gold of the army, the difference heightened by the variety of luxuriant hirsute growths the soldiers sported, adornments which were denied to the traditionally clean-shaven navy. To Lamb's eyes, after so long in exclusively masculine company, the women were a delight, visions in pastel-coloured silk and taffeta and sparkling stones on white flesh; and above all, their eyes, flashing, pensive, darting, missing nothing and nobody, and their graceful, deeply interesting curves of body. A young creature in pale blue drifted past, her low-scooped French inspiration such that he glimpsed the dark rims of her aureoles.

Lamb's heart increased its tempo considerably and in an effort to drag his gaze from those tantalizing half-globes he unthinkingly drained his glass. Tyler nudged him with his elbow.

'Did you catch that glimpse of heaven then?' he whispered. 'My God, such playthings!'

'Oh?' said Lamb, affecting to be puzzled. 'I noticed nothing.'

'Liar!'

The admiral, a tall dark bear of a man, was standing with one hand resting on the marble mantel, talking animatedly to an attentive Cutler. Presently, both men threw back their heads and laughed loudly. The admiral took Cutler by the arm in friendly fashion and headed across the room to the *Sturdy*'s officers. Ignoring the midshipmen, to their great relief, Cutler introduced each of his lieutenants in order of seniority.

'I am pleased to make your acquaintance, Lamb,' said the admiral genially. 'Your little jaunt very nearly went badly wrong, I hear. It would have been extremely embarrassing for Captain Cutler here if it had, would it not, John, eh?' nudging Cutler and thus asserting that he, the admiral, would not have borne any share of the responsibility in the event of such a disaster. Cutler smiled dutifully.

'All's well that ends well, sir, especially when helped by a little luck and a good deal of determination.'

'My sentiments exactly, John, and I repeat my earlier comments. Well done, Mr Lamb, well done indeed.'

Lamb bowed. 'Thank you, sir.'

Supper was a formal affair, taken seated. The dining room was large, but with two long tables, twelve places to a side, very little room between each and a dozen liveried servants, it was cramped for space. Lamb searched for his place-name and found he was seated between an engineer captain and a lady of indeterminate years dressed in pale green. He noticed that Tyler, the lucky hound, was seated next to the young lady in revealing blue.

The captain tucked in his napkin and turned his heavy sidewhiskers in Lamb's direction.

'What ship are you from?' he barked.

'The *Sturdy*, sir.'

'*Sturdy*? Oh, yes, the frigate at the mole. Good, good.'

Satisfied that he had done his duty as a table companion on that side, he turned to his neighbour in scarlet and commenced a conversation that continued without another word for Lamb for the duration of the meal.

A white-gloved hand came over Lamb's shoulder and ladled a little green soup into his plate. He tasted it cautiously; pea, he thought, with just a hint of bacon. It was almost warm.

'The admiral's suppers are such sorry affairs,' said a soft voice in his ear. 'He is such a skinflint that I usually leave as hungry as when I arrive.'

Lamb turned his head and met the gaze of a pair of smiling, blue-green eyes. Her hair was dark, parted in the centre and worked into long, spring-like curls that fell to her shoulders. Small laughter lines etched the corners of her eyes. Her gaze was warm.

Lamb was immediately entranced. He groped for an appropriate answer and could think of nothing.

'Oh, yes?' he said, for want of anything more intelligent, feeling his cheeks begin to glow.

Yes. The admiral was a very jovial man but he was renowned for his meanness. Of course, it was well known that his wife ruled him with a rod of iron and no doubt she had much to do with the household purse-strings and the supper arrangements, but even so, a man was master in his own house, was he not, and it did his reputation no good to be such a miserly host.

'No, I am sure you are right, ma'am,' said Lamb, thinking that he must appear a dull dolt and frantically searching his mind for some bright witticism that would hold her attention. It was not at all necessary; the lady loved a good listener.

She was Mrs Anne Marsden, Lamb learned, wife of Major Marsden, an artilleryman now in St Lucia in the West Indies for an indefinite period. She wished now that she could have persuaded him to take her with him but he had been adamant that the air in those islands was so fever-ridden that he would not take the risk, but, oh, life on this rock was so tedious and tiresome with few ladies of her own class and most of them here tonight. Social evenings such as this, poor affairs that they were, were too rare – she had not caught his name?

'Lieutenant Lamb, ma'am.'

'Oh, quite the poet!' she smiled. 'But were you not christened, Mr Lamb?'

'Your pardon, ma'am. Matthew.'

'I am very pleased to have made your acquaintance, Lieutenant Matthew Lamb,' she said, with a little above-the-waist parody of a curtsey.

'The honour is all mine, Mrs Marsden,' returned Lamb gravely, with a similar diminished bow.

She tinkled merrily and drained her wine glass, not for the first time, Lamb noted. He refilled it for her and did so several more times as she chattered busily through the scanty turbot and the sinewy lamb. By the time the pudding was served, a wet, strawberry concoction, her leg was pressed warmly and firmly against his, to his unutterable delight and some discomfort in his breeches.

She lived at the Villa Rosa, a little red-bricked house not far from the harbour, such a tiny little house but with only her and her old Spanish maid it often felt too large. He must come and admire her garden – it was only a short step from the mole – she worked so hard there, passing the long hours.

The admiral's birthday was warmly toasted, he made a little speech riddled with unnatural modesty, and the ladies retired to the drawing room. They were not left unattended for long – the admiral's suggestion that the men join them after the port had circulated but twice smacked of prior spousely instruction.

Card tables were set up but Lamb, who was an indifferent player and, in any case, had never seen much attraction in card games, begged to be excused. His absence from the tables was not missed – there were more would-be players than there were places. He wandered casually about the room, observing the excited play and smiling as Kennedy made an optimistic and ultimately disastrous bid, briefly joined the small group of officers clustered around Miss Blue-dress and a friend, where he received a conspiratorial wink from Tyler, leaning with some advantage over the lady's chair, and finally halted beside Mrs Marsden, apparently deeply engrossed in the conversation of the two mature ladies seated near her.

She glanced up, seemingly a little surprised at his appearance beside her.

'Oh, you are not playing then, Mr Lamb?'

'Nor you, I see,' said Lamb playfully.

'Well, to be candid, I feel just the tiniest bit indisposed.' She

49

put a hand to her temple and puckered her forehead. 'I have the sharpest pain here – I am sure it was the wine. I felt from the first sip that it was not a healthy vintage and I am grateful now that I took so little of it.'

'I am very sorry for you, ma'am,' said Lamb, rather more sorry for himself as certain ambitions faded sharply. He bowed, preparatory to withdrawing. She held up a slim hand, halting him.

'I am leaving very shortly and I will bid you goodbye now. I feel a slow walk home in the cool air will be sufficient cure for my poor head.'

Lamb bowed again. 'Goodbye then, Mrs Marsden. I trust your indisposition will be a short one.'

'Oh, I am sure it will be. Is it very dark out, have you noticed? I am such a silly creature, so nervous in the dark.'

'I shall be more than happy to escort you home, ma'am,' said Lamb, his dashed hopes suddenly reasserting themselves.

No, no, she would not hear of it, to drag him from his friends just because of her silly fears. She would be perfectly safe, she was sure, once she was past that horribly sinister grove of trees which she was quite certain was haunted. Well, if he was absolutely sure? He was very kind. She would just find her wrap and make her excuses – she would not be a moment.

Lamb made his way through the card tables to Cutler, who was busily engaged in conversation with a colonel who was minus one ear, and waited in silence until he caught the captain's eye.

'Yes, Mr Lamb, what is it?' asked Cutler, a trifle tetchily.

Lamb leaned close and gave his reasons for leaving in a low voice, somewhat over-stressing the lady's indisposition and fear of the dark. Cutler looked at him coldly for a few seconds and then nodded abruptly.

'Very well. I shall make your excuses for you. Be on board by first light at the latest.'

The night was indeed dark, so dark as to make her cling tightly and nervously to his arm as they passed the sinister grove of several stunted trees. The descent was steep and the road badly paved, obliging her to press very close to him for fear of falling. The scent of her perfume was very strong and the grip of her hand on his arm very tight; Lamb's heart soared.

The door to the Villa Rosa was opened by an ancient, toothless Spanish woman who fixed Lamb with a dark frown of immediate hatred. Mrs Marsden stepped across the threshold and turned to smile brightly at Lamb.

'You were so kind to see me safely home, Mr Lamb,' she said sweetly. 'Thank you so much. Goodnight.'

The crone closed the door in Lamb's face, the sound of the bolts slamming home reinforcing the finality of its closure. Lamb stared at the blistered paintwork for several long seconds in stunned amazement, as if unwilling to accept the evidence of his eyes and ears. He breathed a single word with some feeling and turning away from the door, walked back along the path to the road. As he passed the gatepost he gave it a cruel kick and then made his painful, hobbling way to the mole.

Chapter 3

For several days the winds had been light and capricious as the *Sturdy* inched her way southwards with royal topgallantsails and studdingsails set for every minute of the daylight hours. Gibraltar lay many watches astern; over the larboard beam, below the hard-edged horizon, lay the westernmost point of the great bulge of Africa. Many more days ahead lay Cape Town, a recent British acquisition won by Sir George Elphinstone and General Craig and which, together with nearby Simon's Bay, was becoming of growing importance to the Royal Navy, the merchant service and the City of London. It would provide a brief revictualling stop for the frigate in preparation for her long haul across the Indian Ocean; French privateers were roaming free in the Bay of Bengal and playing havoc with the ships and profits of British merchants and the Admiralty had at last been prodded into flexing a tiny muscle in that direction while its main strength was concentrated around Europe and the Channel.

Lamb left the gunroom and made for his stuffy little cell of a cabin, wiping the greasy residue of his breakfast from his lips with the back of his hand. His plans for the next couple of hours were simple; a shave, a change of linen and an hour or so of quiet meditation in the cool isolation of the mainmast cross-trees. There was to be no gun practice today; Maxwell had persuaded the captain to forgo the daily exercise in order that another application of black paint could be added to the many thicknesses of paint already on the guns. Alternate guns on each side would be painted today, the remainder tomorrow – wet, sticky guns would be a hazard if they were to be needed suddenly and the frigate must remain at least half operational as a man-of-war, in spite of Maxwell's zeal for fresh, shining paintwork.

The sound of muffled sobbing caught Lamb's ear as he reached his cabin door. It came from the direction of the cockpit where the midshipmen were berthed. He hesitated, uncertain as to whether or not he should investigate – tears were not uncommon in young midshipmen, as Lamb knew from bitter experience. The sound came again, louder but quickly stifled, the pitiful noise striking a chord in Lamb's memory of his own none-too-happy days in the cockpit. He turned reluctantly from his door and walked forward, to put his head round the half-open door of the cockpit. Blissenden, the youngest of the four midshipmen, undersized even for his scant twelve years, was on his knees in front of his open chest sorting through a little pile of ink-stained, dog-eared exercise books, his small body shuddering from his sobs. Lamb felt a surge of compassion for the boy. He pushed open the door and stepped into the cockpit.

'Hallo, young Blissenden. What's all this, then?'

The midshipman turned his head with a start and scrambled to his feet, wiping his tear-stained cheeks with his sleeve. There was a dark swelling on his cheekbone and a smear of blood at the corner of his mouth.

'Nothing, sir – really, sir, nothing.'

'Hmm,' grunted Lamb suspiciously, eyeing the lad with disbelief. It was quite obvious that the child had been the victim of some heavy-handed bullying and he had a fairly shrewd idea of the identity of the perpetrator. The low-browed, ape-like Cowan was senior midshipman and even if he had not been directly responsible for this physical abuse it could hardly have taken place without his knowledge and connivance. However, there was little Lamb could do about it – the boy must learn to take the hard and often unfair knocks of his calling, as had Lamb in his time, and would eventually grow up tougher and harder because of it. Lamb hoped that Blissenden's present unhappiness was the result of too-vigorous horseplay and not that of someone's sadistic, incessant attention.

'Right,' said Lamb, jerking his head at the door behind him, 'you had better take your books and cut along or you'll be in trouble with Mr Doubleday.'

'Aye aye, sir,' snuffled Blissenden, giving his damp eyes another hasty wipe with his sleeve, and picking up his books he sidled past Lamb and made a dash for the aft companionway.

53

Lamb cast his eyes around the cockpit, breathing the never-forgotten smell of damp clothing, lamp-oil, tallow, ink, blacking, mildewed books and spilled rum suffused into an amalgam that was the essence of all midshipmen's berths. The room was geometrically neat and very clean, as was to be expected when midshipmen shared their quarters with two warrant officers, men who had risen from the forecastle where the habits of spartan cleanliness had been etched deep into them. Lamb dropped the lid of Blissenden's chest and left the cockpit, closing the door behind him. He made his way aft to his own berth, rubbing his hand over his early-morning bristles. He must keep an eye on Cowan and Blissenden, he decided; if he detected any signs of malicious cruelty – or worse, heaven forbid – he could, at the least, discreetly bring the pressure of his authority to bear.

Clad in shirt and breeches, Lamb pulled himself up and over the maintopgallant yard. Admunssen, a quiet man with few words of English, smiled shyly with downcast eyes and made way for Lamb as he lowered himself to squat with his back to the mast and one arm hooked comfortably through the yard's sling. The lower deck was a hotchpotch of different nationalities; Admunssen was one of several Swedes and Norwegians in the ship's crew, in addition to Germans, Hollanders, Poles and a couple of men who claimed to be Americans – but then there were few Britons taken from American ships under the rights of the Navigation Acts who did not claim to be Americans.

The mast performed a lazy dance in the gentle air and above his head the royal bellied and sagged. Looking down, his view of the deck was restricted by the intervening canvas and maintop to a small portion amidships, much of which was taken up the ship's boats. The faint drone of the master's voice, the words indistinguishable at this height, drifted up from where the midshipmen squatted by the larboard rail, heads bent over their slates as they frowned over the complexities of nautical trigonometry. Lamb smiled. It did not seem so long ago since he, too, had sat staring in bewilderment at his slate, certain that he could never master the mysteries scratched on it and praying that the master would not select him to explain the relationship of the angles of a right-angled triangle to its hypotenuse. Lamb had continued to be baffled by much of the esoterics of mathematics, often to the rage and disgust of the several masters and captains who had tried to improve him and even now his skill as a navigator could at best be described as something short of adequate. His very real sympathy for the suffering young gentlemen below was more than outweighed by the relief at the knowledge that such torments were behind him – his commission was a licence to forget.

Lamb tugged his telescope from his belt and put it to his eye. First, he scanned the sea to starboard where, far to the west below the horizon, lay the Cape Verde Islands; then, traversing forward, he brought the instrument round to the other side of the ship and performed the same slow search. Nothing; not even a porpoise or flying fish disturbed the deep blue, slow undulation of the silky surface. He sighed slightly and leaned his head back against the mast with closed eyes, lifting his face to the heat of the sun. His mind went back, as it often had in the past weeks, to Mrs Marsden, and he grimaced again as he recalled the cool way in which she had dismissed him at her door. At breakfast the next morning he had been the subject of much droll comment, ranging from Kennedy's dry non sequiturs to Tyler's more direct and earthier comments. He had not disabused them of their assumptions – in a way, their clear envy had acted as a balm to his suffering ego – and he had responded to their teasing by saying nothing and donning an air of quiet smugness. Tyler, however, was one of those men who liked to wring every last drop out of a good thing and over the past weeks Lamb had found his constant harking on the supposed night of passion increasingly irksome. This very morning Tyler had been particularly playful, launching into a story immediately on relieving Lamb about an acquaintance of his midshipman days who had enraged a lady's husband to the point where it ended in a duel.

'So, they march out their ten paces, turn and level their pistols. My friend, feeling more than a little guilty about the whole affair, deliberately aims wide and fires. The husband, however, has other ideas and takes careful aim at young Romeo's groin, fires and hits him dead centre, neatly removing one of his balls and near killing him into the bargain. What you might call poetic justice – and almost an eye for an eye, eh?'

He dug Lamb in the ribs and laughed exorbitantly.

'Interesting,' said Lamb coldly when Tyler had finished wheezing. 'Was there some point to this story that I might have missed?'

'No, no,' said Tyler airily. 'It happened to come to mind when I was having breakfast and I thought it might interest you.'

'Well, it didn't,' snapped Lamb and stalked from the quarterdeck.

He regretted his sharp answer now – Tyler would be certain to think he had struck home and would no doubt be bringing infidelity and cuckolds into the gunroom conversation at every opportunity over the next week or so until he tired of it and started on a new tack. Ah, well, thought Lamb resignedly, the Tylers of this world are a small cross to bear if it is the price we Lotharios must pay for giving so many women so much pleasure! The thought tickled his imagination and he chuckled aloud, quickly stifling his noise when he realized the astonished eye of the lookout would be upon him.

He wriggled his back into a more comfortable position against the mast and gave a little grunt of contentment. He had been awake since four o'clock and the sun was warm; he felt himself slipping into a doze as his thoughts began to drift and he shook his head and opened his eyes wide. It would not do to fall asleep in this precarious position. Perhaps he would be better employed in going down to his cabin and adding another page or two to the letter he had started to his father a week ago, but there was little in the way of news he could add to it; or he could borrow a book from the surgeon – he must have a good stock of them, his nose was seldom out of one. He considered the idea for a few lazy moments and then swung resolutely into the rigging; a book it would be and maybe he could persuade Surbrown to make a pot of his abominable coffee to go with it.

It was nearly noon. Maxwell, Kennedy, Lamb and the master stood by the taffrail with sextants in hand waiting for the captain to make his appearance.

'What does it say, Mr Doubleday?' asked Maxwell in his hard, harsh voice.

The master glanced at the chronometer in its case. 'It wants but three minutes to the hour, sir.'

Maxwell tightened his lips in exasperation and screwing up one eye, looked briefly at the sun. Lamb followed his example; the ship had sailed due south since yesterday's noon sighting and if she had made no leeway to east or west the sun's highest altitude should coincide fairly closely with the same time today.

The first lieutenant swung round to the duty midshipman. 'My respects to the captain, Mr Cowan, and it wants but three minutes to noon.'

The midshipman darted off and Maxwell resumed his anxious pacing.

'One minute to go, sir,' warned Doubleday.

'Very well,' said Maxwell. 'We won't wait. Carry on.'

The captain mounted the quarterdeck as the master was calculating his latitude on the ebony bar of his quadrant.

'My apologies, Mr Maxwell,' said Cutler. 'I was detained on other duties.'

A certain inflexion in Cutler's voice caused Lamb to give him a curious glance. His face was flushed and he held himself with a stiff, backward slope to his spine as if he was in danger of falling forward. Lord, the man is drunk! thought Lamb, surprised and amused.

Doubleday stepped over to Tyler, the officer of the watch, and read off his pencilled calculations.

'Twelve o'clock, sir, at fourteen degrees, eleven minutes north exactly.'

'Thank you, Mr Doubleday,' said Tyler formally. He turned and walked the three paces to where the captain stood beside the binnacle.

'Twelve o'clock, sir, at fourteen degrees, eleven minutes north exactly.'

'Very good,' said Cutler thickly, squinting slightly. 'Make it twelve.'

'Aye aye, sir,' said Tyler and turning to the quartermaster, sang out: 'Strike eight bells!'

'Turn the glass and strike the bell!' roared the quartermaster to the sentry at the cabin door.

'Pipe to dinner!' bellowed Tyler as the first stroke of the bell sounded. The boatswain's pipe shrilled, the ship's bell continued to sound, the deck thundered to the noise of eager feet and the cook began to roar the numbers of the messes as he gave

57

his tubs a final stir.

Cutler beamed in friendly fashion at his group of officers and descended the ladder to enter his quarters. Maxwell stared thoughtfully at his retreating back and turned in time to see Kennedy raise a quizzical eyebrow at Lamb and close his eye in a meaningful wink.

'Save your grimaces for the gunroom, Mr Kennedy,' he snapped. 'They are out of place on the quarterdeck.'

'Yes, sir. Sorry, sir,' said Kennedy cheerfully, not a whit abashed.

Drunk at noon or not, the captain was his usual quiet, alert self at the start of the first dog-watch, when the ship beat to quarters. Lamb, taking over the watch, gave him a sly glance but could see nothing in his demeanour to suggest that he had been the worse for drink earlier. In the gunroom after dinner, when Maxwell had departed, Tyler had been quite adamant that the captain was in liquor and was vastly amused at the thought of it, but looking at Cutler now, standing still and straight as the hands assembled in their watches and divisions, his face as composed and expressionless as ever, Lamb was not so sure.

The *Sturdy* made her slow way south, life on board settled into the unvarying routine followed in much the same way by all King's ships around the globe, from the ritual cleaning of the decks by men tumbled warm and frowsty from their hammocks to the beating of retreat at the end of the last dog-watch. In between these daily limits came other landmarks, the chief of which were the noon sighting, the hands' dinner and their midday issue of grog; on one side or the other of these, and often on both, came the exercising of the guns and spar- and sail-handling practice. Squeezed into the remaining few intervals came the domestic business of the ship: the shifting of stores, the maintenance of sails and rigging, the renewal of paintwork, the chipping and cleaning of roundshot, perhaps the condemnation and discarding of a cask of beef too rotten even for the purser to declare it wholesome. Time had also to be found, once or twice a week according to the length of Maxwell's list, for the hands to assemble aft to witness punishment.

The *Sturdy*'s hands, remarkably, were a law-abiding lot on the whole, apart from the inevitable cases of drunkenness.

These, because there had so far been no insolence accompanying the offence, had invariably been dealt with by curtailment of the sinner's grog entitlement. Occasionally, a man was charged with idleness on duty or with being slow to report on watch or similar crimes, nothing very heinous but which nevertheless called for a stern lecture from the captain and the imposition of extra duties.

Today, at six bells in the forenoon watch, the boatswain piped the hands aft to witness punishment. The hands were well aware of the nature of the main charge to be heard this morning and there was a rush for the places where the evidence could be clearly heard. Armed Marines stood on the quarterdeck facing aft; at the foot of the quarterdeck ladder the lieutenants, dressed in full uniform complete with swords, gathered with the midshipmen, the purser and the surgeon; on the quarterdeck the captain and the first lieutenant awaited the arrival of the accused, brought from below in the company of the master-at-arms and an escort of Marines.

The master-at-arms, a corpulent, heavy-featured man named Rolf, much detested by the hands, strode forward through the press of men followed by the two accused men and the Marines. The group halted in front of the quarterdeck ladder; the master-at-arms placed his cane beneath his left armpit and waited for Cutler to start the proceedings.

The two seamen between their red-coated escorts were pale-faced and clearly very nervous. Lamb noticed that one of them, Lloyd, had a dark swelling over his right eye and his lips were bruised and puffy. Wantage, the other, was a good deal older than Lloyd with a long, narrow face and heavy eyebrows that merged above his nose. His tongue constantly flickered about his lips.

'What are the charges, master-at-arms?' asked Cutler.

'Conduct contravening Article Twenty-Nine, sir,' said Rolf in a loud, hard voice.

A low buzz of excited sound came from the watching men. Maxwell took a step forward, his face dark with anger.

'Silence on deck!' he bellowed. 'The next man to open his mouth will have me to answer to.'

The silence was instant and total but the excitement which had brought on the outburst continued to manifest itself by way

59

of nods and winks and meaningful nudges. The hands had listened to the captain reciting the Articles of War on many a Sunday morning and Article Twenty-Nine was as familiar to them as the Lord's Prayer in which they joined two Sundays out of four. The Article dealt with the crime of sodomy, promising death to any man found guilty of it. The hands knew well that if the captain deemed there was sufficient evidence of guilt then a court martial would be convened as soon as a sufficient number of post-captains could be gathered in one place, and a hanging would almost inevitably follow.

The master-at-arms gave his evidence; his voice was slow and deliberate and clearly heard by every man on the deck.

'Last night, sir, just after two bells in the first watch, I was in the course of my duties, making my evening rounds, when I was approached by a certain man who informed me he suspected that criminal activities were taking place in the cable-tiers, sir.'

Cutler did not ask for the identity of the 'certain man' nor did he expect the master-at-arms to volunteer it. He would be, as every man knew, one of Rolf's narks, a petty informer who delighted, for obscure reasons of his own, in bringing to the master-at-arms' attention minor breaches of Admiralty regulations or ship's standing orders. In a crew of over two hundred seamen and Marines there would always be one or two of these miserable creatures, nurtured with a few shillings and small favours by the master-at-arms but heartily detested by officers and men alike.

'I proceeded to the cable-tiers without delay, sir, and there I found the two accused men engaged in certain activities, sir. I immediately placed them in irons and informed the first lieutenant, sir.'

'And the nature of these activities you witnessed, Mr Rolf?' asked Cutler.

'One of the men, Lloyd, was in a state of near nakedness, sir. The other, Wantage, had his arm around Lloyd's shoulders, embracing him, like, sir.'

'That's a filthy lie!' Wantage took a pace forward, his eyes blazing with anger. 'He's lying, sir – I wasn't doing nothing of the sort!'

'Hold your tongue!' snapped Cutler. 'You will get your chance to speak later. Carry on, Mr Rolf.'

'That is all there is, really, sir. As I say, I then arrested them and placed them in irons.'

'I see. Were there any other witnesses, apart from yourself, to what you saw?'

'Yes, sir, Millington, sir, ship's corporal. I ordered him to accompany me when I went to investigate, sir.'

'Step forward, Millington.'

Millington, a member of the afterguard when on watch and a ship's corporal during the dark hours, shambled forward to stand beside the master-at-arms. A large, low-browed, untidy-faced man, he received a few extra shillings for his policing duties and enjoyed much the same degree of popularity amongst the hands as was accorded to Rolf. His account of what he had seen tallied closely with that of the master-at-arms; but then, thought Lamb, watching him closely as he spoke, it would be surprising if he'd said otherwise, being in Rolf's pocket, as it were.

Cutler frowned. 'Millington,' he said slowly, staring keenly at the man's face, 'think carefully before you answer. Did you actually see sodomy taking place? Were the men's organs or buttocks exposed?'

Millington knitted his brow and glanced nervously at the master-at-arms before he spoke.

'Well, no, sir, not actually taking place, sir. As for organs and – and buttocks, I can't actually recall seeing any, sir, but the light warn't none too good and it wouldn't 've taken 'em a second to pull their trousis up, sir. What I'm saying is, sir, it was obvious to me and Mr Rolf what was going on there, sir, being undressed and hugging each other, like. We didn't need no pictures drawed, sir.'

'Perhaps not,' said Cutler. 'Mr Rolf, do you bear out what Millington has just said – that sodomy was not actually being committed?'

Rolf hastily removed his baleful glare from the ship's corporal.

'Not as such, sir, no, the act itself, that is, but I am quite convinced –'

Cutler cut him short. 'Just bear in mind before you go any further, Mr Rolf, that it will not take the surgeon more than a few minutes to determine whether or not the act took place.

Now, do we have to go that far?'

The master-at-arms took a deep breath and tightened his grip on his cane. 'Perhaps not, sir,' he admitted. 'But he couldn't prove the act had not been attempted, in any case, sir, could he?' he added craftily.

Cutler gave him a cold look. 'That is not for you to say, Mr Rolf. Very well, on your own admission, then, what we have here is not a charge of sodomy but one of attempted sodomy. It is still a very serious charge. Thank you, Mr Rolf.' He directed his gaze at Wantage. 'Right, Wantage, now is your chance to speak. What have you to say?'

Wantage may have had a mean, unprepossessing face but he did not lack courage. He turned his head and looked the master-at-arms squarely in the face before turning his eyes back to the captain.

'He's lying, sir. We weren't embracing, like he said. I don't go for that sort of carry-on – it turns my stomach as much as the next man's, sir. Lloyd had just taken a tumble and near knocked hisself silly, as you can see from the marks on his face, sir. I'd just picked him up and was sort of supporting him, like.'

Cutler glanced briefly at Lloyd's pale face. 'I see. What were you doing in the cable-tiers at that time of day, then?'

'Catching rats, sir,' said Wantage.

Cutler nodded slowly. 'Catching rats, eh? And Lloyd, he had to get undressed to catch rats?'

'He weren't undressed, sir, leastways, only his shirt, like, to catch the rats in.'

'Well, what have you to say, Lloyd?' asked Cutler, turning his attention to that terrified seaman, whose eyes had been switching nervously between Wantage and the captain as they spoke. 'Is this business of rat-catching the truth?'

Lloyd nodded his head rapidly. 'Oh, yes, sir, that's all we was doing, sir, catching rats, sir.'

Cutler took a slow pace or two along the front of the quarterdeck, his hands behind his back and his head bowed as if in deep thought. Lamb wondered whether the captain was playing the actor – he suspected that Cutler had made up his mind already about the action he would take and this impression of slow and careful consideration was a dramatic touch entirely for the benefit of the crew. Lamb had no doubts himself about the truth of the men's story – rat-catching was a popular sport on a man-of-war and the little animals, alive or dead, could be put to all sorts of uses. It was true that he had never eaten a rat himself but he had known many men and boys who swore that a fat, bread-fed rat was a tasty delicacy. Their skins were not wasted, either; half a dozen such would make a warm, waterproof fur cap or, in the hands of a clever needleman, a splendid pair of gloves. Alive, the rats could be put to more sporting purposes such as rat-baiting, in which the terrier was replaced by a kneeling man with his hands bound behind his back, with only his teeth and the quickness of his head set against the viciousness of the rats. A dangerous game, this – Lamb had seen men with fearful bites on their faces and necks as a result of such an evening's illegal sport. A less dangerous but no less illegal variation was the rat version of the cockfight, although rats were not so instantly aggressive as cock-birds and had to be prodded and goaded into the attack. A very popular sport, this one, with much money or the promises of money changing hands. Seamen were inveterate gamblers and Lamb had known of a whole year's future pay riding on the back of a likely-looking fighting rat.

Cutler stopped his careful pacing and turned to face the accused men.

'I have given deep thought to what I have heard. The first thing I must say to you two is that I do not care to hear my master-at-arms being called a liar to his face in my hearing. The evidence he gave, supported by the corporal, differs in very little respects from your own testimony. Mr Rolf drew certain conclusions from what he saw and in my opinion, those conclusions were not unreasonable.'

He paused. The silence from the attentive audience was intense as the men hung on his every word.

'However, the charge of attempted sodomy cannot be upheld, in spite of that. Conclusions alone are not sufficient and without further evidence I am not prepared to commit you two men to trial by court martial. Nevertheless, from what the master-at-arms has said, you both came close to brushing with Article Twenty-Nine, on the face of it; if your own story of rat-catching is true, then on your own admission you were in a place which is forbidden to you, for purposes which would

63

almost certainly have resulted in illegal sport – I did not miss the point that you were catching the rats alive. Punishment is certainly called for.'

He glanced at his small group of officers.

'Is there any officer willing to speak for these men before I announce punishment?'

Tyler and Lamb stepped forward half a pace and touched their hats. Both had known they might be called upon and their little speeches had been carefully rehearsed and polished.

'Yes, Mr Tyler,' said Cutler.

'Wantage is in my division, sir. He is a first-class fo'c'sle man and has always been willing and courteous, sir.'

'Thank you, Mr Tyler. Mr Lamb?'

'Lloyd is in my division, sir. He has always performed his duties cheerfully and well, sir, and is in training to be a topman. I would also like to remind you, sir, that he is a volunteer and not a pressed man.'

'Thank you, Mr Lamb. Now, you two; your officers have spoken well of you and I take that into account. You will each receive six lashes. Quartermaster, seize them up!'

There was no need for further orders; the ritual was long established and the participants knew their parts well. The carpenter and his mates ran to the nearest hatch on hearing Cutler's last words and carried a grating to the break of the quarterdeck, scattering seamen left and right. The quarter-master advanced on the prisoners, pulling short lengths of cord ready prepared for their purpose from his pocket as the miscreants, set-faced, began to remove their shirts. In a trice, Wantage was bound to the upright grating by his outspread arms and Regan, a square-built boatswain's mate, was tenderly removing the cat-o'-nine-tails from its red baize bag.

Wantage took his half-dozen well. Apart from an involuntary grunt as the first blow knocked the breath from his lungs he made no sound. Once cut down, he draped his shirt over his weal-ridden back, gave Regan a polite nod and walked quickly forward. Lloyd, younger and without Wantage's hard, extra years to stiffen him, was whimpering in fright before the first blow, screaming in pain from the second and sagging from his wrists at the sixth. As he was cut loose from the grating he fell to his knees and then rolled over on to his side. The surgeon knelt beside him and Maxwell walked over to stare at the limp figure with a look of disgust on his face.

'Leave him be, Mr Meadows,' he growled. 'A bucket of sea water over him is all he needs, the spineless bugger.' He crooked a finger at a couple of nearby seamen. 'Get this mess off the deck and below, out of my sight.'

Maxwell's feelings were plainly shared by the watching seamen. They had witnessed Lloyd's performance with something close to embarrassment and heads had been shaken in disbelief that a mere six lashes could produce such a song and dance. The older hands, not unused to seeing a man's back cut to butcher's meat by many times six lashes, eyed Lloyd sadly as he was half-carried, half-dragged away forward. What was the service coming to when a well-fed lad couldn't take his half-dozen and walk away whistling?

Lamb was surprised and disturbed by the sentence – he was familiar with the spectacle of the grating and the lash and it no longer affected him as it had when he was a very young midshipman, but in this case he was convinced that the captain's verdict was unfair and unjust, a point he later made with some heat as the officers took their midday meal.

'Well,' Tyler was saying as Lamb took his place at the table. 'I've often wondered whether our dear captain was a flogger. It seems he is – but only just. On my last ship it was a rare day when we didn't hear the cat whistling – the captain thought a touch of the lash did the men more good than all the physic in the surgeon's chest could. That was Sandy Shore – you knew him, did you not, Sam?'

'Aye, I did,' replied Doubleday. 'He put up his blue flag last year, you know. I knew him before he made post. I never liked him then and I doubt if I would like him now. He was one of those who got pleasure from watching men bleed. No, I prefer John Cutler's way – let the men know you are prepared to use the cat when it is necessary but until then keep it in its bag.'

Lamb looked up from his plate. 'And you think it was necessary today, then?' he asked.

The other officers looked at him in surprise, startled by his earnest tone.

'Aye, of course it was,' growled Doubleday. 'Don't you think so?'

'No, I do not.'

Maxwell put down his glass and gave Lamb a cold stare. 'Why not?'

Lamb laid down his knife and ticked off the points on his outstretched fingers. One, the story the two men gave clearly rang true. Two, the master-at-arms and his weasel of a corporal were not above stretching the truth in order to press their case. Three, the captain had found the charge unproven and that being the case, then, four, the men were flogged for mere rat-hunting, a punishment which far exceeded the crime. He sat back in his chair, feeling flushed and conscious that he had sounded pompous and over-earnest.

'He rests his case, m'lud,' intoned Tyler from the end of the table.

Maxwell gave Lamb a hard, narrow-eyed look. 'You are not squeamish, are you, Lamb?' he asked. 'Did the sight of a few bloody weals upset you?'

'You miss my point entirely,' said Lamb heatedly. 'Six lashes or a hundred – I have seen too many to be bothered by the sight. No, the essence of my argument is that if the men were clearly innocent of sodomy or unnatural behaviour and that was accepted by the captain, then by imposing punishment, especially of that nature, he was not only being heavy-handed, he was being unjust.'

Maxwell leaned forward over the table and pointed his raised forefinger at Lamb. His voice was hard. 'It seems to me you miss the greater point. On this ship, on any ship in the King's service, you will find on the lower deck men who are not much more than animals – gaol-birds, thieves, scum from the London stews, villains of all types – aye, and a few murderers, too, no doubt – and the master-at-arms is the man who keeps law and order amongst that rabble. He may not be popular, he may be over-zealous at times, but he is feared. Take away that fear and you will have crime, disobedience and disorder. Now, if the captain had laid aside the testimony of the master-at-arms in favour of those two men he would have stripped Rolf of some of his authority and influence. As it is, he compromised – and those two men got off lightly, in my opinion. It was all for the good of the service.'

Lamb stared back at the angular features of the first

lieutenant in silence. The words 'for the good of the service' had touched a chord in him. As a midshipman on his first ship, one of the first things he had seen and which had stuck in his memory ever since, had been a sampler beautifully worked in coloured threads hanging on the cockpit bulkhead. It read: 'Midshipmen must be flogged for the good of the service' – a wry but not completely untrue statement lovingly stitched by one of the cockpit's warrant officers. He had soon learned that the ship's captain, first lieutenant and senior midshipman thoroughly approved of the sampler's dictate; it had been the most painful and miserable year of his young life. 'For the good of the service' was a ready phrase which was too often used to mask a multitude of evils without which the good of the service would not suffer at all; and yet, in this instance, he knew that Maxwell was right – the captain's judgement had a wiser and wider dimension than Lamb had observed.

'Well, young Lamb,' said Maxwell. 'Are you still of the same opinion?'

'No, sir. I must admit I had not looked at the question in those terms. My viewpoint, I fear, was too narrow.'

'Handsomely said!' cried Maxwell, leaning back in his chair with a wide grin. 'What it is to open a young man's eyes – I do believe I could see the scales falling then, pitter-patter into his plate.'

He chuckled at his wit as he beamed around the table and pushed back his chair. His little triumph had clearly delighted him and he was smiling broadly as he left the gunroom.

'I must get myself some spectacles,' said Tyler, rubbing his eyes. 'I think my sight is playing tricks – I could have sworn I saw our dear first lieutenant smiling just then.'

The surgeon, who had not uttered a word during his dinner, brushed the crumbs from his book and rose from the table. He paused by Lamb's shoulder on his way to the door.

'You disappointed me then, sir,' he said in his high, nasal tone. 'You should have stuck to your first opinion. Whatever Maxwell said, to flog innocent men is a clear injustice and should not be excused. It is a barbarous enough punishment even for the guilty.'

He thrust his book into a sagging side pocket and left the gunroom, leaving Lamb feeling foolishly confused and wishing he had kept his mouth shut in the first place.

Doubleday glared at the surgeon's disappearing back. 'Pompous little shit,' he muttered.

Chapter 4

Simon's Bay, the newly formed British naval base near to Cape Town, was almost deserted of shipping when the *Sturdy* made her salute to the flag flying from the old Dutch-built seventy-four. Cutler set off to pay his respects, huddled under his cape in the stern sheets of his gig. It was the first rain the men in the frigate had seen in weeks and as if to make up for its tardiness it was falling so hard that the scuppers could not cope and at the bulwarks the water was inches deep. The captain was on the flagship for a few moments only and when his gig returned to the frigate he came up the side in a rush. From that instant it was bustle, bustle for all hands. The admiral was ill – close to death, his flag lieutenant informed Cutler – and unable to see visitors or perform his duties. His second-in-command, the captain of the seventy-four, had taken the admiral's place on a trip inland but was expected back shortly, perhaps even today; he might well have fresh orders for the *Sturdy*, the young flag lieutenant suggested diffidently – perhaps Captain Cutler would care to wait on his return? No, Captain Cutler would not – his orders would brook no delay; he would top up his water and get under way the moment the hoy removed itself. He would be obliged if the flag lieutenant would present his warmest wishes to the admiral at the earliest opportunity and his regrets to the captain for being unable to wait.

Cutler had no wish to wait on the whims of the returning officer – his frigate might well be kept in these waters as the flagship's errand boy, a prospect which he viewed with no delight.

Directly the water-hoy had left the *Sturdy*'s side the frigate up-anchored and left the bay, a scant six hours since she had entered it. The junior officers were glum; their wine stock was low and they were eating nothing but ship's rations. Their hopes of buying a few delicacies at Simon's Bay had been dashed by Cutler's refusal, with no reason given, to allow even the gunroom steward ashore. The thought of a long voyage with the plainest of dull fare supplied solely by courtesy of the Admiralty brought no joy to their hearts.

As the frigate beat out of the bay, broad-reached under clearing skies, Tyler stepped into the gunroom, shook the raindrops from his sou'wester and announced that they were now heading for Cape Town.

'Are we indeed?' said Lamb with a pleased smile. 'I was certain our next port of call would be Calcutta.'

'Yes, so did we all. Either John Cutler intended to call at Cape Town all along or Watson has pointed out that his liquor supply is getting low.'

Whatever the reason, the frigate duly anchored in the wide waters of Table Bay under a sky so blue it seemed unreal. In contrast to the neighbouring Simon's Bay the anchorage was well-covered with ships; Cape Town was thriving and growing fast and now that it was a British possession it was a firm port of call for merchant ships en route to and from India and China. Lamb went ashore on his own – Kennedy was suffering from running bowels and Tyler, who had visited the place once before, had no wish to see it again.

'It's a dreary little place, built for church-going farmers,' he said disparagingly.

Lamb shared a boat with the captain's steward.

'He's very partial to cheese, sir,' said Watson as they were rowed ashore. 'I have to eke it out or he'd eat a month's supply in a week. Cheese is a weakness with him, sir.'

'I hope he likes Cape Town cheese, commented Lamb, smiling at the garrulous little man.

'Oh, he ain't none too fussy what sort he has, sir, purwiding it's strong and there's enough of it. Cigars, too, he wants, fresh fruit, ham, pickles, coffee, wine, soap – I've got a list as long as your arm, sir, and woe betide me if I don't get all of it.'

The town was a disappointment to Lamb. It was small and laid out in depressingly straight lines, the roads geometrically parallel and crossed by other straight roads at precise right angles, as if the town had been laid out by dividers and set square. He quickly cut through the settlement and began to climb the hill behind the town that led to the great, flat-topped mountain beyond. Walking was no chore to Lamb; he loved to stretch his legs and after the confines of a frigate's quarterdeck with no more than eleven strides between turns, the sight of the road reaching out before him was an absolute delight. The air was warm and still, filled with the sounds of birds and crickets, and his eye eagerly took in the bright splashes of colour glowing from the shrubs and wild flowers beside the dusty road. The land on either side of the road was well cultivated and fields of corn and vegetables and neat orchards alternated with pastures of grazing cattle. A man on horseback cantered towards him, raising his crop to his hat as he passed by; a short while afterwards a wagon pulled by two massive oxen also passed by. It was driven by a stout woman in a plain blue dress and large bonnet; she smiled as he raised his hat and called out something he did not catch. At the back of the wagon, legs dangling, sat two lissom young black girls; they eyed Lamb slyly as he stood in the grass at the side of the road and bent their heads together and giggled softly at his smile.

Lamb walked on, perspiring more than somewhat but with contentment bubbling gently within him, breathing deep of the scented air and revelling in the solitude and the firm ground beneath his striding feet. An hour from the sea, happily placed at the point where he decided he must retrace his steps, stood a little tavern and here he sat on a bench beside the door with a solemn, bearded farmer beside him, washing his throat with a tankard of warm, bitter beer, gazing down the road to the little town and the ships in the blue water beyond, as quietly happy as he ever remembered.

He arrived back at the boat hot and breathless, clutching a plaited straw basket filled with fruit for the gunroom. Watson was seated with his legs protectively astride the captain's hamper. He smiled at the perspiring Lamb as he scrambled into the boat and nodded his bald head appreciatively at the basket of fruit.

'Wery nice, the fruit here, sir. I bought a few oranges and the like for the capting.'

'And plenty of cheese?' smiled Lamb.

'Oh, yes, sir – I wouldn't dare show my face without that. Yes, sir, I got cheese and a nice ham, pickles, fresh bread, coffee beans. And I found him some cheroots – nasty, smelly things, stink the cabin out they do, but he's wery partial to a smoke in the evening. Course, sir, I shall have to keep my eye on the going of 'em, else they'll disappear as fast as his cheese, if I let him.'

Lamb was tempted to ask the little man if he had also purchased much in the way of liquor, remembering Tyler's acid comment, but looking at his cheerful face and knowing of his fierce loyalty to the captain he decided against it. He noted, however, that when the hamper was swayed on board, it appeared to be remarkably heavy for those few comestibles that the steward had mentioned.

Lieutenant Potter, Royal Marines, had few very onerous duties on board ship but one of these was the responsibility for the wardroom's wine and extra delicacies and he spent a busy hour with Surbrown listing and stowing the supplies which the steward had purchased. He emerged from the pantry with his list and conferred briefly with Maxwell, who then announced to the gunroom at large that the officers could now, with decency, invite the captain to a supper that would not shame them. His suggestion was met with unanimous approval by those officers present; the idea had been mooted several times in the past few weeks but the gunroom's provisions had been much too basic to allow them to put up a meal that would not give them deep embarrassment at its poor fare. An invitation to the captain to dine with his officers was not given lightly or too frequently – the wardroom's privilege to seclusion was long established and jealously guarded and it would be an arrogant captain indeed who lightly set aside convention by failing to beg permission to enter; moreover, an unpopular captain would find the intervals between such invitations uncommonly long. Cutler, however, was not one of these captains and it was with a great deal of pleasure that Maxwell's suggestion was endorsed.

Cutler was anxious not to remain in the bay a moment longer than he needed – the holding was not of the firmest and the anchorage was notoriously vulnerable to north-westerly gales. Early the next morning the *Sturdy* set sail in the grey light of an overcast sky, heeling under the influence of a cold south-westerly wind which brought with it temperatures lower than they had been for many a day.

It was Lamb's watch and he was glad of his heavy jacket as he stood huddled beneath its warmth on the lee side of the quarterdeck close to the wheel, from where he could keep a watchful eye on the shipping anchored haphazardly about the bay and also give any necessary orders to the helmsmen. Cutler had been on deck since the anchor was lifted from its soft holding at first light and was now standing by the weather rail, arms folded across his chest and gazing, apparently deep in thought, at the wind-snatched waves, leaving the progress of the frigate entirely in Lamb's hands. As the arms of the bay widened to the open sea a ship, on which Lamb had been keeping an eye since it had been a blur of white canvas far ahead, passed about a cable to larboard, heading for the anchorage. She was an American schooner, a light and graceful thing, her sails full-bodied in the following wind, her slim hull cutting through the green water with the ease of a knife-blade.

Lamb heard a loud exclamation from the captain and he turned his head to see him staring fixedly at the schooner as she passed abeam. He was uncertain as to whether Cutler had been addressing him or not, but acting on the wise assumption that no captain takes kindly to being ignored, even by way of a misunderstanding, took a pace or two towards the starboard rail and gave a tentative 'Sir?'

To his surprise, Cutler's face showed every evidence of anger. He looked sharply at Lamb and banged the rail with his fist.

'Did you not notice anything remarkable about that schooner, Mr Lamb?' he demanded, frowning.

Lamb hastily searched his memory of the schooner's approach and cast a quick glance over his shoulder at her retreating stern. No, he was certain he had not seen anything amiss – a lovely craft, certainly, but otherwise unremarkable.

'Not that I can recall, sir,' he answered warily.

'Then you disappoint me, sir,' snapped Cutler. 'Is not this ship a British man-of-war?'

'She is, sir,' replied Lamb, realizing at once the drift of the captain's question.

'And is it not accustomed practice for merchant ships to show their respect when passing a British man-of-war? Well, it may be outside your short experience, Mr Lamb, but certainly not mine.' He turned and glared at the fast-receding schooner.

'Arrogant bastard! It would have cost him nothing to display a little courtesy.'

Lamb maintained a diplomatic silence. Cutler, he knew, had served on the American station during the War of Independence, and the failure of the British army which led to the humiliating defeat of the mother country had left a bitter aftertaste in the Royal Navy. The present alliance between the two countries was an uneasy one and was based almost entirely on trade alone. As for the custom of showing respect for the navy, usually by letting fly the topgallant sheet or lowering a topsail, while British merchantmen rarely failed to do so, many foreign ships silently cocked a snook and ignored the practice, no doubt with wide grins on the faces of their masters. Lamb strongly suspected that had it been a ship of any other nationality Cutler would have shown little reaction – from an American ship, however, the implied insult was like rubbing salt into a still-tender wound.

Cutler stared after the receding schooner, grunted something unintelligible and paced the quarterdeck until the frigate had taken the heading that would keep her clear of the Agulhas Bank at the southern extremity of the cape, and then vanished into his quarters without a word. When Lamb was relieved shortly afterwards, the *Sturdy* was rolling heavily in an ugly, lumpy sea.

Breakfast in the gunroom was usually a quiet affair – the natural surliness of the newly risen Englishman was in no way lightened by the fare he was normally offered at the mess-table and conversation was invariably limited to requests for the coffee-pot or muttered complaints about over-active biscuits. Today, however, a noisy buzz of talk filled the gunroom as Lamb entered; fresh bread and firm butter might have had an influence, and perhaps the new supply of quince preserve, but it was also apparent that two separate conversations were going on at opposite ends of the table, one noisily conducted between Maxwell and the surgeon and the other, more soberly, between the master, Kennedy and the purser. Lamb seated himself between the two and reached for the coffee-pot.

Maxwell, senior of the gunroom, had definite ideas as to what food should be offered the captain that evening; the surgeon's suggestions were different but tendered with equal

74

firmness. The pair were arguing with some heat but, Lamb was glad to note, fairly good-humouredly. Meadow's position on the ship, as for all surgeons, was rather curious; his status and authority were not as hard-edged and firmly limited as they were for the other officers. He was not commissioned as were the lieutenants, but he held the right to walk the quarterdeck; he held his warrant as a surgeon from the Transport Board and took his place in the wardroom with the master and the purser. He wore no uniform and was independent of the watch system and the day-to-day routine of the ship and yet was subject to ship's discipline and naval law. Lamb, the most junior of the commissioned officers, was certainly superior in rank to Meadows and yet he would never have dared to talk to the first lieutenant in the manner in which the surgeon was now holding forth.

'Yes,' he was saying, 'your notion of an attractive and well-balanced meal might have great appeal to the sophisticates of the Highland crofts where you were – um – reared, but in more civilized –'

'Bollocks!' interrupted Maxwell rudely. 'You nancy boys south of the border are fine at crooking your finger with a cup of tea and mincing about with a biscuit but put a good, honest meal in front of you and your dainty stomachs would squeal in protest.'

Meadows took a deep breath and valiantly returned to the attack. 'It may be that we English were not brought up to regard raw herring and lumpy oatmeal as the ultimate in table delights but nevertheless our more refined palates –'

'Bollocks!' repeated Maxwell, happy in the knowledge that this one word could bring the surgeon's eloquent flow to a sudden halt and not at all concerned at the pained expression it brought to his face.

The surgeon knew he was outgunned and sought for an honourable escape. 'Why you persist in repeating that un-necessary word is quite beyond me – I really have no interest in the contents of your cranium,' he said with a righteous sniff, and made a dignified retreat from the gunroom.

'Ha, ha! Well done, sir!' shouted the master, who had not missed a word of this exchange and was delighted at the discomfiture of his old enemy. He clapped his hands to show his appreciation.

Maxwell grinned. 'Perhaps I should try my hand at politics and give up the sea,' he mused.

'What was that all about?' asked Lamb, curious.

'Oh, he had the ridiculous notion that we should not have plum duff tonight – said it was too commonplace and we should set our sights higher. I disagreed, naturally – how can you finish a meal without plum duff?'

'And that is what you were arguing about?'

Maxwell looked surprised. 'Isn't that enough?' he said indignantly and went off in search of Surbrown, to shower upon that unfortunate individual blood-curdling threats of hanging, keel-hauling and castration if the forthcoming meal was one whisker's width short of perfection.

Lamb smiled and refilled his cup, turning his attention to the talk at the other end of the table, where the purser was explaining to an attentive Kennedy the implications of the recent Compulsory Convoy Act. The purser was a vast pear-shaped man with a large, round head which merged without apparent narrowing into a neck corrugated with rolls of fat. Appearances notwithstanding, a keen and informed mind sat atop that gross body and his opinions, often given with some wit, were given weight seldom accorded to a purser. Lamb sipped his coffee and munched the delicious fresh bread as he listened to the purser discourse on a subject about which he knew very little.

The Act, the purser explained, was brought about by pressure on a reluctant Admiralty from Lloyds' underwriters after a long series of successful attacks on British shipping by French privateers in the Channel, the West Indies and the Indian Ocean. In the Straits of Malacca and the Bay of Bengal, areas of immediate interest to the *Sturdy*, privateers had made such ravages amongst merchantmen homeward bound from China and India that their insurance rates had increased enormously, so much so that alarming strains were showing in the City of London. Frigates of the French navy, based at Mauritius, had recently added to the toll of ships captured and Lloyds' losses had become so great that the Admiralty had been forced to introduce the convoy system.

'Mind you, the Act ain't popular with the owners, it may

76

surprise you to know. The convoy has to travel at the pace of the slowest vessel, naturally, which means a slower passage for most of them. And of course, if a dozen ships arrive in London at the same time carrying the same goods, then the price drops – and shipowners don't take kindly to dropping prices. East Indiamen, though, I do believe, don't come under the Act. They are supposed to be fast enough and well-armed enough to be able to take care of themselves.'

'Oh, are they?' said Doubleday. 'Well, I shall tell you a little story about an Indiaman – something that happened not so long ago. The *Triton*, she was – twenty-six guns and more'n a hundred and fifty men. Well gunned, you might think, for a merchantman, perhaps a trifle undermanned by our standards. Anyway, she meets with a French privateer – Surcouf, you've heard of him, I don't doubt. Well, Surcouf had a brig, four guns and less than twenty men – and he took the *Triton*.'

Lamb raised his eyebrows. 'In a brig, with less than twenty men? I can scarcely believe it.'

'You would if you'd served on an Indiaman,' growled Doubleday. 'Big, flash ships, most of 'em, lots of guns but little idea how to use 'em and not enough men to man 'em, in any case. But then, what can you expect? They are not navy, d'you see, they are not run in navy fashion.'

Leaving his table companions to ponder on this enormous flaw in the running of Indiamen, the master levered his large bulk from his chair and left the gunroom, shortly followed by the larger bulk of the purser.

Kennedy grinned at Lamb. 'How are you off for clean shirts?' he asked.

It may well have been that Surbrown had taken the first lieutenant's threats seriously – more likely, being an independent-minded individual, he had thumbed his nose at Maxwell's back – but in any event the meal he served in the gunroom that evening was received with acclaim. He and his Marine helpers brought in a huge joint of beef – *fresh* beef that had not so much as sniffed at a cask – chicken, kidney pie, steaming hot vegetables, plum duff and fruit, washed down with rough, dry Cape Town wine and topped up with port. The presence of the captain introduced a certain stiffness into the early part of the evening, with each officer anxiously intent on guarding his

77

tongue. The convention of the service demanded that junior officers did not initiate conversations with their captains and much of the early table talk consisted of polite responses to Cutler's comments and questions. However, the captain was an amiable man and worked hard in his attempts to ease the atmosphere. In this he was assisted by the surgeon who, in his ignorant, semi-civilian way, blithely treated Cutler as just one more face at the table and at one point shocked the other officers by waving his fork across the table at the captain as he underlined a comment. The wine, too, had its effect and before the plum duff was brought in the gunroom was filled with the loud and cheerful cross-chat of men fully at ease. The plum duff was greeted with welcome shouts, bottles were drained, replaced and drained again and as the air grew thicker and warmer, buttons were slyly loosened and faces grew shiny with perspiration. The master so far forgot himself as to ask the surgeon to drink a glass with him and for a moment the old enemies beamed at each other through their upheld glasses.

'Come, sir, no heel-taps!' cried Doubleday, his sharp eye detecting a half-inch of liquid remaining in the surgeon's glass. Meadows thought he heard a hint of hectoring in the master's tone and in a flash the brief truce was over. He thrust his thin face forward and glared at Doubleday.

'I am not a sot, sir. I am not a toper, sir. I shall drink at my own moderate pace, sir, in accordance with my principles of abstemious-ousness, an example you would do – do – do well to follow.'

The surgeon's principles had shown little evidence of themselves that evening and he finished his stumbling sentence with a loud hiccup. The master opened his mouth to deliver a blast of invective but was checked by the voice of the captain.

'A glass with you, Mr Doubleday,' he called down the table.

'An honour and a pleasure, sir,' replied the master, raising his glass, and the threatening squall had passed.

Towards the end of the evening the captain, who had barely moistened his lips with wine throughout, made a short speech in which he expressed his pleasure at his officers' hospitality and his greater pleasure and satisfaction in his ship, his officers and his men. He outlined the *Sturdy*'s expected duties when she reached her port of call – she would be sailing direct to the

Hooghly River at Calcutta to rendezvous with the *Lord Warden*, a seventy-four, and another frigate already making its own way there independently. As he understood it, the first part of the convoy would be shepherded to Madras and then on to Trincomalee, picking up more merchantmen at each port.

'And then home, gentlemen, a long, slow haul to the Port of London. However, there is always hope of excitement on the way – Frenchmen, privateers, perhaps a fat prize or two, who knows? Let us raise our glasses and drink to a happy and successful voyage.'

'Hear him! Hear him!'

Feet were stamped loudly on the deck in enthusiastic support to the toast and glasses were drained. Looking around the table at the flushed faces, Cutler decided it was not too soon for him to leave; tongues loosened by wine could too easily stray over the border between informality and familiarity and a sensible captain avoided those situations in which such embarrassment could occur. The officers rose unsteadily to their feet as he made his departure and then sank thankfully back into their seats.

Lieutenant Potter, whose face now exactly matched the colour of his jacket, initiated his colleagues into a drinking game which he swore was performed at every Marine dinner and consisted largely of round-the-table, non-stop emptying of glasses. For Lamb, the rest of the evening and the early hours of the morning were extremely vague. At one time, in a lucid moment, he found himself being addressed by Tyler – a bright, fresh and sober Tyler – and he realized that Kennedy must have left to take over his watch. Minutes or hours later he opened his eyes to see the surgeon being dragged from beneath the table, the stench of vomit strong in the close air. Then, somehow, he was in his cot, leaning over a bucket, the thick, upward rush of vomit startling in its powerful surge.

At four in the morning he was on the quarterdeck feeling close to death, unsure of how he had arrived there. Someone must have awakened him – he remembered splashing his face with water, discovering he was still fully dressed, complete with shoes – and he remembered nodding gravely as Kennedy handed over the watch, but what instructions had been passed to him he could not now recall. He could see, however, that it was a fine, clear night and he knew that the ship was in absolute safety in the hands of Bennet, a quartermaster who had been at sea since before Lamb was born and was now standing watchfully abaft the helm.

Lamb wandered slowly to and fro, blinking his gritty eyes and taking deep breaths of the cool night air in an effort to clear his head. He did not remember ever feeling so ill; he felt as if someone with a vicious sense of humour had crept to his cot while he slept and fastened an iron strap very tightly around his forehead, sprinkled sand into his eyes and stuffed some of the contents of the bilge into his mouth. An hour of slow, solitary pacing and deep breathing gradually lessened the pain in his head and reduced the wretched churning in his stomach, and at two bells – when Surbrown would be rolling out of his hammock to commence his duties in the wardroom pantry – he sent the duty midshipman down to him to beg for hot coffee. The coffee duly arrived, hot and strong, a full half-pint; he downed it gratefully and uttered silent thanks to Surbrown for saving his life. The morning watch quickened its pace from then on, the sky lightening to reveal a fine, clear morning and the maindeck suddenly a-bustle as the ship's day began. Sly probing of the quartermaster produced the instructions Lamb had failed to register from Kennedy and when the captain stepped from his quarters and mounted the ladder to the quarterdeck Lamb was confident that he presented the image of an alert and capable young officer.

Cutler nodded politely to Lamb, performed his customary early morning sniff of the air, glanced up at the set of the sails and in at the binnacle, walked briskly along the length of the ship and back and disappeared into his cabin without a word. Hammocks were brought up and stowed, the men were piped to breakfast and suddenly, although he would not have thought it possible an hour back, Lamb was hungry, ravenously so. When Tyler stepped on to the quarterdeck to relieve him, he was almost his normal self again; four hours of clean, cool air had left him with no more than a slight pain behind the eyes and a vague discomfort in his stomach. He made his way below, eager for his breakfast.

The *Sturdy* crept along the toe of Africa, the southernmost point of the voyage, in fair weather and light winds and it was several days before her figurehead was pointing to the north-east, a direction that would take her up the eastern coast and through the Mozambique Channel, past the equator and on to latitude 8°N, where she would turn eastward across the southern limits of the Arabian Sea, skirt the nothernmost Maldive Islands, enter the Gulf of Manaar and pass through the straits into the Bay of Bengal. Such were the firm instructions laid down in Cutler's orders – a course designed to keep a lone ship clear of patrolling squadrons of French frigates.

The weather grew rapidly warmer as watch succeeded watch and the frigate made her slow way towards the equator, keeping well clear of the African coast and its hordes of fishing craft and long-ranging dhows. The daily exercising of the guns continued in spite of the heat, with Cutler taking a close personal interest, often descending to the maindeck to check or correct a man and on occasion taking his place to demonstrate how he wished a thing to be done. The handling of the guns and their implements became second nature to the men and with the spur of competition between gun-captains seconds were daily shaved off practice times until the guns on both sides were regularly achieving three broadsides in less than five minutes.

Tyler and Lamb had responsibility for each forward division of guns, the larboard and starboard sides respectively, while the after, larger divisions came under Maxwell and Kennedy. During an exercise one oppressively hot forenoon, with the men's shadows extending no more than a few inches from their feet, Lamb caught a glimpse of Cutler's white-shirted figure moving amongst the crew of one of Kennedy's guns. When that lieutenant entered the gunroom later he was grinning broadly.

'Did you see John Cutler making a fool of himself up there?' he asked, as he fell limply into a chair. 'It was all I could do to keep a straight face.'

'Why, what happened?' asked Lamb.

Kennedy opened his shirt front and blew cooling air over his sweating chest. 'I think he had a very liquid breakfast, that's what happened. He was falling about all over the crew – insisted on taking the rammer's place because he thought the man's actions could be improved and promptly dropped the rammer over the side. How I stopped myself from laughing, I don't know, and why he –'

81

'That will do, Mr Kennedy!'

Maxwell stood in the doorway, his face grim, glaring at Kennedy. He went to his favourite chair and collapsed into it with a grunt. He wiped the sweat from his forehead and gave Kennedy a weary, narrow-eyed look. 'While I am in charge of this mess there will be no derogatory talk of the captain. Is that quite clear?'

'Yes, sir,' said Kennedy, for once subdued.

'Good. You will do well to remember it.'

A little north of the equator, in heat that softened the deck seams and created a minor hell below, a sail was sighted almost dead ahead. Within the hour the ship had been identified as an Indiaman and by the end of the first dog-watch Cutler was being pulled across to her side in response to an invitation from her master. She was the *Madras Queen*; the officers and men of the *Sturdy* crowded the sides to stare at her.

The Indiaman appeared enormous when viewed close-to from the deck of the frigate. Lamb raised his telescope to his eye and moved it slowly along the length of the vessel, from the large, gilt figurehead to the high, crowded poop deck. There were people in plenty milling about her decks; some were congregated about the entry port awaiting Cutler's arrival and many more were lining the ship's rail, gazing with equal interest at the *Sturdy* and her people. The pale colours of women's dresses mingled with the blues and scarlets of the uniforms of homeward-bound army officers and the bare, brown torsos of native seamen. A large dog pushed its way between the legs that blocked its view and stuck its head beneath the lower rail, its pink tongue lolling sideways as it panted in the heat. The merchantman appeared to be well-gunned – Lamb counted thirteen on its near side, including the bow-chaser and two carronades on the quarterdeck. He also saw what appeared to be a large chicken-coop erected between two of the forward long-guns – yes, it was definitely a chicken-coop, he could see the hens through the bars quite distinctly. The odd sight caused him to give a chuckle and he pointed it out to Kennedy.

'I am not surprised,' said Kennedy, shaking his head wryly. 'The gun barrels are probably chock full of chicken-feed.'

Cutler appeared at the entry port and shook hands with the

Indiaman's master, a short, stout figure whose lack of hair above was more than compensated by the vigorous growth below, flowing over his lapels. This was no reception for Cutler as he would be accorded when going on board a Royal Navy ship, with boatswain's pipe, sideboys with white gloves, Marines at the present and hatless officers standing in line; here it was an untidy press of men and women pushing forward in the hope of an introduction in order to confirm their status. The merchant captain gave the names of a few select persons, there were bows and handshakes and the two captains moved off along the crowded deck towards the privacy of the master's quarters.

An hour later, after more bows and handshakes, Cutler was rowed back to his frigate, to be welcomed aboard with considerably more ceremony than he had received aboard the Indiaman. A certain stiffness in his gait and a cheerful loudness in his voice pointed to a happy hour in the merchant captain's cabin. The two vessels resumed their respective courses amid much waving – particularly intense between Tyler and a group of young ladies on the *Madras Queen*'s quarterdeck – but in the light airs it was several hours before the Indiaman was hull down.

Cutler talked with Maxwell that evening and the first lieutenant duly passed on the information to the officers of the gunroom. Surcouf was still active in the Bay of Bengal, it seemed. A few weeks earlier an Indiaman and a fast merchantman had been attacked off Calcutta by the Frenchman in company with another privateer. The Indiaman had fought off the attack but the smaller merchantman had been trapped between the two privateers and boarded. The Indiaman, putting prudence before valour, had fled, returning to Calcutta with several dead and many injured on board.

The master of the *Madras Queen* had twice postponed sailing from Calcutta after hearing reports of privateers so thick in the bay that it amounted to a veritable blockade of the river mouth. Finally, more in desperation than with courage, he had taken his ship down to the mouth of the Hooghly, waited until dark and then sailed west, hugging the ragged Bengal coastline. He had made his way down to Madras, where he waited several days before nerving himself for the dash to the narrow straits between Ceylon and the mainland. He had happily told Cutler that he had not seen the smallest sign of a privateer since leaving Calcutta and it was his firm opinion that reports of privateers and French frigates patrolling the waters of the Bay of Bengal like packs of hungry wolves were much exaggerated.

This last produced long faces and glum looks in the gunroom; fat merchantmen might welcome peaceful waters and quiet voyages but not ambitious naval officers, anxious for promotion, prize money and fame.

'Shiny-headed old fool!' said Tyler. 'What would he know, anyway, creeping along the coastline on tip-toe, practically on the beach?'

Early one morning, after examining the log-board and making certain calculations, the master announced that the ship had reached latitude 8°N and Lamb, who had the watch, sent Midshipman Cowan to inform the captain. The hands were at their breakfast and Cutler was considerate enough to allow them to finish their meal before changing course. The *Sturdy* duly turned towards the climbing sun and for several hours enjoyed a strong following wind but at noon, in the space of a few minutes, the wind had veered round to blow hard from the south and the sky in that direction showed rapidly building dark storm clouds. Kennedy was on watch, sharing the quarterdeck with Maxwell who had just completed one of his restless prowls around the deck.

Maxwell cocked an eye at the fast-climbing clouds and an ear to the rising note of the wind in the rigging.

'The royals would do well to be taken in, Mr Kennedy,' he said, glancing aloft.

'Aye aye, sir.' Kennedy crooked a finger at the duty midshipman. 'My respects to the captain, Mr Blissenden, and weather is building up from the south. Request permission to take in the royals.'

Blissenden was back within the minute. 'Please, sir,' he reported to Kennedy, 'the captain sends his compliments, sir, and you are to do as you think fit.'

Kennedy raised his eyebrows at this. Permission to take in sail was not given lightly on the *Sturdy* and never without Cutler personally determining that it was necessary.

'Are you certain that is what he said?' demanded Maxwell,

looking sternly down at the little midshipman.

'Well, sir,' piped Blissenden cheerfully, 'what he *actually* said was, "Tell Mr Kennedy to please his bloody self and not to bother him with trifles", sir!'

Maxwell's frown deepened, Kennedy's eyebrows shot even higher and the quartermaster exchanged expressive glances with the helmsmen.

'Take in the royals, Mr Kennedy,' growled Maxwell. The deck heeled suddenly as the wind gusted and the two officers staggered, clutching at the mizzen shrouds. 'Belay that. Take in royals and t'gallants and double-reef the tops'ls.'

Kennedy stepped forward to the quarterdeck rail and bellowed over the wind.

'All hands! All hands!'

The hands swarmed aloft. Ten minutes later the frigate's masts were bare above the topsails but in the space of those few minutes the sky darkened dramatically as black clouds raced up from the south and the wind increased sufficiently to lay the ship over at a sharp angle on to her starboard side.

Tyler and Lamb, at ease with a coffee-pot in the gunroom, noticed the deepening roll of the ship as the wind whipped up the waves. Tyler was about to speak when the ship, hit by a strong gust, suddenly rolled sharply to starboard until she lay almost on her beam, sending the coffee-pot leaping over the fiddle and crashing to the deck. Both men made for the aft companionway at a run.

They arrived on deck to witness a loud altercation between the captain and the master. Both were clinging to the mizzen-shrouds in order to keep their footing on the steeply sloping deck. Their voices were raised as they faced each other, the master's round face set stubbornly and the captain's eyes narrowed beneath lowered brows.

'Do you dare to argue with me, sir?' thundered Cutler in a voice that carried over the wind the length of the ship, drawing the intense attention of fifty pairs of eyes and almost the same number of ears. (Vernon, mizzenmast topman, had but one ear remaining to him.)

'No, sir,' bawled Doubleday, 'I am but doing my duty, sir, as master of this ship, to point out that this will be no short-lived squall, sir. We must take in more sail and turn into the wind,

85

sir, otherwise –'

'Must, sir, must? Do you presume to give me orders, Doubleday? Need I remind you –?'

Cutler's enraged words were cut short by a dazzling flash of lightning that stretched from cloud to sea, and a simultaneous thunderclap that shook the ship as if she had been hit by a broadside from close range. With the thunder came the rain, instant, hard-driving rain in a screaming wind that ripped the main course from top to bottom.

Tyler and Lamb reacted together, running forward by way of the raised larboard side, clutching a hold where they could and drenched to the skin before they had gone three paces. Maxwell was already beneath the mainmast shrouds, lank, black hair plastered over his forehead as he chivvied the hands aloft to the mainyard. He caught sight of Lamb and Tyler making their way towards him.

'Mr Tyler! Take over here, if you please. Mr Lamb, my compliments to the captain and beg permission to clew up the foresail.'

Lamb turned and hurried aft, to be cannoned into by Little, the second youngest but smallest of the midshipmen.

'Hold hard, Mr Little,' growled Lamb, winded, swinging the infant up by his collar so that his legs dangled a foot above the deck. 'What do you mean by assaulting me and where are you off to?'

'Sorry, sir,' piped the boy. 'Message for Mr Maxwell, sir. The captain would like the foresail clewed up, sir, and the foremast staysail taken in, sir.'

'Right, I'll tell him. Cut back to your station and keep a tight hold on the way.'

Lamb grinned to himself as he made his way forward again. The captain had heeded part of the master's counsel, at least, he thought, and with the thought the angle of the deck eased as the ship's bow was brought round into the wind. His smile broadened.

The torn, wildly flapping remnants of the mainsail were being gathered in as Lamb made his way to the foremast. Maxwell and the foremast men were standing by and the moment Lamb passed on his message they sprang to work, hauling at the clew-garnets.

Lamb made his way to the aft companionway and descended to his cabin, where he changed his saturated shirt and donned his tarpaulins. He was not due on watch for another two hours but in this weather he preferred to be on deck where he could see what was happening and make himself useful. The ship's motion was easier now that Cutler had brought her before the wind and reduced her canvas, but even so she was far from comfortable. The oncoming waves, rushing past the frigate in steep, foam-streaked ranks, lifted the bow high in the air before they rolled beneath her, lifting her stern and plunging her nose in the troughs, bringing on board tons of green water.

The lee side of the quarterdeck was crowded when he came back on deck. All the lieutenants and the duty midshipman were there, together with the surgeon, the purser and the Marine lieutenant, taking a rare opportunity to exercise their right to walk the quarterdeck, although little walking was possible on the wet and heaving deck and very little was intended, from the way they clung grimly to the mizzenmast shrouds. Amidships, two helmsmen and a quartermaster were at the wheel, struggling to hold the frigate into the wind and on the weather side stood Cutler, shapeless in his tarpaulins, facing forward with one arm hooked through the ratlines. Maxwell had cleared the duty watch below – there was no sense in needlessly risking men's lives – and the maindeck was deserted; but from time to time, as the afternoon wore on, he and the boatswain made their perilous round of the deck, checking on gun-lashings and boats and hatch-covers.

With the coming of dark the weather appeared to worsen. The baying of the wind became shriller, giving a sound that was threatening and fiendish; the tormented motion of the ship as she was constantly lifted and dropped was such that Lamb feared for her timbers. The rain lashed across the deck as it had for the past six hours and Lamb was soaked and numb beneath his tarpaulins. Officially, it was his watch and he had formally relieved Kennedy at the end of the afternoon watch but Kennedy – like Tyler, who was due to relieve Lamb in two hours – remained on the quarterdeck. A rumbling noise came from the darkness of the maindeck, followed by a crash and the sound of splintering timber.

'Jesus Christ!' shouted Maxwell. 'One of the guns is loose!'

He flung himself down the dancing ladder and disappeared into the darkness, yelling for the boatswain, with Kennedy and Tyler hard on his heels. Lamb had taken two paces forward before he remembered he was the officer of the watch and as such his duty was to remain on the quarterdeck. Another crash came from forward, followed by the sound of Maxwell's voice bellowing a mixture of orders and curses, only snatches of which came back to Lamb. Lamb peered into the rain-swept blackness – a hint of movement came from the waist but it was impossible to see anything clearly. From the sound of breaking timber he judged that the ship's boats, nestling one inside the other and wedged and lashed amidships, had provided a temporary check to the passage of the rogue gun across the deck. He became aware of the captain standing beside him, peering forward, his eyes slitted against the hard-driven rain.

'Can you see what's going on from up there, Mr Lamb?' he shouted.

Lamb was accustomed to taunts about his height but so far Cutler had never alluded to it. He was surprised that Cutler could spare a thought for humour at a time like this and not a little flattered that he should be the cause of it.

'I think it's one of the middle starboard guns, sir,' he yelled, bending his neck to bring his head nearly on a level with the captain's ear. 'By the sound of it, it has damaged the boats.'

'Damaged?' bawled Cutler. 'Made firewood of them, more like! Don't just stand there, looking useless – get for'ard and give a hand!'

Lamb opened his mouth to remind Cutler that he was officer of the watch but thought better of it.

'Aye aye, sir,' he shouted and plunged down the ladder and into the wet darkness of the maindeck.

The squeal and rumble of wooden wheels on the deck came again as he groped his way forward, snatching a quick handhold where he could. He expected to hear another crash of breaking timber as the gun ploughed into the remains of the boats but instead there came a thud that vibrated through the soles of his shoes. Several dark figures came into view, dancing back from the gun as it began to roll away from the centre of the deck with the lift of the larboard side. One of them stepped close and gripped Lamb by the arm.

'Is that you, Lamb?' bawled Maxwell. 'Look, we've lashed baulks of timber to the midships ring-bolts and against the side, to try to contain the fucking thing. What we've got to do now is to trip it – nip across and see Tyler, he's got some hammocks. And don't fall under the bloody gun!'

A resounding thud and the sound of breaking timber came hard on his words. Lamb ran to the gun, laid a quick hand on the breech as he peered at the side and leaped away as the starboard side began to rise. The wheels of the gun-carriage had ridden up over the baulk of timber and the muzzle of the gun had been driven through the inward-sloping timbers of the tumblehome. He joined the dark group of men on the far side of the gun's path.

Kennedy's sou'wester had gone and his fair hair was spread wetly over his ears and forehead. He grinned as he saw Lamb's unmistakable, tall figure loom up.

'You are just in time for the fun,' he shouted. 'We are going to try to trip the bastard. When Tyler throws his hammock beneath the truck, we'll rush it. Don't move until I shout.'

The deck heeled to larboard and the wooden wheels began their loud grumble on the deck again.

'Stand by!' bellowed Kennedy.

One and three-quarters of a ton of iron on wheels trundled down the slope of the deck. Tyler took a quick pace forward and thrust the tightly-lashed hammock in front of the carriage.

'Now!' screamed Kennedy.

The gun, awkward, brutish and wilful, slewed sideways as the wheels nipped the canvas on the wet deck and slid with a jarring crash into the midships baulk of timber, one set of wheels lifting up and then coming down again with a shock that threw off the men clinging to it. Lamb leaped to his feet as if on springs, his body cringing at the thought of being run down by the rampaging monster.

'Quick!' It was Maxwell, looming up out of the darkness. 'Where are those bloody hammocks? We've got to stop the thing – its pointing fore and aft now.'

He snatched a hammock from the pile on the deck; the others followed his example and hurried after him as another crash told of damage to somewhere further aft. The rogue had struck the carriage of another gun, glanced off and was now beginning to roll forward as the bows dipped. The boatswain and several hands appeared from somewhere amidships, armed with crossbars and lengths of timber. They rushed the gun, jamming their bars and levers beneath the wheels and under the carriage. Like a wild bull the gun shrugged off its assailants and slewed again, bearing down on Maxwell. The first lieutenant went to spring aside, but his foot slipped on the wet deck and he came crashing down in the path of the wicked little wooden wheels. Lamb flung himself forward as Maxwell rose unsteadily to his hands and knees, far too late to save himself. His outstretched hand found the first lieutenant's collar and he yanked back hard. Maxwell landed on his back with a bone-jarring thud, the trundling wheels missing his legs by a whisker. Lamb went down equally hard, his head smacking against the breech of the passing gun. For the briefest of instants intense agony flared through his skull and then he was floating in blackness, swimming up towards a distant light and an insistent voice.

'Mr Lamb! Mr Lamb! Come, sir, wake up! Do you intend to lay there all night because of a little bump? Wake up, sir!'

He opened his eyes warily; for a moment the face of the surgeon and the lantern hanging from the deck beam behind him swam hazily, unfocused. He was startled to discover he was stretched out on the captain's window bench. His head thumped with a regular, sickening ache and when he put a hand up to investigate he found a bandaged pad wrapped around his temples.

'Yes, a little contusion there,' said Meadows. 'I have put in a couple of sutures – you will probably have a sick head for a day or two.'

Lamb swung his legs off the bench and sat upright. The world teetered wildly for a moment and then steadied itself. God, his head ached!

Meadows thrust three fingers in front of Lamb's nose. 'How many fingers can you see?' he demanded.

'Three, of course,' snapped Lamb, testily. 'What is this, some sort of game?'

'You'll live,' said Meadows, and stuffing his bits and pieces into his bag he left the cabin.

Lamb rose gingerly to his feet and stood, swaying, for a

moment. He gently pressed the pad on his temple and winced. Suddenly, the memory of the long-gun careering about the wild deck came back with a rush. He recalled plunging forward to grip Maxwell's collar – and then nothing. The thought crossed his mind that Maxwell might be badly injured – even dead. He must get back on deck. His sou'wester was lying at his feet and he bent with a groan to retrieve it, placing it carefully on top of his turbanned head.

On deck, the night was as wild and wet as ever. Clinging grimly, Lamb made his way up the ladder to the quarterdeck.

'Mr Lamb!' The call came from Cutler, still huddled darkly beneath the weather shrouds.

'Sir?' said Lamb, bringing his hand to his sou'wester in salute as he approached.

'I am pleased to see you on your feet again. I thought for a moment we had lost you. How is the head?'

'A trifle sore, sir, but I am quite fit for duty.'

'Very good.' Cutler nodded in dismissal and Lamb made his way across the sharply pitching deck to where Tyler stood, shoulders hunched against the lashing rain.

'Hallo!' said Tyler cheerfully. 'How is the head?'

'Ringing like a bell. What o'clock is it?'

Tyler laughed. 'Your watch finished ten minutes ago, while you were snoring in the old man's cabin.'

'How is Maxwell?'

'Maxwell? Oh, he's for'ard somewhere, checking on the breechings. He owes you a vote of thanks – if you hadn't moved so fast he'd be pulp by now.'

'Do you think I'll get one?'

Tyler grinned and shook his head. 'No!'

'Nor do I! You secured the gun, then?'

'Yes, all snug, though the carpenter will be busy tomorrow. It made its mark on the side before we put it to bed.'

'And that is where I am off to,' said Lamb. 'Goodnight.'

He turned back as a thought struck him.

'That business earlier, between John Cutler and Doubleday. What on earth brought that on?'

Tyler shot a wary look across the deck at the indistinct figure of the captain.

'Need you ask?' he said quietly, nodding his head in Cutler's direction. 'He reeked of brandy, according to Kennedy. When Doubleday suggested we take in more sail he flew off the handle – seemed to take it as a personal slight on his judgement. He soon sobered up, though, when we lost the mains'l and now I think that little squall between him and Doubleday is quite blown over and forgotten.'

Lamb's thoughts were sombre as he made his way below. An outburst of temper from a captain on his quarterdeck was certainly no rarity – in Lamb's experience, irascibility was as much a part of a captain as was his epaulette (doubly so when he had the seniority to wear two) – and a captain the worse for drink was no uncommon animal, either, but for Cutler, for whom Lamb had always had the greatest respect, to endanger his ship in a drunken rage was another thing entirely. His esteem of Cutler had taken a hard knock.

When Lamb took over the morning watch the wind and sea had declined considerably and, mercifully, the rain had ceased. A strong swell was still rolling the ship heavily but the cloud had broken sufficiently to give occasional glimpses of a sliver of a moon and the odd, bright star. The topsails were still fully reefed but the torn mainsail had been removed and another bent on in its place. At some time in the night the frigate had been eased round to her original course and as a consequence the wind, although less strong, was laying the ship over at a moderate angle.

Lamb considered himself fortunate to have the morning watch. In these latitudes the sun's heat was fierce by breakfast time and savage by noon. Conditions on deck were made bearable by the movement of air and wind cooled by its passage over the sea; below decks, the stifling heat and fetid atmosphere were such that few of the officers cared to remain there for long and spent many of their off-duty hours in the open air. For the hands, however, with their system of watches which allowed for no more than four hours' sleep at a time and on occasion not even that, conditions were more unpleasant. Some of them curled up to sleep in odd corners of the maindeck and forecastle but most were unwilling to risk disturbance to their precious sleep by the noise and movement of the duty watch and clung stubbornly to their hammocks, slung from their hooks at the allotted intervals of fourteen inches. The fore and main hatches were left open and a canvas contrivance rigged in an attempt to funnel a movement of air between decks but it would have needed a polar blast to have dispelled the stench of stale sweat from the tightly-packed bodies and clothing of nearly two hundred men and the malodorous and lingering effects of the dried peas they consumed on five days out of seven.

This morning, with the shreds of the storm prevailing, the air was pleasantly cool, almost chill, and Lamb hummed quietly to himself as he paced back and forth along the heaving quarter-deck. His temple was still painfully sore but the agony of his earlier headache was almost gone after nearly seven hours of deep sleep. His thoughts flowed aimlessly from one subject to another as he walked – women, India, promotion, Cutler, his laundry, women, breakfast – and suddenly the sun was dazzling his eyes off the water as it rose in clear skies almost dead ahead and the boatswain's mates were piping and bellowing, rousing the hands with their customary cheerful courtesy. Another day had started as days always started on board a man-of-war, with water and brooms, sand and holystones, and sleepy, frowsty men in bare feet on damp decks. Lamb stretched and yawned and yearned for coffee.

Chapter 5

The *Sturdy* crept slowly eastward across the brilliant, blue, empty sea, the little landmarks of shipboard life entered in bald, laconic sentences in the ship's log. For several days the entries for mid-September differed in the main only in the day of the month and the ship's position; the wind and weather remained much the same and the details that followed recorded nothing more startling than the replacement of a deadeye on the starboard chainplates and the breaking of a Marine's shin. On the seventeenth, Captain Cutler dipped his pen and wrote: 'Winds southerly, light. AM sighted northernmost Maldive Islands 7 miles to starboard. Set royal topgallants fore and main. Rebuked first officer for loose gammoning on bowsprit. Hands at guns AM, employed cleaning shot PM. Sighted sail south-east just before dark.'

Cutler glanced about him at his officers on the quarterdeck and selected Cowan, the large and very stupid midshipman whose chances of passing for lieutenant were marginally greater than those of the one-legged cook.

'Mr Cowan, up you go with your glass and see what you make of her.'

'Aye aye, sir,' roared Cowan and almost before his words had reached the captain's ears he was swarming with great strength and ape-like agility up the mainmast ratlines. The sun had already sunk its lower two-thirds into the horizon and the pink-streaked violet sky was rapidly darkening to the east.

Cowan's voice came down from his perch on the maintopgallant yard.

'It looks like a brig or a brigantine, sir. It's square-rigged on the foremast at least, but the light's none too good, sir.'

'How does she bear, man?' yelled Maxwell impatiently.

'Bows-on, sir, I think.'

'He thinks!' muttered Maxwell disgustedly to no-one in particular.

'It's getting too dark – I've lost her now, sir,' roared Cowan.

Cutler considered the situation. His orders were to avoid unnecessary engagements but it was an order which did not bear too heavily on him; should a chance occur for him to exercise his guns in earnest he would snatch at it, orders notwithstanding. His men were trained and as ready for action as they ever would be. In any case, he had no intention of diverting from his course during the night in order to shake off the stranger – he would lose too much of his hard-won eastings.

'We will maintain our course, Mr Maxwell. Keep an extra lookout aloft tonight and inform me the moment anything is sighted.'

'Aye aye, sir,' said Maxwell, eyeing the captain coldly as he descended to his quarters for his supper.

Lamb gave Maxwell a sly look and smiled inwardly, careful to keep a rigid countenance. It would not do for the first lieutenant to catch a smirk on anyone's face today. He had been in a foul mood since this morning when Cutler, in one of his periodic, keen-eyed tours of the deck, had noticed a slight, a very slight, decrease in tension on one of the lashings of the bowsprit. He had returned to the quarterdeck and ordered the duty midshipman to present his compliments to the first lieutenant and he would be obliged for a moment of his time. Maxwell had been at breakfast and a trace of bacon grease shone at the corner of his mouth as he hurried up the ladder to the quarterdeck.

'You sent for me, sir?' he asked, touching his hat in salute.

'Yes, Mr Maxwell. The bowsprit is in danger of falling off. Kindly see to the gammoning.'

With that Cutler left the quarterdeck for his own breakfast, leaving Maxwell staring after him, a red flush of anger and mortification racing up his cheeks. Lamb, on watch a few feet away, had heard every word and was astonished at Cutler's public, coldly-uttered rebuke and the way he had summoned Maxwell in order to deliver it. It was not typical of Cutler – he was generally cold, stern, but discreet when dealing with his officers. Lamb stared tactfully out to sea and pondered on the reasons for the captain's uncharacteristic behaviour. The bottle again? No, he thought not – his speech and manner had shown no signs of that. Liver, migraine? Unlikely again – his

95

morning greeting of Lamb had been pleasant and cheerful enough. Perhaps it was his way of keeping his officers on their toes by showing the occasional flash of steel. If that was so, then Lamb must expect his own turn to come in time – he must make sure that he gave no good reason to deserve it.

Maxwell had eventually closed his mouth, given Lamb a hard look as that officer gazed with great interest over the side and stalked off in search of the boatswain, to deliver to that indignant individual a verbal savaging. He, in his turn, had passed it on at a usurious rate of interest to his mates who, knowing Moriarty of old and being well acquainted with his histrionic rages, had nodded stolidly until he had finished and then spent ten minutes putting matters right at the gammoning.

'Put an extra man aloft, Mr Lamb,' growled Maxwell, 'and make sure he keeps alert.'

'Aye aye, sir. I'll send up young McKenna – he's got a sharp pair of eyes.'

'Please your damn self,' said Maxwell gracelessly as he moved towards the ladder.

At three bells in the morning watch, as the sky to the east was changing from black to pale green to lemon all in the space of a moment, the lookout hailed the deck: a sail was in sight off the starboard beam.

''Bout t'ree, four miles, I t'ink. A brig, sir.'

'How's her head?' shouted Lamb.

'Iss comming at our bow, sir.'

Lamb turned to the duty midshipman. 'My compliments to the captain, Mr Blissenden. There is a brig in sight, four miles off the starboard beam, heading north-east.'

'Aye aye, sir,' said Blissenden and scuttled down the ladder. 'Stand aside, sentry,' Lamb heard him pipe importantly. 'I have orders to wake the captain.'

Lamb clambered into the mizzen-shrouds and stared out over the paling sea. Ah, there she was! He caught the white flash of her topsails as the unseen sun thrust back the darkness. He raised his telescope to his eye. A brig, certainly, square-rigged on both masts – a fair-sized one, too. As he looked her topsails appeared to stretch upwards, first on one mast, then the other. She had set her topgallants! There could be no mistaking her intentions now – she was clearly determined to come up to the frigate with all possible speed.

Cutler appeared at the top of the quarterdeck ladder, hatless and in shirtsleeves, his hair tousled from his pillow.

'Let me have your glass,' he said to Lamb, holding out his hand.

He levelled the telescope at the brig and studied her for a long minute.

'She has just set her t'gallants, sir,' said Lamb.

Cutler grunted in reply, snapped shut the telescope and handed it back to Lamb.

'Beat to quarters, Mr Lamb,' he said as he walked away. 'Clear for action.'

Like a stick poked into an ants' nest, the magic call, the purpose and aim of every seagoing officer, stirred up an explosion of activity. The ship thundered to the noise of hundreds of feet as men scampered to their action stations, to their guns, forward and aft, aloft and below, urged on by the shouts of the petty officers and the belated alarm of the Marine drummer, frowsty of face and with buttons askew. The preparations, so often rehearsed in the past weeks, were carried out with an urgency and enthusiasm never attained in practice. The carpenter's mates swept through the captain's quarters like little hurricanes, ignoring Cutler as he scraped at his chin with razor and cold water and bearing off his furniture to the safety of the hold. The galley fires, not long blown into life, were doused; the decks were strewn with damp sand and the hatch leading to the magazine was screened with damp fearnought. Aloft, the boatswain and his mates secured the yards with chains and below, in the magazine, the gunner in his felt slippers began to serve the cartridges to the waiting powder-boys. The Marines clattered to their stations clutching their muskets, some to climb aloft to the tops to act as marksmen and man the swivel-guns and others running to their places at the long guns.

Lamb watched from the quarterdeck as the guns were run inboard and primed and loaded, Maxwell, Kennedy and Tyler striding about their divisions, pointing, shouting, conferring with their quarter-gunners. As officer of the watch he was unable to leave the quarterdeck until the captain returned and he paced the boards in a fever of impatience.

The brig, now plainly visible from the quarterdeck in the low light of the early sun, was maintaining her course, driving for the frigate's bow. Lamb estimated her distance to be no more than three miles. Clearly, she had put about after sighting the *Sturdy* in the dusk and had followed a parallel course, calculating that the frigate would not deviate from her line in the dark hours. Lamb was puzzled. While a well-armed brig with a good crew would be more than a match for most armed merchantmen, taking on a thirty-six gun frigate could only be classed as foolhardy.

Cowan, who had been keeping his telescope trained on the brig, spoke from the starboard rail.

'She is turning away, sir.'

Lamb put his own glass to his eye. Yes, Cowan was right. The gap between her masts appeared to widen as her bow was turned away from the frigate and then steadied to follow the same course. A movement at her mast-tops caught his eye – her topgallants were being furled. Lamb studied the brig, frowning. It appeared that she had no wish to come to grips with the *Sturdy* but for some reason was anxious to dog her footsteps. She had placed herself well out of harm's way; Lamb guessed her distance to be about two miles, perhaps twice the maximum range of the frigate's long-guns. She flew no flag but her nationality was beyond doubt; her black-painted masts and narrow yards were as French as the tricolour.

Cutler mounted the quarterdeck wearing his best hat, coat and sword. He was freshly shaved and appeared trim and spruce. Lamb approached, saluted and reported the latest movements of the brig. Cutler did not appear to be surprised.

'Perhaps she is playing a waiting game,' he commented. He pushed at his lip with a thoughtful finger and stared at the Frenchman for a second or two. 'Waiting for what, I wonder? I think we should edge a little closer and see what she does.' He called over his shoulder. 'Helm a-lee, quartermaster.'

The deck heeled sharply as the bow swung towards the privateer. Cutler and Lamb kept their gaze on the brig, as did every man on the ship – there was no need for telescopes now in the crystal air at this range. The brig responded within seconds, her bow turning away to the south. Cutler grunted and ordered the helm put back to the original course. Again, the privateer followed suit. Cutler smiled and gave a knowing nod. He turned to Lamb.

'Well, Mr Lamb, what conclusions did you draw from that little exercise?'

Lamb hastily arranged his thoughts. 'Well, sir, it is obvious that she has no wish to come within reach of our guns and yet she has shortened sail to keep pace with us. I imagine that she could show us a clean pair of heels without too much trouble, if she wished. It must be, sir, that she has friends in the offing and is hopeful of meeting them.'

'My thoughts exactly,' said Cutler. 'Now stretch your imagination further – a good deal further! – and imagine you are captain of this frigate. What would your next move be?'

Lamb heard the warning clang of alarm bells in his mind; this is where he would make an absolute ass of himself, of that he was sure. Ah, well, ass or not, the captain was waiting for an answer.

'Um, as captain, sir, I would find it infinitely preferable to fight one vessel at a time, rather than two or more, but knowing that fellow out there can give us several knots, I cannot see us readily coming to grips with him. We could settle down into a chase but that might last for days and take us many miles out of our way. So, as I see it, sir, we should continue as we are and see what that Frenchman leads us to.'

Cutler smiled. 'Excellent, Mr Lamb, excellent. You have summed up the situation very nicely. I shall act on your advice and do nothing at all. Meanwhile, I shall strip you of your epaulette and ask you to step along to the first officer with my compliments. He can stand the men down from action stations for the time being. I doubt if we shall see any action this side of noon, at least.'

'Aye aye, sir,' said Lamb, turning to the ladder – but he had not taken two paces when the deck was hailed by the mainmast lookout. A sail!

'Belay that order!' snapped Cutler and turning his head aloft, cupped his hands. 'Where away?'

Magnesson was a shy man and in the sudden silence that followed the captain's bellow he was conscious that he was the centre of attention of some two hundred pairs of ears (give or take the odd ear). The stammered reply that he sent down sounded like a rattling drumstick.

'D – d – d – dead ahead, sir. Hull d – d– d – down. Iss all I c – c – can see, sir.'

Cutler despatched Cowan aloft with his glass and as the midshipman pulled himself up the rigging with his long arms and hairy hands, the captain turned to Lamb with a grim smile.

'Those friends in the offing perhaps, Mr Lamb. Well, plenty of time yet. We shall see, we shall see.'

'Yes, sir,' said Lamb. 'May I have leave to attend my station, sir?'

Cutler assented with an abstracted nod and Lamb hurriedly made his way forward along the starboard row of guns. The men were grinning, happy and excited, their heads bound with coloured handkerchiefs to keep the sweat from their eyes. He paused for a moment with Maxwell, the Scot as grim and dour as ever but with a certain wild spark deep in his eyes. Lamb passed on the gist of the captain's comment but Maxwell had already arrived at the same conclusion and said as much.

Lamb reached his division of guns as Cowan hailed the deck. A frigate, almost certainly, and by the cut of her jib, French. He could tell no more at this distance except that she was almost bows-on to the *Sturdy*. He was ordered to stay where he was and to report as and when he had anything definite to say.

Lamb received the reports of his quarter-gunners and made a quick inspection of his charges and their crews. Everything was as it should be – guns and men were primed and ready, the one with powder and roundshot, the other with evident enthusiasm and keen anticipation. He bent his back to speak with Ayers, one of his gun-captains, squatting by the breech of his gun and a constant reminder of his bloody excursion ashore in Portugal. Ayers grinned shyly and put a knuckle to the striped handkerchief around his forehead.

'How's your head, Ayers?' asked Lamb, a question he had put so often it now almost took the form of a greeting.

'Fine, sir, thankee,' rumbled the gunner, as always. 'How be your'n?' he added slyly.

Lamb touched his temple, feeling the slight ridge left by the surgeon's sutures.

'Fine, thank you, Ayers,' he grinned and the pair of them

chuckled together for a moment.

Another hail came from Cowan. The distant frigate had luffed, her heading now south-west.

Cutler smiled; if the Frenchman wanted the weather gauge, then he would have to struggle for it. He snapped an order over his shoulder and the *Sturdy* luffed, bringing her bow nearer to the wind and heading south-east, so that the two frigates were now racing towards the same distant point. The shadowing brig sheered off as the *Sturdy*'s head swung towards her and settled down again on a parallel course, keeping the same safe distance.

Cutler turned to the quartermaster. 'Hands to breakfast, Bennet.'

'Hands to breakfast, aye, sir,' said Bennet and strode forward to call down to a boatswain's mate. The welcome pipe sounded and the men rattled down from aloft and trotted from their guns. There would be no burgoo this morning, with cold galley stoves, but to hungry men biscuit and beer was a feast. Lamb took his breakfast in the shade of the foresail, chatting quietly with Kennedy and Tyler while Maxwell roamed restlessly up and down the lines of guns, tugging at the boarding-nets, peering into buckets, lifting the lids of the arms-chests and casting critical glances aloft. The men returned to their stations and a silence settled over the ship.

With the advantage of his height, Lamb was able to see clear over the netted hammocks along the side merely by stepping up on to a gun-carriage. The approaching frigate had not deviated from her line since she had turned into the wind and before long she was close enough for Lamb to count her gun-ports. Of much the same size as the *Sturdy*, she carried only thirty-two guns. Lamb was not surprised; the French, he knew, considered British ships to be generally over-gunned, sacrificing speed for fire power, and studying the oncoming vessel as she lifted and dipped over the water with a graceful lightness, he privately agreed. Close-hauled, she was still moving at an impressive rate, a white moustache of foam showing at her cutwater. The *Sturdy*, with more canvas set and a slight advantage from the wind, was travelling no faster, he judged, and if they both maintained their respective courses, they would – and he smiled at the thought – cross bowsprits in about half an hour.

Pacing slowly beside his guns, he tried to envisage the scene from above; the two frigates and their wakes were forming the two sides of an obtuse angle, the apex yet to be determined but needing only an onward shift of the eye to fix its position. The parallel line to one side, added by the brig, complicated the simple configuration in his mind and as he could think of no geometric shape that would encompass all three lines he abandoned the imagery and returned to the deck of the *Sturdy*.

The other frigate was little more than a mile away when her gun-ports lifted and the snouts of her guns appeared along her side. They were painted a bright red, Lamb was interested to note. The instant they appeared Cutler's voice rang out from the quarterdeck.

'Larboard guns, open ports! Run out your guns!'

With ready fists already closed around lanyards, the gun-ports rose as one. Preventer tackles were whipped free from the ring-bolts amidships and the guns trundled their little wheels down the slope of the deck as their crews heaved on the side-tackles, bringing the trucks hard up to the side and extending the black barrels out over the water.

A puff of gunsmoke drifted up from the Frenchman's foremost gun, followed a few seconds later by the flat report of the explosion. A line of white splashes appeared on the water as the shot skipped, pointing directly at the *Sturdy*, but the final splash was at least two cables distant. A lone, derisive cheer sounded from one of the aftermost guns but was cut short by Maxwell's angry bellow.

'Silence on deck! Mr Blissenden, take that man's name.'

Cutler's voice rang out. 'Stand by the starboard guns! Open ports! Run out your guns!'

The men ran across from the larboard side and within the minute the starboard guns were poking their muzzles through the ports, their captains squatting at the breeches.

'Mr Tyler! Mr Lamb!'

Maxwell was standing amidships between the guns of the two lieutenants. The two men crossed the deck to stand before him. The first lieutenant's voice was forceful, urgent.

'In a moment the captain intends to swing to starboard, as if we are going to cut between the frigate and the brig. As soon as your guns bear you will commence firing without further orders, Mr Tyler. Clear?'

Tyler nodded. 'Yes, sir.'

'At the right moment we will tack again, to larboard, hopefully to cut across his stern. You, Mr Lamb, must make the most of the opportunity. Double-shot your guns with round-shot and canister. Understood?'

'Yes, sir.'

Maxwell hurried away to his station aft of the mainmast and Lamb and Tyler crossed back to their guns. Lamb roared his orders and had a quick word with his quarter-gunners as the guns were hauled briefly inboard to have the canisters of case shot rammed down the barrels.

'Haul sheets and tacks!' bellowed Doubleday from the quarterdeck.

'Haul sheets and tacks!' echoed the master's mates from the maindeck.

The French frigate fired again as the *Sturdy*'s head began to swing, a single, ranging shot that grazed the mizzen chain-plates before plunging into the curving wake, doing no more damage than severing the aftermost lanyard. Seconds later, Tyler's guns erupted as they came to bear, followed almost immediately by the aftermost battery under Kennedy's command. Lamb, excitement bubbling white-hot within him, attempted to keep one eye on the fall of shot and the other eye on the brig, which had now come before the wind and would shortly be within reach of his guns if she kept on the same tack.

As a result of the *Sturdy*'s turn to starboard the French frigate now presented a bows-on target which, while making her less vulnerable to the British guns, effectively limited her useful guns to the bow-chasers. Her captain was quick to remedy this and her head was already turning away as the first shots hit her. Splinters flew from the forward bulwarks, her figurehead disappeared in a shower of debris and her spritsail and foremast staysail sagged towards the foremast as a lucky shot severed the bowsprit. A loud, ragged cheer went up from the *Sturdy*'s deck and this time there was no reprimand from Maxwell, although Lamb heard one of Tyler's quarter-gunners savagely requesting that his gunners 'keep their fucking eyes inboard, the swabs'.

The Frenchmen were quick, their broadside sounding before the larboard guns were run out again. Aimed high, in the hope of crippling the *Sturdy* by damaging her spars and rigging, the shot tore a dozen holes in the sails and the foremast lost the support of one of her backstays with the same roundshot that removed the head of a Marine in the foretop.

The two frigates were now about three hundred yards apart, point-blank range for their twelve-pounders, and Lamb was on tenterhooks as he awaited the expected tack to larboard. The brig was approaching fast from the starboard beam and in a few moments she would be in a position to add her fire power to that of her compatriot. The larboard guns roared again and before the echoes had died away Lamb heard through his numbed ears the voice of the master raised in a tremendous bellow to the sail-handlers. Helmsmen and hands had evidently been well prepared for the move; the ship swung violently in almost her own length to point her bowsprit at the Frenchman's stern, her deck heeling sharply as she turned and then steadying as the helmsmen checked the swing. With the sudden advantage of the wind abaft her starboard quarter, the frigate rushed down on her opponent, the French captain caught flat-footed.

'Stand by, my lads!' yelled Lamb, his voice cracking with excitement. 'Fire as you bear!'

Another cheer rang out, from the larboard gunners and the men in the tops. Lamb had his eyes fixed on the Frenchman's stern but he risked a quick glance along her decks. To his delight he saw that the wheel and the helmsmen had disappeared, smashed by a truly lucky shot, leaving her captain with only his sails with which to manoeuvre.

The bowsprit swept past the enemy's stern, with perhaps only thirty yards between the two hulls. Lamb glimpsed her name – the *Réunion*, picked out in gold – a bare half-second before the first of his guns fired. Her wide stern windows were instantly blown inwards as roundshot and case shot blasted through the captain's quarters, tore through the bulkhead beyond and swept the length of her deck. The taffrail was lined with men armed with muskets – Lamb could see the sparks and flashes from the priming pans but the musket fire went unheard in the greater noise of the *Sturdy*'s guns, firing at intervals so close that a continuous thundering roll ran down her starboard side as she passed the shattered stern of the frigate. Lamb turned to keep his eyes on the *Réunion* as the first of the starboard guns were being frantically swabbed and reloaded. Her stern was already a ruin, the windows a gaping hole and the rudder shattered; he could only guess at the damage and carnage along her deck, where shot after shot continued to blast its length. A few brave souls were still aiming their muskets over the taffrail and from between them the *Réunion*'s stern-chasers suddenly belched smoke and flame as they fired together. They were a trifle premature; a second later and they would have swept the *Sturdy*'s quarterdeck but as it was the shots passed over her waist, doing no more than maltreating a little canvas and rigging and shortening Kennedy's life some-what as his hat was snatched from his head by the wind of a passing shot.

The instant the last starboard gun had fired Doubleday's voice boomed out and the frigate wore, swinging her stern through the wind, away from the *Réunion* and her so-far-silent larboard guns. As the *Sturdy* swept round in a wide circle in order to bring her larboard guns to bear again, Lamb snatched the chance to study the *Réunion* through his telescope. She was a sorry, bloody sight as she squatted helpless in the water unable to steer, her lower rigging hanging in strands and the mainmast leaning wearily against the foremast. He moved his glass along her deck, picking out overturned guns, sprawled bodies and the wreckage of her boats. On the quarterdeck a small group of men bent over a figure lying beside the stump of the shattered wheel – her captain, he guessed, from the attention he was receiving. He lowered his glass and tucked it beneath his belt as he turned his attention to his guns and their crews.

A shout from Tyler made him spin round. 'Look, Matthew, I think she's afire!'

Lamb raised his telescope again. A tendril of black smoke was rising into the air between her foremast and mainmast and bending with the wind over her starboard side. A flash of movement from the far side of the *Réunion* caught his eye – it was the brig, turning into the wind half a cable from her ally, gallantly intent on assistance.

A wild mixture of shouts and cheers burst from the *Sturdy*'s deck, the men waving their arms and leaping up and down in excitement.

'She's struck! She's struck!'

Lambs eyes flashed to her mizzen peak. It was true; her colours were jerking and fluttering in descent. He gave a broad grin and resisted the urge to join his men in their shouting and waving. Something struck him between the shoulder blades and he turned to see the laughing face of Tyler about to clap him on the back again. Instead, he stuck out his hand and the two men shook each other's fist and smacked one another on the shoulder.

'That will do! Silence on deck! Silence, I say!' It was Maxwell, striding along the deck, his face dark with fury. The cheers and shouts faltered and died away. 'This is a King's ship, not a bloody kindergarten! Get back to your posts – every man-jack of you,' he added, his furious eye resting significantly on Tyler.

Tyler gave Lamb a surreptitious wink and trotted back to his battery. Lamb suppressed a grin and turned away to see the brig wearing, sheering away from the *Réunion* as if the sight of her lowering colours was enough to remove all thoughts of assistance. He watched her set off with the wind astern – goodbye and good riddance, he thought.

Cutler allowed the *Sturdy* to continue her curving course until she luffed, hanging in the eye of the wind about three hundred yards from the *Réunion* with her larboard guns trained across the gap. Lamb wondered which of the officers would be given the honour of boarding the Frenchman to receive the surrender and entertained himself with thoughts of his name being selected, but he was disappointed. Kennedy was summoned to the quarterdeck and Lamb eyed him with a little envy as Cutler gave his instructions. His eyes were still on the quarterdeck as Kennedy saluted and turned away and the enormous explosion which smashed into the still air caused his heart to lurch and his heels to leave the deck in shock.

He whirled round to see a great ball of smoke and debris expanding up and out from the remains of the *Réunion* and hastily grabbed at a foremast shroud as the *Sturdy* rolled sharply in the blast of air and disturbed water. Solid objects – broken timbers, hammocks, bodies – seemed to hang in the air for a long moment before they fell, splashing into the area of angry sea surrounding the shattered frigate. Her forward and after parts were in two separate pieces, as if a giant axe had chopped through her waist. As Lamb watched, motionless with shock and horror, the larger aft section rolled on to its side, showing the torn keel, and then quickly settled as the water rushed into the exposed compartments, leaving the hulk floating and awash amidst the wreckage surrounding it. The smaller bows section must have slipped under at the same time – when Lamb looked for it, it had gone.

For several long seconds there was absolute silence on the deck of the *Sturdy*. The end of the frigate had been so sudden, so cataclysmic, so final, as to almost suspend belief of eyes and ears; then Lamb heard, through his ringing ears, the voice of one of the quarter-gunners.

'Well, if you've got a job to do, then you might as well do it properly, I always say!'

A low ripple of uncertain laughter came from the men about him and they stirred, dragging their reluctant gaze from the grave of the *Réunion*.

'Secure the guns!' roared Maxwell. 'Douse your matches! Get those men moving, Mr Tyler, Mr Lamb!'

Cutler brought the frigate as close to the barely visible hulk of the *Réunion*'s afterpart as he dared but in spite of careful scanning of the floating rubbish and bodies, not a single survivor was found and the *Sturdy* resumed her course eastwards. With the ports and guns of his battery secured and the men busy with brooms and shovels retrieving the precious sand from the deck, Lamb made his way to the aft companionway, intent on washing the greasy gunsmoke from his face and the bitter, gritty taste of it from his tongue. The boatswain and the sailmaker and their mates were already hard at work repairing and replacing the torn canvas and the damaged rigging. It was not yet noon.

The next day was Sunday and as the hands assembled in their divisions on the maindeck Cutler was below, dragging a small retinue of warrant and petty officers behind him as he moved from compartment to compartment, satisfying himself that the ship was not in immediate danger of falling apart, that the boatswain had not sold the entire contents of the cable-tiers and that the midshipmen were not secreting naked ladies in the cockpit. Having completed his inspection of the ship below and then of the men above, he moved to the quarterdeck. Today, he chose to read the Articles of War, speaking in a loud, sonorous voice, the words so familiar to him that he needed but to cast an occasional glance at the page.

Lamb noted, with some amusement, that Cutler had a habit of pausing after uttering the words '– shall suffer death' and scanning the silent assembly below him, as if to impress on them the awful warning in that particular Article. It was, he thought, a theatrical trick which he had seen practised by other captains, a significant little silence designed to add an extra measure of menace to the sombre words. He doubted if the men were impressed by it one iota – the Articles had been read to them so often that in all probability they no longer heard them, in spite of their apparent quiet attentiveness.

Cutler finished reading and closed the leather-bound Articles. At this point he would normally have given Maxwell a nod as a signal to dismiss the hands to their dinners but today he advanced to the edge of the quarterdeck, leaned his hands on the rail and surveyed the silent faces below.

'Yesterday,' said Cutler, 'this ship sank a French frigate and caused an armed brig to turn and run. On the face of it we should all be very pleased with ourselves. The issue, of course, was never in doubt and I was gratified at the way you conducted yourselves. However, if any of you have the notion that we won a great victory, then let me disabuse you of it. Leaving aside the brig for the moment, this frigate, in terms of number of guns and weight of metal, was much superior to the Frenchman. Even so, we might have been badly mauled if an early fortunate shot had not destroyed her wheel. It was that and that alone which gave us such a quick and easy victory. We buried two men yesterday; had circumstances been slightly different, we could have buried a good many more. Bear that in mind the next time we exercise the guns – it might fire you with a little more enthusiasm. That is all. Carry on, Mr Maxwell.'

Chapter 6

Calcutta, a hot, noisy, dirty, crowded city, sprawled to the west of the Ganges delta, where the great river is split into a dozen meandering waterways that make their way across the unhealthy lowlands to the Bay of Bengal. The city was situated a considerable distance from the coast and the Hooghly was not an easy river to navigate. Fortunately, the *Sturdy* had no need to sail as far as the city – the commodore's ship, the old *Lord Warden*, was anchored in a wide reach south of the docks. The twenty-eight gun frigate *Rapier* was moored close to her and stretching upriver was a small forest of spars belonging to the assembled convoy – merchantmen of various sizes and conditions of paintwork, and, like royalty amongst peasants, two Indiamen.

The broad, blue pennant that hung limply from the mast of the seventy-four denoted a second-class commodore and as such deserved the honour of a nine-gun salute. The last flat echo had barely died away when signal flags were hoisted on the *Lord Warden*.

'Our number, sir,' squeaked Blissenden, nervously clutching the signals book. 'Captain to repair on board, sir.'

'Acknowledge,' said Cutler. He had anticipated the order the moment he saw the blue pendant and was now sweating uncomfortably beneath his best, broadcloth coat, his report tucked beneath his arm.

He was rowed across to the two-decker and piped aboard with due ceremony. Two hours later he was back, beaming widely and dispensing brandy fumes generously about the deck.

'The officers to my quarters in five minutes, Mr Maxwell,' he said in passing and disappeared into his cabin.

For once, Cutler was in an expansive mood and was at pains to put his officers at their ease.

'Sit, gentlemen, sit. Make yourselves comfortable, please.

Watson, a glass of wine for the officers, if you please, and if it is warm I shall dangle you from the yardarm by your balls.'

Watson's manhood was saved; the wine was no more than tepid and of considerably better quality than Lamb was accustomed to drinking in the gunroom. He sipped it gratefully, sitting stiffly upright in his chair; a junior officer might be invited to sit in the captain's presence but a prudent one took care to show he was not lounging.

The commodore, it turned out, was one Captain Peabody, an old acquaintance of Cutler's – indeed, one of his former captains in his days as a lieutenant. He was, said Cutler, in a fever of impatience to set off and was only awaiting the arrival of a third Indiaman now loading cargo and embarking passengers upriver. She was expected to join the convoy in a day or so and the *Sturdy* must be ready for sea in all respects by that time.

So far as French frigates and privateers were concerned, the news was mixed. Surcouf, who had made this part of the world ring with his exploits, was as busy as ever in the Bay of Bengal, his favourite hunting ground. He was not alone. Reports of attacks from other privateers – Lememe, Duterol, Mallerousse, all of them infamous – were brought to Calcutta almost daily. As for the reported squadrons of French frigates roaming the Indian Ocean, little had been heard or seen of such for many weeks. It was Peabody's contention that they had been recalled to home waters or perhaps the West Indies, where their services could be put to better use than attacking the odd merchant-man.

With regard to the disposition of the convoy, Peabody's plan was simple and straightforward enough even for merchant masters to comprehend. He expected to sail with fourteen merchant ships, including the three Indiamen, and it was his intention to form three columns, with an Indiaman at the head of each. The *Lord Warden* would lead the convoy, the *Sturdy* would be deployed to windward and the *Rapier* would look after the tail.

'Captain Peabody confided that another sixth-rate would make our task very much easier but as he cannot pluck sixth-rates out of the air we must make do with what we have. I cannot promise you an easy voyage home, gentlemen. For the immediate time, then, our task is clear – we must be ready to sail the moment the Indiaman joins us. We will take on water this afternoon and gunpowder tomorrow morning. By that time, Mr Maxwell, you will no doubt have completed your overhaul of the rigging – every inch, that is. There will be no shore leave granted – the men will have to forgo the dubious delights of the Calcutta brothels. You gentlemen, however, are more fortunate. I cannot allow you shore leave but I can allow you to accept the commodore's kind invitation to the officers of both frigates to dine with him tonight – in fact, I have already accepted on your behalf. It will be a splendid opportunity for you to become acquainted with each other.'

Lamb and his fellow officers were given ample time to become acquainted not only with the officers of the *Rapier* and the *Lord Warden* but also, over the next few days, with the officers and masters of many of the merchantmen. Dinner on the flagship was followed by dinner on the Indiaman *Maid of Kent* and then by dinner on the Indiaman *Orion* as Peabody waited with growing impatience for the *Bengal Star* to join his convoy. Boats plied daily up the river to the Indiaman bearing notes from the commodore; acid queries, sharp reminders and eventually open threats were politely handed to her master; the boats returned bearing apologies, complaints of delayed goods and passengers, details of urgent work being carried out on the hull and repeated promises of imminent sailing. After six days and as many promises, Peabody summoned Cutler and gave him orders to confront the captain of the *Bengal Star* with an ultimatum – to join the convoy by noon the next day, because with him or without him, Peabody intended to weigh anchor at that time.

It was an awkward situation for Peabody; Indiamen were not bound by the Compulsory Convoy Act and he had no legal authority over them. The master of the *Bengal Star*, however, like the masters of the other two Indiamen, had requested that she sail with the convoy and having assented, there was little that Peabody could do except to curse all merchant masters and their civilian ideas of urgency.

The officers of the *Sturdy* did not keep watch in harbour – that duty was given to the ship's petty officers – but Lamb happened to emerge from the aft companionway as Cutler made for his cabin on his return from his briefing by the commodore. Lamb politely touched his hat and stood aside as Cutler strode past. The captain nodded absently and then checked his stride.

'What are your plans for the next hour or two, Mr Lamb?' he demanded.

Lamb indicated the shoe in his hand. The buckle had come adrift and he was intending to seek out the sailmaker.

'Just to beg a few stitches from the sailmaker, sir, and then to spend an hour or so with a book.' This last was a lie; he had planned to sleep throughout the afternoon in an attempt to recover from the previous evening's lively hospitality on board the *Orion*, but he had no intention of admitting such idle intentions to the captain.

'In that case you may accompany me upriver to visit the *Bengal Star*. It will be more entertaining for you than your book. I will give you three minutes to change out of those rags you are wearing.'

The river was crowded with native craft and the silt-laden water was flowing fast as the gig was pulled upriver. The crew was in a muck sweat before the boat had travelled half a mile and Lamb, sitting at his ease, was also sweating heavily beneath the weight of his heavy coat. Cutler made no attempt at conversation during the journey and sat in apparent gloom, moodily puffing at a cheroot.

Cutler was welcomed on board the Indiaman by her master, a round-faced, merry-eyed little man of some sixty years and the pair of them disappeared into his quarters beneath the poopdeck, leaving Lamb in the care of the third officer. He was a confident, cheerful young man, his freckled face beneath bright red hair showing the effects of the strong sun – the skin was peeling from his nose and forehead. He shook Lamb by the hand and glanced up at his face.

'Is it as warm up there as it is down here?' he asked with a grin. He saw a certain coolness come into Lamb's eye and went on hurriedly: 'Forgive me; no doubt you have too many remarks of that sort. I have some fruit and a bottle of Holland below – what say we make ourselves comfortable out of this sun?'

Lamb was impressed with the size of Steele's cabin and not a little envious; he estimated it to be at least twice the size of his own cramped little canvas-sided cell on the *Sturdy*. The fruit was refreshing and the gin stimulating and inside ten minutes Lamb's shyness had thawed under the twin influences of the alcohol and Steele's friendly chatter. He shed his coat, loosened his stock and stretched out his legs.

Steele was a one-time midshipman, he told Lamb, and had circumstances been different he would have been a lieutenant some years ago. He had disgraced himself a few weeks before he was due to take his examination – he gave a lewd wink, suggesting female involvement in his fall from grace – and he had been turned off the ship by the captain there and then.

'I was angry at the time, of course – dumped ashore in Portsmouth with my sea-chest at my feet, no money to speak of, no prospects, no hope of another berth. I felt my life was shattered. Still, looking back, the pious old bastard did me a good turn, unknowingly.' He waved his hand around the cabin. 'Look at me now. I live better, I'm paid better and a little investment at one end of the voyage gives me a handsome profit at the other.'

'Yes,' said Lamb, looking around the neat, well-furnished cabin, 'you appear to be very comfortable.'

'Have you never thought of leaving the service?' asked Steele with a sly grin.

'No, never,' said Lamb, taking a long pull at his glass.

'You could do very well for yourself, if you found the right berth. With a little luck, I should clear close on five hundred pounds on the round voyage this time.'

Lamb smiled. 'With a little luck I could make ten times that on one prize-ship!'

'Maybe, maybe not,' said Steele, refilling their glasses. 'My prospects are at least steady. You could go for years without taking a prize that would give you as much as I make in a year.'

'Perhaps you are right,' said Lamb, tiring of the argument. 'If we meet in twenty years' time, when you are master of your own brig and I am a mere admiral of the blue, you will be at perfect liberty to scoff at me!'

Steele chuckled and reached beneath his pillow. 'What do you think of my art collection? I bought these yesterday, in the town.'

They were pornographic pictures, cleverly drawn and with

much attention to detail. Lamb's experience in the activities they depicted was next to nil but he was in no mind to admit this to Steele and chuckled lightly in an easy, man-of-the-world manner as he examined them, suppressing the tendency of his eyes to bulge.

'Very good,' he said lightly as he passed them back to Steele.

'I shall sell them for five times the price I paid, when we reach London,' confided Steele. He looked at Lamb and winked. 'The ladies like this sort of thing, you know. A glimpse of these can do wonders, very often.'

He laughed, more than a little drunk, and began to boast of past conquests and the demands that had been made on him by lonely women inflamed by the heat of long tropical voyages. Lamb laughed politely at his lies and felt that Steele was becoming tiresome. He was pleased to hear a rap at the door and a shout that he was keeping his captain waiting.

He bade Steele a hasty goodbye and raced up to the deck in time to beat Cutler into the gig, as naval convention demanded. Cutler descended very slowly and carefully and seated himself with a bump, the air in the gig suddenly rich with the smell of brandy.

'Shove off,' ordered Lamb. 'Give way together.'

The boat moved out into the stream of boats and made its way downriver. Cutler leaned back against the transom and fell asleep, snoring loudly.

Whether by reason of the commodore's ultimatum or by the persuasive force of Cutler's charm was not forthcoming but the *Bengal Star* duly made its precarious way down the treacherous reaches of the river and joined the convoy at anchor shortly before noon the next morning. A single gun fired from the flagship was the signal to get under way and the *Sturdy* led the long line of ships downriver to the open sea. The masters had been well briefed regarding their respective positions in the convoy and had each been supplied with a neat diagram but, being strong-minded, independent individuals with their own firm ideas as to the best positions for their vessels they gave scant regard to the commodore's orders or his diagrams and it took the remainder of the daylight hours for the escorts to bully, cajole and threaten the masters to take up the places laid down for them. Signals came thick and fast from the commodore and the frigates dashed to and fro like sheepdogs around an unruly flock, snapping at the heels of recalcitrant ships and leading lost ones back to their places, almost by the scruff of the neck. It was dusk before the three straggling lines were in roughly the order accorded them on the convoy plan and the flow of signals from the commodore slowed and finally ceased, signifying either Peabody's grudging satisfaction or his apoplectic collapse.

Convoy orders stipulated that at night ships would maintain a distance of two cables from the vessel in front and three cables from those abeam. On paper, this gave a block of ships neatly dispersed over an area of sea three-quarters of a mile wide and almost a mile long. Stern lanterns were to be shown to assist following ships to maintain the correct distance and dire warnings had been issued regarding the dangers of breaking formation.

The *Sturdy* patrolled to windward of the convoy. Cutler, hoarse from shouting, gave his final orders to the officer of the watch before he went to his quarters for his supper.

'Keep a close eye on the buggers, Mr Lamb,' he whispered. 'If any fall out of line, chase them back again. You know what to do – call me only if you think it is necessary.'

It was a fine, clear night. The moon was a thin, silver crescent and the sky was ablaze with a myriad stars shining like diamonds strewn across black velvet. Lamb paced the quarterdeck, pausing at every turn to peer anxiously at the indistinct lines of merchantmen to larboard. He stopped short, crossed to the side and narrowed his eyes into the darkness. Was that brig turning out of line? Yes, she was! He turned to the quartermaster and pointed.

'Lay the ship alongside that brig, quartermaster,' he ordered.

'Down helm,' muttered the quartermaster.

The frigate slipped through the black water and came within hailing distance of the fat, little brig ghosting along in a short column of one.

'Ahoy there, *Constance*!' shouted Lamb.

A dark figure materialized at her rail and hailed back.

'Yes, what do you want?'

'You are out of line. Resume your proper station.'

'Can't help that,' returned the voice. 'I nearly ran my

bowsprit up the arse of the stupid bastard ahead.'

'You must maintain your station – keep two cables astern of him.'

'Yes? Well, tell him to show his fucking stern light then. We ain't got fucking cats' eyes, you know.'

The man turned from the rail and disappeared into the darkness of the brig's deck.

Lamb swore softly and turned away. The expressions on the faces of the quartermaster, the helmsman and the duty midshipman as he turned round were so serious, so solemn and rigidly grave that he knew at once that a bare instant before they had all been split by wide grins. Midshipman Blissenden in particular was in danger of bursting with the effort of keeping his breath from exploding from between his tight-pressed lips as he stared steadfastly over the starboard rail.

'You heard the man, quartermaster,' snapped Lamb. 'The next ship in line, if you please.'

It took several loud hails before an answering shout came from the three-masted barque and Lamb was beginning to wonder if her master had dispensed with the formality of keeping a night watch. He pointed out, with some shortness, that the barque was showing no stern lights.

'Oh, are we not? So sorry!'

Lamb kept the frigate hovering off the barque's stern until the lanterns were lit and then allowed the brig to come up alongside. The brig gave no answer when Lamb shouted across but after a moment or two she moved, sulkily, it seemed, back into line.

During the night the formation of the convoy slackened as ships from the lee pulled out of line and the distance between them lengthened. Some masters, accustomed to shortening sail as dusk fell and content with a speed of two or three knots until morning, objected to the speed of the convoy, reduced as it was to that of the slowest vessel. Others, who liked nothing better than to crack on day and night and suffered agonies if adverse weather necessitated taking in a single reef in the mainsail, slyly overtook their more cautious brothers in the night and crowded up behind the sterns of the leading Indiamen. As a consequence, at first light, in Lamb's morning watch, he was horrified to see ships spread untidily far and wide over a distance of several miles, at the rear of which was the *Rapier*, desperately trying to round up a couple of vessels which had dropped astern of her during the night.

This was the pattern set for the next few days; early morning, widespread confusion followed by a gradual shrinkage in convoy area as the ships were bullied back into formation again. It was hard work for the frigates, acting as sheepdogs to such an undisciplined flock, and called for constant sail-handling as they tacked and wore and came about and tacked again. The hands were left exhausted at the end of their watch and the officers almost voiceless from shouting at stubborn masters.

'My God!' exclaimed Kennedy hoarsely as Lamb relieved him from watch on the second evening out from Calcutta. 'We've got weeks of this to look forward to.'

The commodore, inevitably, gave up the wearying struggle to keep the merchantmen in any sort of tight order and after a few days he was content with a loose formation of ships in no set order following the three Indiamen. The masters were happier with this arrangement and for the two frigates it meant an altogether easier life.

The first of the privateers appeared after four days and some six-hundred-odd miles out of Calcutta. The *Sturdy*, to windward of the convoy, sighted the sail approaching from the south at first light. A submission from Cutler that he investigate was answered from the flagship with a brief negative and the convoy ploughed doggedly on as the stranger came into view. It was a slim brigantine, fast enough to give three knots to both frigates and sufficiently gunned and manned to take any armed merchantman with the ease of a cat snatching up a mouse.

The brigantine closed to about a mile and a half and settled on a parallel course. The distance was a good half-mile beyond the range of the *Sturdy*'s long-guns but just at the limit of the *Lord Warden*'s twenty-four-pounders at their maximum elevation. The flat crack of the report reached the quarterdeck of the *Sturdy* two seconds after the shot left the barrel and every telescope to hand was immediately raised and trained on the privateer. The shot was well aimed and only a little unlucky; a small plume of white water arose, dead ahead of the brigantine's bow. Her reaction was immediate, sheering away as if stung. She kept pace with the convoy from a more prudent distance for another hour before turning away to the south from whence she had come.

'Well, we have seen the last of her, I think,' commented Lamb as he stood by the lee rail with the first lieutenant.

'Don't you believe it,' grunted Maxwell. 'I'll wager we'll see her back before long with a few of her friends in tow. She's weighed up the opposition pretty well – two frigates and a third-rate won't put them off.'

Maxwell was right. At first light the lookout reported two sail to windward, hull down, four points off the larboard bow. And two more, both fine on the larboard quarter – and another, dead ahead.

Cutler was on the quarterdeck before the last sighting was reported; shaved and fully dressed, he had clearly been expecting this.

'Mr Cowan, make to the commodore "Five ships to windward", and then take your glass aloft and keep us informed as to what you see. Mr Lamb, beat to quarters, if you please. Ah, good morning, Mr Maxwell – we are in for a busy time, I think.'

'Good morning, sir. Yes, a busy and bloody one, I shouldn't wonder, sir,' replied Maxwell dourly.

'Very possibly. We must endeavour to make it more bloody for them than for us, though, eh?'

'Quite, sir.'

The commodore acknowledged the *Sturdy*'s signal, which had certainly been unnecessary in the sense of passing information – the *Lord Warden*'s mainmast was higher than the *Sturdy*'s and her lookouts just as keen-eyed – but it had been absolutely necessary in hierarchical terms. Recognition of subordinate rank and status was held more jealously from above than from below and the withholding of information, plain as it might have been to both ships, would have earned the frigate a swift rebuke.

News from Cowan came down piecemeal as his glass picked out details from the approaching vessels: yesterday's brigantine, two gun-brigs, another brigantine, a *chasse-marée*. They were apparently converging on the first brigantine, the northernmost vessel, now directly to windward and square on the beam.

118

Cutler was in high spirits, smiling, talking to Lamb and Maxwell, passing comments to the men as they pattered about the quarterdeck seeing to the carronades and the stern-chasers.

'They will approach to near gunshot range and then split, I shouldn't wonder, to keep the three escorts as far apart as they can. Careful with that crow, Beamish, you will ruin Mr Maxwell's paint. Their intention will be to keep us busy while their comrades pick out a nice fat ship from the lee side. Good morning, Mr Moriarty – have a care for my poor head with those chains, won't you? There is really little we can do until they get a good deal closer – it would suit them very well for us to break away and challenge them. Mr Blissenden, perhaps you would be good enough to nip down and inform my servant that his captain is dying for want of coffee – you will join me, Mr Maxwell, Mr Lamb? – a large pot, enough for three, if you please, Mr Blissenden. I expect the commodore will remove himself from the van soon and place himself to windward – the three Indiamen should be able to cope with any attack, providing they remain together. Call Mr Cowan down, Mr Lamb, we can see well enough from the deck and his observations are becoming superfluous. Ah, coffee! What would life be without our morning brew, eh, Mr Maxwell?'

Lamb sipped his coffee gratefully. The bitter brew, steaming hot, warmed his empty stomach and sent its invigorating tendrils throughout his body. Watson, he thought, had shown commendable initiative in boiling his kettle before the galley fires were doused. The captain, Maxwell and he stood in a companionable little group drinking their coffee and looking out to larboard. The privateers were now in a body, cracking on at a fine pace and heading for the convoy's beam – twenty minutes or so would bring them within range, he thought.

Sturdy's number was flying from the *Lord Warden*.

'Take station one mile to windward of van, sir,' reported Blissenden, his finger still pointing at the flag book.

'Acknowledge,' said Cutler.

'Execute, sir.'

'Very good. Down helm! The ship is yours, Mr Doubleday.'

'Thank you, sir,' said the master formally and stepped forward to take his place in the centre of the quarterdeck, forward of the wheel. From now on, the responsibility for executing the ship's movements would be his, leaving the captain to concentrate his mind on tactics and his guns.

The *Lord Warden* heeled ponderously out of line and into the wind, luffing while the convoy sailed past her until she had gained the position vacated by the *Sturdy*. The convoy was showing its tightest, neatest formation since leaving Calcutta. Merchant masters who had hitherto felt cramped with a quarter of a mile of clear water around them now crowded up close enough to their colleagues to endanger their yards; Lamb glanced over his shoulder at the mass of close-packed ships and received a distinct impression of hunched shoulders. The five privateers, coming on in line abreast, were now little more than two miles away.

Maxwell had a brief word with the captain and went down to the maindeck to see to his guns. Lamb approached Cutler and touched his hat.

'Have I your leave to join my guns, sir?'

'Bide awhile, Mr Lamb. I may have need of you here yet. Mr Kennedy will look to your guns.'

The *Lord Warden*'s larboard guns fired their broadside, a tremendous grumbling roar vibrating through the air, dirty yellow-grey smoke billowing up and washing away to leeward, shadowing the bright sea. Perhaps Peabody hoped to hit the privateers while they still presented a broad target but the range was extreme, even for his guns with their quoins fully out and fired on the uproll. Lamb kept his eyes on the water around the privateers and curled his lip as a ragged line of little fountains showed momentarily, well short of their target. It might have been better, he thought, had the commodore held his fire for a minute or so longer – as it was, he had now shot his main bolt because the vessels were dispersing to left and right, spreading like an opening fan.

Two of the privateers, both brigs, headed in the direction of the *Sturdy*, to windward of the Indiamen; the other three made for the rear of the convoy, giving the seventy-four a wide berth. As the brigs came round in a great circle ahead of the *Lord Warden* they came within range of her guns and she tacked in order to bring her starboard guns to bear. Lamb raised his telescope as the broadside sounded and saw the mainsail of the rearmost brig suddenly split; a mass of white water thrown up in the brig's wake showed that the bulk of the broadside had gone wide.

'Our number, sir,' cried Blissenden. 'Chase – engage, sir.'

'Acknowledge,' said Cutler crisply. 'Mr Doubleday, wear ship and put me alongside that leading brig. Mr Cowan, my compliments to Mr Maxwell and he is to engage, as and when, directly we are within range. Mr Lamb, keep your eyes on the convoy and inform me of developments there – we may have to break off and return if things get too hot for them.'

'Aye aye, sir,' said Lamb, casting a sorrowful look at his battery of guns. 'The *Lord Warden* is wearing, sir.'

The *Lord Warden* was turning away from the convoy, her head coming into the wind. Clearly, she was going to the assistance of the little *Rapier*, which was standing bravely out to cut off the three privateers circling round to the rear and lee of the convoy. As Lamb watched, the three separated, the *chasse-marée* making directly for the *Rapier* and the two brigantines racing for the convoy's lee quarter with the wind behind them.

Lamb passed this information on to the captain, who threw a quick glance over his shoulder and grunted before turning his attention back to the rapidly approaching brig. It was now bows-on to the frigate, both vessels moving along the same arc with the wind abeam.

'Luff, Mr Doubleday,' cried Cutler. 'Give me the weather gauge.'

The frigate came nearer to the wind, losing a little headway. The brig maintained her course, her black hull with two thin yellow lines running along the sides and her black-painted masts giving Lamb the impression of a large and angry wasp.

Maxwell's forward larboard guns were now able to bear; the range was perhaps half a mile and with each passing moment more of his guns, trained hard forward, would bear. He had to judge the moment when the maximum number of guns to bear was balanced against the shrinking range and that instant now arrived. Both ships fired their guns at exactly the same moment; the brig's six- and nine-pound roundshot, bar-shot and chain-shot ripped through the lower sails and rigging of the *Sturdy*, parting stays and shrouds and bringing down a tangle of sheets, halyards and blocks into the netting rigged above the deck. The heavier shot of the frigate, at almost point-blank range, smashed into the foremast chains and larboard bow of the brig which, at the instant of firing, had wore, spinning on its heel to shoot across the frigate's bows and immediately tacking to bring her starboard guns to bear on the *Sturdy*'s beam.

'Lord!' exclaimed Cutler in admiration. 'She handles like a cutter in —'

The rest of his words were extinguished by the crash of gunfire from both ships as starboard engaged starboard across a stretch of water some seventy yards wide. For a brief, stretched instant Lamb glimpsed the deck of the brig, her men crouched over the guns behind the low bulwark, the captain by the wheel with his arm outstretched towards the frigate and a packed mass of men along the length of the deck with their faces all seemingly turned towards Lamb, axes, cutlasses and pistols in their hands. An overturned gun and a length of shattered bulwark told of some of the damage of the *Sturdy*'s first hits before the image vanished in a rolling cloud of smoke as the brig let fly its starboard guns. Iron screamed low over the frigate's deck and Lamb staggered in the wind of a passing shot which neatly plucked the epaulette from Cutler's right shoulder before ploughing through the upper torso of one of the helmsmen, hurling his body wide and drenching his mate in blood. One of the guns from Lamb's own battery was on its side behind its shattered gun-port and screams came from the waist as splinters from the side whirled murderously through the air. But the brig was being hit hard, too, as roundshot and canister smashed through her side, iron and timber shards scything through the gunners and waiting boarding party. The exchange was brief; the ships were passing each other too rapidly and too closely and the *Sturdy* heeled as Doubleday brought her head round to cut across the brig's wake in order to give the guns the chance of a crack at her stern. The brig's master was too awake for that; she, too, was turning sharply and as the *Sturdy* came into the wind so the brig wore, shooting off towards the convoy with the wind at her stern.

Lamb had been careful to keep a watchful eye on the activities going on elsewhere and he had passed the information on to Cutler, mostly in a bellow, receiving a preoccupied nod or grunt in return. The wasp-like brig's sister had turned towards the convoy before the *Sturdy* fired her first shots and was now lost from sight after passing through the mass of merchantmen to find a plum on the more favourable lee side. The *Rapier* and the *chasse-marée* were exchanging shots as they chased each other's tail and were falling rapidly astern of the convoy – clearly, a deliberate ploy on the part of the privateer. The *Lord Warden*, having given ponderous chase to the two brigantines, was now enveloped in gunsmoke off the convoy's lee quarter, the flashes of her guns showing yellow through the dirty grey smoke. The black and yellow brig headed for the centre of the convoy – a wolf let loose at a pack of sheep, thought Lamb.

The convoy was no longer the cohesive, close-packed mass of shipping it had been earlier; the three Indiamen still forged steadily ahead in the van but behind them the other ships were milling about in confusion. Some of them had taken fright at the approach of the privateers and had sheered away to leeward, leaving large gaps in the untidy lines. Several ships were hovering uncertainly outside the main mass of merchantmen and one schooner had reversed her direction and was weaving through the convoy as if determined to return to the safety of Calcutta.

The *Sturdy* had almost missed stays as Doubleday brought her head through the wind in pursuit of the brig and for a moment Lamb thought she was in irons, unable to continue her swing or to reverse it. The master was almost dancing on the deck in his rage, leaning over the quarterdeck rail and brandishing his fist at the sail-handlers as they leaned back on their sheets and tacks.

'Haul! Haul, you poxy bastards!' he screamed.

The canvas suddenly caught the wind and the frigate came to life again, nodding her head and heeling as she came round.

'Meet her, meet her, for Christ's sake!' shouted Doubleday excitedly at the helmsman. He needed no unnecessary orders of this sort and his blood-splashed lips moved fractionally as he spun the great double wheel in order to check the frigate's swing. The *Sturdy* put her stern to the wind and set her bow at the black and yellow brig. The small delay and the advantage of wind and speed had taken her close to the edge of the convoy and some sparse gunfire came from a few brave merchantmen as the brig drew near. This was ignored by the privateer and

123

she plunged into the centre of the loose convoy, before the *Sturdy* had half-way covered the same distance.

Cutler slammed his fist into his hand and swore in disgust, using language so foul that Lamb raised his eyebrows in surprise. Apart from the occasional 'damn' and 'bugger' he had never heard Cutler swear seriously and had hitherto considered him something of a prig in this respect, unlike his previous captain who could strip paint with the foulness of his tongue.

'Take her round the rear of the convoy, Mr Doubleday,' ordered Cutler. 'We will see what is happening on the other side.'

'The *Rapier*'s number, sir,' said little Blissenden, who had faithfully kept his eye on the flagship during the noise and turmoil of the past skirmish. 'Disengage, sir.'

'Ah, easier ordered than executed, I suspect,' said Cutler, shading his eyes at the distant frigate and her opponent.

Lamb trained his telescope in that direction and was in time to see the dipped acknowledgement from the *Rapier*'s masthead. Aided by the wind the privateer had lured the frigate several miles astern of the convoy and he knew that her captain would have a difficult time beating back against the wind, at the same time fending off the attentions of the privateer.

The sound of gunfire which had been heard from the far side of the convoy suddenly ceased and only the rumbling grumble of the flagship's guns and the distant noise of the running fight between the *Rapier* and her insistent opponent could be heard. As the *Sturdy* rounded the rear of the convoy the *Lord Warden*'s guns fell silent.

A haze of gunsmoke hung about her as she came into view from the *Sturdy*. Nearby, dismasted, wallowing in wreckage and awash to her chains, was one of the brigantines. Her masts, enveloped in a tangle of canvas and rigging, lay at crazy angles across her hulk, and bodies were littered over her deck and in the surrounding water. She had put up a bitter fight; the flagship had been badly mauled and her great stern-windows and quarter-gallery were a mass of splintered timber, and the stern-post and the upper, visible part of her rudder were a sorry sight. Lamb doubted if she could steer.

To leeward, perhaps half a mile distant, the black and yellow brig was racing to join her sister brig and the remaining brigantine, both of whom were pulling away from the sides of two merchantmen. Through his glass Lamb could see the decks of the merchant ships swarming with armed men and as he watched, reefs were shaken out, topsails sheeted home and the ships turned to bring the wind on their larboard quarters. Within moments of the *Sturdy* sighting them they were running north-east flanked by their two captors, with black and yellow coming up fast astern. As if it had been waiting for this moment, the *chasse-marée* broke off her action with the *Rapier* and putting her stern to the wind, headed north to the sound of a few, last desperate shots from the frigate.

The instant the group of privateers and their captives had come into view Cutler had put the *Sturdy* on a course designed to intercept and she was now running before the wind with men scampering aloft to shake out the topgallant royals and set the studdingsails. It would be a hard chase thought Lamb as, freed from the quarterdeck at last, he made his way forward to his battery.

'Signal from the commodore, sir,' reported Blissenden. 'Our number, sir. Disengage. Take up proper station, sir.'

Cutler said nothing for a long moment, his face expressionless as he stared at the escaping privateers and their prizes.

'Acknowledge,' he said at last. 'Come about, Mr Doubleday.'

The carpenter, the boatswain and their mates, under Maxwell's urgent and strident supervision, began to make good the damage to the timberwork and rigging as the *Sturdy* made her way back to her station windward of the widely scattered convoy. The shattered privateer, Lamb saw through his glass, was on the verge of sinking and the flagship's boats were dragging men from the water. The general signal to lay-to flew from the *Lord Warden* and the merchantmen began the slow process of reforming behind the stationary Indiamen, the more widespread ships receiving scornful attention from their more steadfast colleagues as they sidled back into position.

The ships squatted on the gently heaving sea throughout the long, hot day while the damage was made good and the flagship's carpenters sweated to free and repair her rudder. Despondency and depression were the order of the day in the *Sturdy*'s wardroom and the conversation was bitter. The service had been made to look foolish, rings had been run around them, merchantmen had been snatched from under their very noses – the French had out-smarted and out-manoeuvred them at every stage with their quick-footed, divisive, hit-and-run, keep-'em-occupied tactics.

The *Sturdy*'s bill for the morning's work was five dead and as many badly injured and Meadows and his assistant worked on into the evening patching and stitching. The *Rapier*'s account was much higher; both frigates took the opportunity while hove-to of committing their dead to the sea and Lamb counted twenty-two separate splashes at the side of the smaller frigate.

A sour and sullen mood hung about the *Sturdy* during the few days it took to reach Madras; everyone was affected, it seemed, from the captain to the cook. Maxwell was in a permanent foul temper from which no-one was safe; a virulent and savage attack on Kennedy's competence which followed a mis-heard order left that officer white-faced and shaking with rage and humiliation. Young Little, the smallest midshipman, an undersized, twelve-year-old scrap of a boy, lost control of his bladder in sheer terror while being loudly and brutally rebuked for a minor misdemeanour; Maxwell had eyed the growing stain on the youngster's breeches with disgust, seized a rattan cane from a boatswain's mate, stretched the lad over the breech of the nearest gun and laid into him so savagely that he was carried below in a dead faint.

On the day following the attack by the privateers, as dusk was falling towards the end of Lamb's watch, Cutler slowly climbed the ladder to the quarterdeck. Lamb saw at a glance that he was very drunk. The whisper had already reached him that the captain had been drinking heavily all day – he had not stirred from his cabin since his usual first-light promenade – and he was alarmed at Cutler's appearance. The captain staggered to the weather mizzenmast shrouds and clung, swaying unsteadily, his eyes fixed on the deck. He was unshaven, his shirt was stained with drink and cigar ash and his normally taut, alert expression had been replaced by a slack, inebriated grin. He gave a loud belch, muttered: 'Par'n me!' and looked around him. He crooked a finger at Lamb. Lamb crossed the deck and touched his hat. 'Yes, sir?'

'Everything – everything all right, Mr Lamb?'

'Yes, sir.'

'Good, good.' He belched again. 'Par'n me.' He waved a hand around him. 'It all looks very quiet. That's how it should be, on a well-wun – well-run ship with a competent officer like you on watch, Mr Lamb.' He patted the horrified Lamb on the shoulder. 'You are a good officer, Mr Lamb, a credit to the service. I've kept my eye on you – up at you, I should say, ha, ha!'

'Thank you, sir,' said Lamb. He shot a quick look at the quartermaster and the helmsman and was thankful to see their stolid faces staring stonily forward, apparently completely deaf to the slurred speech of their captain some nine feet away. A short, rotund figure appeared at the top of the quarterdeck ladder and approached quietly. It was Watson. He touched his bald head to Lamb in salute.

' 'Scuse me, sir,' he said and turned to peer into the captain's face. 'Your coffee's all ready, sir, just as you ordered, sir.'

Cutler frowned down at the little man, swaying back to get him in focus. 'Coffee? I didn't order any bloody coffee.'

'Yes, sir, course you did, sir. It's just as you like it, sir, nice and hot and strong. Come along with me, sir, 'fore it gets cold.'

To Lamb's horrified astonishment Watson stretched out his hand and gripped Cutler by the arm, pulling him gently away from his hold on the shrouds; to Lamb's equal surprise, Cutler did not explode in outraged fury but meekly allowed himself to be urged towards the quarterdeck ladder, his steward chattering nonsense all the while about hot coffee and a nice wash and fresh sheets. The captain was guided down the steps ('The ship's rolling a bit, sir, I'll go first, sir, shall I?') and the pair disappeared into Cutler's quarters. The door banged firmly shut behind them.

Lamb stood bemused in the gathering darkness and sudden quiet of the quarterdeck. He turned and walked slowly back to his usual station on the other side of the deck, debating whether he should warn the quartermaster and the helmsman to forget what they had seen and heard, but decided against it; to order was one thing – to expect the order to be obeyed was another. In any case, Cutler's periodic bouts with the bottle must by now be common knowledge to all on board.

The captain was his customary alert self the next morning, a little dark-eyed but neat and spruce. If he remembered anything of his visit to the quarterdeck the evening before he gave no sign of it as he gave his usual polite nod to Lamb on his return from his early-morning brisk walk around the deck.

The convoy anchored in the Madras roads for twenty-four hours waiting for several more merchantmen to join it, and during this time the commodore, the captains and the first lieutenants of the escort ships were entertained to dinner on board the *Maid of Kent.* At breakfast the next morning Maxwell entered the gunroom with an uncharacteristic smile on his normally dour, pre-breakfast face. He was also cheerfully expansive.

At dinner on board the Indiaman the assembled merchant masters had been kindness itself to their uniformed guests and their praise at the way in which the escorts had defended the convoy was unstinting. For three men-of-war to take on five fast, heavily-armed privateers, disable one and chase off the remainder with the loss of only two merchantmen was, in their collective opinion, an action worthy of the highest traditions of the navy. The commodore's polite demurs were brushed aside. They were convinced nobody could have done better or more bravely and they intended to inform their Lordships of the Admiralty of their admiration and gratitude at the earliest opportunity.

'I thought I caught a whisper about an engraved sword for the commodore,' said Maxwell, 'but I think that is pitching it a bit high.'

Spirits in the wardroom suddenly lifted and excited chatter broke out. Why yes, looking at things from that point of view, perhaps they had not done so badly – it took an outsider to put things in proper perspective, of course, to give a truly objective opinion. It might be coming it a bit strong to call it an overwhelming victory, perhaps, but yes, on reflection, there was certainly cause for praise.

Looking into his shaving mirror after breakfast, Lamb found his reflection smiling wryly at him as he considered how easily are the moods of men blown from one tack to another by a few windy words. And yet – and yet, he had not been unaffected, had he? His reflection shook its head and closed one eye.

Five merchantmen and a sloop under the command of a

fresh-faced, perpetually beaming young lieutenant no older than Lamb joined the convoy at Madras. At Trincomalee, their last port of call before heading across the Indian Ocean, they collected another three merchant ships and in addition, a fourth-rate, the fifty-gun *Sentinel*. The *Sentinel* was on her way from the China station to England and had suffered damage during a violent storm shortly after passing through the Straits of Malacca, causing her to divert to Trincomalee, limping across the Bay of Bengal with a badly sprung mainmast and the pumps working day and night to keep in check the water coming in through her strained timbers and rotting tree-nails. Now, patched up and declared seaworthy again, she was a welcome addition to the escorts.

In the event, neither her guns nor those of the other men-of-war were needed on the long haul to the Cape. The weather was the enemy; strong, adverse winds, gales, squalls and continual heavy seas were the convoy's lot throughout its long journey across the Indian Ocean. Time and again the ships were scattered and each time the convoy was re-formed it was a little smaller, the missing ships either having gone their own way or gone to the bottom. The sun was rarely glimpsed and their daily position a subject of some discussion but it was at a point reckoned to be some thirty miles west of the Seychelles, at the height of a storm that had been blowing for two days, that disaster struck the *Sentinel*.

The convoy was scattered over many miles of sea; in the deepening gloom of the late afternoon Lamb could see a few ships running under scraps of canvas to the south and south-west. Astern, within half a mile of the *Sturdy*'s starboard quarter, was the *Sentinel*. She was an old ship, built long before Lamb was born, and she was a crank ship, apt to dip her lower gun-ports in the mildest of swells. In the seas that were running now she was rolling heavily and her near-naked masts were performing a wild dance. As on the *Sturdy*, her sails had been reduced so that her spars were almost bare and her weakened mainmast, fished and fished again, was carrying no more than a fully-reefed topsail.

Lamb had been idly watching her for some minutes, using her as a point of reference in the grey waste of heaving, spume-swept water. He turned his gaze to the merchantmen in view and methodically counted them; there were seven in sight from the quarterdeck, as there had been when he took over the watch twenty minutes ago. The flagship, unseen since the previous day, was presumably still in the van of the convoy several miles to the south and out of sight in this murk. A cry from the quartermaster made him spin round. The man was pointing over the starboard quarter.

'Look, sir, look!'

Lamb's heart lurched. The *Sentinel*'s mainmast had snapped some ten feet below the mainyard and was hanging over the starboard side in a tangle of canvas and rigging, the topsail in the water and the massive, broken end of the mast thumping against her side like a huge hammer. Her head was slewing away from the wind; the delicate balance of wind, sails and rudder had been instantly destroyed with the fall of the mast, and the topsail, thrust deep into the water by the captive spar, was acting as a brake to the ship's forward movement on that side. As she presented her beam to the wind a huge roller swept up and over her in a weltering smother of white water. In the twinkling of an eye she was on her side, wallowing helplessly with her larboard gun-ports looking at the sky and her weed-covered bottom exposed to Lamb's horrified gaze. It had happened so quickly that the quartermaster's arm was still outstretched, his shout still resounding in Lamb's ears.

Lamb snapped himself alert. 'Mr Blissenden, inform the captain!' He sprang to the forward rail. 'All hands! All hands!'

Cutler came up the quarterdeck ladder at a run, closely followed by Maxwell and the master. The captain clung to the shrouds, his hair blowing wildly in the fierce wind as he followed the line of Lamb's pointing hand.

'Mr Doubleday!' he snapped. 'Bring her about, as quick as you possibly can.'

The master leaned out over the quarterdeck rail and bellowed to his mate as the sail-handlers ran to their ropes.

'Stand by to go about! Get those creeping caterpillars hauling as soon as I sing out.'

He glanced at the wheel and at the sea, judging the moment. Cutler looked at him, saying nothing, leaving the manoeuvre to him.

'Down helm!' bawled Doubleday. 'Bring her round, handsomely now! About ship! Mains' haul!'

The frigate's head, obeying the thrust of the sea against the rudder, began to fall off from the wind, the deck tilting sharply as the ship put her beam to the run of the waves; then, as the yards were shifted and the sails picked up the wind again, her bows swung faster in response to the increasing thrust on her canvas.

'Meet her, damn you!' cried Doubleday but the wheel was already turning the other way and the frigate was plunging northward with the wind across her quarter.

It was now almost dark, low clouds covering the sky and the sea a tumbling waste of black water flecked with white as the wind whipped the tops off the waves. The frigate fairly flew along, bouncing and rolling, crashing through the waves, her waist awash with green water and spray flung high over the forecastle. Lamb cast an anxious eye astern as an occasional roller, higher and steeper than usual, lifted the stern alarmingly.

Cutler had no way of pinpointing the position of the *Sentinel* but sharp eyes were on the water from the shrouds and tops and suddenly a dozen simultaneous shouts told of wreckage to starboard. Lamb sprang to the side and peered out over the dark sea.

'There's an upturned boat, sir,' he reported. 'And a hatch-cover – some timber – a hammock – and another.'

'We must have passed her,' said Cutler. 'Bring her about again, Mr Doubleday.'

The precarious manoeuvre was repeated, this time in total darkness, and the *Sturdy* crept back along her previous track, close-hauled, with the wind over her starboard bow. Wreckage there was in plenty but although the frigate searched, tacking and wearing, beating against the wind, firing five-minute guns, there was no sign of the *Sentinel*. The *Sturdy* lay-to, hanging in the eye of the wind, a dropping wind that continued to slacken during the night. When Lamb took over the morning watch the weather had improved sufficiently for him to catch an occasional glimpse of the low moon through ragged clouds. Cutler was on deck at first light; the sea had subsided to no more than a heavy swell and the rising sun brought a cheerful golden warmth not felt for some days.

The search continued throughout the morning, Cutler taking the ship round in ever-widening circles from its night-time position. There was no hope now of finding the *Sentinel* afloat but there was a chance – a very slim chance – that men might be found alive. From time to time a shout would go up from one or other of the lookouts, to bring the frigate swooping down to investigate a length of timber or a spar or a cask or a water-logged hammock. One man was found, a corpse, and the crew watched in silence as it floated past face-down, rising and falling with the waves, bumping along the ship's side, its hair floating wide and a bald patch on the crown of its head giving it a curious, living look.

At six bells in the forenoon watch Cutler called off the search.

'We can do no more, Mr Maxwell. It is time we rejoined the convoy. Set the courses and shake the reefs out of the tops'ls. Steer sou'-sou'-west and let me know the instant the convoy is sighted.'

Lamb crossed to the lee rail and looked out over the dancing, glittering water. Yesterday, half a mile astern of the *Sturdy*, there had been a fine old ship and perhaps three hundred and fifty men. Today – a few scraps of wreckage and a floating corpse. He pursed his lips and gave a slow, thoughtful shake of his head. Ah, well, here today and gone tomorrow – perhaps one day I shall go like that. He gave the rail a valedictory slap and went below.

'I served in her once, you know,' said Doubleday, closely inspecting the shred of beef on the end of his silver toothpick. 'I was a midshipman, spent a year and a half in the West Indies. She was neaped on a sandbank one time – I forget where now, but I remember the devil of a job we had getting her off. The captain had every man on board jumping up and down on the poop and quarterdeck trying to rock her free – didn't work, though. Winched her off in the end, with cables through the hawse-hole. What was the captain's name now? A foreign sort of name, I seem to recall. Well, it doesn't matter. He was a real tartar, though, would flog the last man down the mast as a matter of course. He'd be dead long ago now, he was an old man then – aye, a wicked old man, too. French, that was his name, Captain French. He caused me a few tears, I can tell you.'

He fell silent and busied himself with his toothpick, lost in his old memories.

'She was a cow of a ship, roll on a damp rag and leaked like a sieve. Her knees were rotten then – God knows what they were like before she went down. She must have fallen to pieces the moment she broached-to.'

'Well, let us hope it was a quick end for the brave Jacks aboard her,' said the purser.

'Brave Jacks? That's as good an epitaph as any they are likely to get,' said Doubleday.

Chapter 7

Simon's Bay was bathed in late-morning sunshine. The light wind, coming off the warm land, was gentle and caressing, barely stirring the sparkling surface of the anchorage or the escort vessels that had arrived shortly after first light. The merchantmen were safely tucked up in neighbouring Table Bay, except for the three Indiamen; they had not felt the necessity to break their journey home and had dipped their topsails and sailed on as the remainder of the depleted convoy headed for the comfort of Table Bay.

There were other ships anchored in Simon's Bay; two frigates, the *Swiftsure*, thirty-eight, and the *Martin*, thirty-two, and the *Fountainebleau*, a fine seventy-four built by the French some ten years previously and now flying the square, blue flag of Rear-Admiral Shillington, newly arrived from England to find his predecessor dead.

On board the *Sturdy* the hands were busy restoring the frigate to the degree of perfection which had been lost during her storm-ravaged journey across the Indian Ocean and which was now demanded again by the first lieutenant. The rigging, standing and running, had been overhauled and anointed with galley slush and the rancid remains of a keg of condemned butter. In the waist, the sailmaker and his mates were sitting in the sun, busy with needle and palm, patching and roping. Sitting in a loop of rope slung from the bowsprit was Aldridge, a grey and wrinkled waister and one-time gun-captain who was acknowledged to be the best man on board with a paint brush. He clutched a small and precious tin of gilt paint in one hand as he delicately applied his brush to the helmet of the centurion, forever staring ahead with jutting chin and wide-set, bright blue eyes. Along the bulwarks the less gifted painters were happily slapping red paint on the sides, the deck and themselves with no particular bias, the black-painted guns having been wisely hauled well inboard.

Captain Cutler sat in the large and plainly furnished stateroom of the admiral's quarters on the *Fontainebleau*. With him were the captains of the frigates *Swiftsure* and *Martin* and for the past ten minutes they had been sitting in silence listening to the polished and effortless flow of words coming from the admiral. Shillington was young for his rank – his hair was barely touched with grey and his face was plumply unlined – but he was well-connected. His wife was the niece of the First Sea Lord and her father the owner of a vast estate in Norfolk. Shillington had stood unsuccessfully as a Whig for the present Parliament but with the promise of a safe borough in London for the next election did not expect to remain at the Cape for long. He had swiftly made it apparent to the three captains, however, that he intended to make his presence felt whilst he was here. He was a forceful, aggressive, hold-your-damned-tongue, sir, sort of speaker and had bluntly informed Cutler in his first sentence that the frigate *Sturdy* was no longer on escort duties and was now attached to his station.

Parliament was angry, said the admiral. The Cabinet was worried, London shipowners were outraged and Lloyds were insistent. The Admiralty was stretched for ships but had bowed to pressure. Ships of the line were out of the question but a squadron of frigates would be found.

'Your frigates are that squadron, gentlemen. Our losses in the last twelve months have been enormous, scandalous, eleven ships in one week alone. It simply cannot be allowed to continue – the economy of the country is threatened. Action has been called for and action is what I intend to achieve. You, Captain Cutler, have recently had a brush with these vermin and can bear me out here – no merchant ship is safe, even in convoy. Some of these privateer fellows are making quite a name for themselves and a fortune into the bargain, all at Britain's expense. It must stop, gentlemen, and I intend to stop it, with your assistance. Your task is simple and straight-forward. You will sail into and patrol the Indian Ocean in general and the Bay of Bengal in particular. You will make your presence felt among those privateers, those corsairs, those licensed pirates. Sink them, burn them, destroy them!'

He banged the table with his clenched fist and thrust out his jaw pugnaciously, glaring at each captain in turn as if defying them to raise the smallest point of criticism. Cutler shifted uneasily in his chair, a trifle uncomfortable at the admiral's extravagant speech. None of the captains spoke – there was little they could say in response to this dramatic exhortation without appearing to be sycophantic.

Shillington leaned back in his chair, spread his hands and smiled. 'I do not expect miracles, of course, gentlemen. Three small ships to scour such a vast area? But I am convinced that if you stick closely to the trade routes for much of the time you are bound to come across the scum. Give them no mercy. I want no prizes sent back, do you understand?'

The three captains nodded. 'Yes, sir,' said Beamish, captain of the *Swiftsure*.

'Good. It should be a very pleasant mission for the three of you. I only wish that my duties would allow me to accompany you, but alas, it is not possible.'

Thank God! breathed Cutler silently.

'Now, as to details. Captain Beamish, as senior, will command the squadron. Your three ships will act as a squadron unless Captain Beamish decides otherwise. I see from your fitness reports that there is nothing to prevent you weighing at first light tomorrow and with that in mind I will bid you, Captain Cutler and you, Captain Blake, good day. Captain Beamish, I will beg your indulgence for a few minutes while your orders are completed.'

Many miles to the north-east lay Ceylon; as many miles to the south-west lay the islands of Mauritius and Bourbon. From the masthead of the *Sturdy* all that could be seen in the vast, blue, shimmering ocean that surrounded her was a scrap of white far to the west – the topgallant sails of the commodore's frigate *Swiftsure*. Further west still, out of sight of the *Sturdy*, was the *Martin*. Between them, the three ships were able to scan hundreds of square miles of sea and today, as they had done yesterday and the day before, the lookouts reported nothing.

Beamish had taken the squadron through the Mozambique Channel and northwards along the African coastline as far as the equator. They had met a few merchant ships along the way – a lone Indiaman off Dar es Salaam running before a light wind with every possible inch of canvas she could carry, flying past with a courteous dip of her topsails, a couple of 'runners' – fast merchantmen, well-gunned, with a good chance of beating off most privateers – and an American barque, sailing blithely past without acknowledgement; but apart from these and dozens of Arab dhows, nothing. The Convoy Act was keeping most merchantmen in harbour, waiting for a convoy, and the trade routes were remarkably empty.

The squadron had turned east at the equator and had struck out across the huge expanse of the Indian Ocean, with the intention of sweeping the privateer routes between Mauritius and their favourite hunting ground, the Bay of Bengal. It was as if the sea had been swept clean of ships – ever since the frigates had turned east the ocean had been theirs alone.

Lamb sat in the sun on the main hatch-cover. The heat in this early part of the afternoon was fierce – the timber beneath his haunches had been hot enough to cause him to whistle in surprise as he seated himself. Beside him, where he caught the shade of the mainsail, sat the surgeon, silently immersed in a book. Forward, beneath the forecastle, some of the younger, more energetic hands larked in the sun, walking on their hands and turning cartwheels, their bare torsos browned by the constant sunshine. Lamb envied them the comfort and freedom of their bare feet and naked chests – he would dearly have loved to copy them. He glanced at the surgeon, sitting with one leg cocked up beneath his haunch, a bead of perspiration running down his long, sharp nose. The bead dropped on to his page and with a tut of annoyance the surgeon dabbed at it with his sleeve.

'What are you reading, Bones?' asked Lamb.

Meadows gave a little sigh of exasperation and held the book out sideways without bothering to answer. Lamb cocked his head and squinted at the title. He read it aloud. *'Some Observations on the Causes of Hernia or Rupture among Seamen and a Discussion on the Various Treatments Thereof.'*

The surgeon returned the book to his lap.

'That sounds a fascinating topic,' said Lamb.

'I find it so,' said Meadows coldly, without looking up from his page.

Lamb stretched his arms wide and yawned. He turned his mind to the serious question of whether he should continue

137

sitting in the sun, getting sleepier by the minute, or face the heat and discomfort of his airless little cabin and settle down to sleep in earnest. He was in the middle of another huge yawn, the problem still unresolved, when a shout of 'Sail ho!' made him snap his teeth shut.

'One point off the larboard bow,' roared the lookout.

Lamb raced for the quarterdeck, snatched a battered telescope from its rack, ran back to the mainmast shrouds and pulled himself up to the maintopgallant yard. My God, the man has good eyes! he thought – the sail was the merest suggestion of a faint discontinuity at the hard edge of the horizon and if he had not known where to look he was sure he would have missed it. He levelled his telescope and tried to focus his glass on the distant ship. It was not easy; the sea shimmered and danced in his eye and the white canvas of the sails merged their separate segments into one. It was impossible to detect the number of masts she carried but he was able to determine that no other ships were near her.

'What do you see, Mr Lamb?' came Maxwell's voice from the deck.

'Not very much, sir. Just the one ship, too far as yet to pick out any detail.'

'Very well. Stay there, if you please.'

A flash of colour caught at the corner of Lamb's eye and he glanced over his shoulder to see a row of signal flags jerking their way upward. That would be Cutler's signal to the commodore – he, no doubt, would order the *Sturdy* to turn to starboard, to gain the weather gauge and keep the stranger between the two frigates. He settled back against the mast and waited.

A few minutes later the mast leaned as the deck heeled and the *Sturdy* tacked to starboard. Lamb allowed himself a little smile and lifted his telescope again. The tack had put the distant sail four points off the larboard bow and in the few minutes since he last looked, the image was perceptibly clearer. Two masts, one square-rigged, the other –? He lowered his glass, wiped the sweat from his eyes and tried again. Yes, both square-rigged – a brig. Was there not something familiar about her? For a second there his brain had given a recollective twitch but whatever it was, his memory refused to tell him.

138

'Deck there!' he shouted down. 'It's a brig, heading south-west.'

South-west would take it directly to Mauritius – there was little doubt in his mind that she was a privateer. But could she be cornered? The *Sturdy* was sailing south-east with the wind on her starboard beam and on this course would soon be cutting across the brig's bows a mile or two ahead of her. The privateer would be a fast ship, of that he was certain, and the next thirty minutes or so would be crucial. Cutler's immediate task was to keep to windward of her and turn her head towards the north and west. The brig had certainly seen the *Sturdy*, but had she sighted the *Swiftsure*? He kept his glass trained on the privateer, pausing every few moments to wipe his sleeve across his eyes and forehead. A small suspicion nagged at the edge of his mind and suddenly, as she turned to the north-west and showed him her side, it became a certainty. It was the black and yellow brig which they had encountered with the convoy. Lamb grinned and gave a little grunt of satisfaction. Now, you bastard – now it's your turn.

He hailed the deck. 'She's tacked to the north-west, sir. She can't have sighted the *Swiftsure*, by the look of it.'

'Thank you, Mr Lamb,' bellowed Maxwell. 'Just report what you see – gratuitous comments we can do without.'

'Aye aye, sir,' muttered Lamb to himself, feeling his face flushing at the public rebuke.

The *Sturdy* wore, putting the wind at her stern and her bowsprit pointed at the brig, and presently a gang of young topmen appeared at Lamb's perch and busied themselves setting the topgallant royals. They were polite but cheerful.

'Par'n me, sir.'

''Scuse me, sir.'

'Good day for a chase, sir,' remarked one nut-brown lad, nodding his head in the direction of the brig. 'Pity the wind's a mite lazy.'

'Yes, drooping in the heat, I expect,' said Lamb, still a little too sulky and preoccupied to make a proper attempt at wit and was surprised at the laughter that went up.

Below him the studdingsails suddenly bellied out and with these and the topgallant royals blossoming above him, the frigate picked up her heels with a sudden surge. It was clear that Cutler intended to convince the brig that she was being chased in earnest – she must be persuaded to flee downwind, or within a few points of it, directly into the arms of the other frigates.

Lamb gave a thought to the disposition of the *Martin*, the most leeward of the three. The privateer was now heading straight for the *Swiftsure* and if she had not sighted her already, it would not be many minutes before she did. Would she turn east or west? The southerly wind would be on her beam whichever way she turned. If she chose east she would lose precious moments coming round; she would almost certainly prefer to tack slightly and head west. In that case, thought Lamb, if I was commodore I would order the *Martin* to come about and position herself off the *Swiftsure*'s larboard quarter, ready to block the brig's bolthole. She would be trapped between the converging frigates like a rat between terriers.

'Beat to quarters!'

The noisy summons galvanized Lamb into action and he descended hastily to the deck, all thoughts of tactics driven from his mind by the urgent rush of men about the decks and the blood-stirring rat-tat-tat of the Marine drum. The guns of his battery were already being run inboard as he reached his station and the gunners, their movements honed to a fine art by constant practice, were busy priming and loading. Lamb paced to and fro beside his guns, keeping a careful eye on what was going on and glancing forward over the bow from time to time at the brig, running with full sail in the direction of the distant *Swiftsure*. The *Sturdy*, flying every scrap of canvas she could, appeared to be making no headway on her and he wondered how the brig would sail close-hauled – rather better than the *Sturdy*, he guessed. The privateer tacked sharply to larboard, heading west, and the deck beneath Lamb's feet tilted suddenly as Cutler brought the frigate on to the same tack in grim pursuit.

The frigate was not at her happiest close-hauled but neither, it appeared, did the brig give of her best on a broad reach because it seemed that not an inch was lost or gained between the two of them for the next six or eight minutes. The frigate was prepared for battle; the guns were loaded and the men were ready and now every pair of eyes on board was fixed on the fleeing brig.

'Sail ho!' sang out the mainmast lookout. 'Fine on the starboard bow!'

Aha! thought Lamb; the *Martin* is where she should be, about to slam the gate on the brig.

Tyler stepped over from his battery and stood at Lamb's elbow, staring out over the starboard bow.

'Well, if she gets away now we want our arses kicking,' he said.

'I cannot see how she can,' said Lamb. 'With us astern and holding the weather gauge, the *Swiftsure* guarding the lee and the *Martin* driving hard to head her off, she will have to wriggle a good deal to get off the hook.'

'Oh, I don't doubt but she'll wriggle, and I would too, in her place. But providing the *Martin* cracks on, she is as good as ours.'

Yes, thought Lamb, the *Martin* would be the deciding factor in whether or not the brig escaped. Having come about very early, she had managed to get into a position to approach the brig almost bows-on. However, she was sailing into the wind and although Lamb knew that she performed very well close-hauled, it would be touch and go. If the privateer reached the intersection of their converging courses before the *Martin* she stood an excellent chance of escaping; likewise, if the *Martin* reached the same spot first, then the brig was trapped. Any move to the south or west would bring her under the guns of the *Sturdy*; if she turned to the north, she would come up against the *Swiftsure*.

Cutler's voice rang out from the quarterdeck. 'Mr Tyler! See what your bow-chasers can do.'

'Aye aye, sir,' roared the delighted Tyler and sprinted up to the forecastle guns. Lamb, anxious to see some action but not daring to leave his station, compromised by mounting two steps of the forecastle ladder. The little six-pounders were already trained on the brig and it only needed the quoins to be removed in order to lift the muzzles to give them their maximum elevation. Tyler used his authority to usurp the gun-captain on the starboard side, much to that gentleman's fury, and bent over the breech with the smouldering slow-match in his hand. He blew gently on the glowing end of the match as he waited for the frigate's bows to rise.

'Fire!' he shouted and touched the match to the priming-tube in the touch-hole. Both guns fired at the same instant and Lamb shielded his eyes as he watched for the fall of shot. The range was extreme for the small guns and one roundshot plunged harmlessly into the brig's wake; the other passed through the lower corner of her mainsail and grazed her side, leaving a small hole in her canvas and some damaged paint abaft her foremast chains. A cheer went up from both gun-crews.

'That was mine,' claimed Tyler loudly.

'It bloody weren't,' muttered the larboard gun-captain beneath his breath.

The guns were swabbed, reloaded and fired again – and again. No more hits were observed but their purpose was achieved – to discourage the brig from turning into the wind away from the oncoming frigates.

The *Swiftsure* was now a couple of miles off the privateer's starboard quarter, almost abeam of the *Sturdy*, while the *Martin*, which Lamb had observed tacking and wearing like a thing possessed for the last twenty minutes, were now poised to cut across the brig's bows a mile or so distant.

Lamb grinned and rubbed his hands in anticipation. We've got her! he thought and dropped down to the maindeck and his guns.

The sound of gunfire boomed out. 'The *Martin*'s firing,' shouted someone and Lamb stretched to peer over the hammock nettings. He could not see much of the *Martin* – the brig was in the way – but he could see the gunsmoke drifting away to leeward. She must be trying her bow-chasers too, he thought.

The brig suddenly tacked, coming into the wind, sheering away from the *Martin* and presenting her beam to the *Sturdy*. No, Lamb realized, in a surge of excitement, she was not tacking, she was coming about, heading for the gap between the *Sturdy* and the *Swiftsure*.

'Stand by!' he roared at his battery, almost hopping with excitement. The privateer completed her turn, coming round so fast that it seemed as if she had spun in her own wake, and drove fast for the diminishing gap. Cutler was not going to allow her to reach it without a struggle and the helm was put over to cut her off.

'Stand by the larboard guns!' shouted Maxwell as the guns on that side came to bear.

The *Swiftsure*, Lamb saw, had also tacked and the two frigates now formed the jaws of a rapidly closing pair of pincers with the brig in between.

The privateer was the first to fire, the sound of her guns overlaying Maxwell's strident order. Bar-shot and chain-shot screamed low over the *Sturdy*'s deck, tearing through the lower sails and rigging, doing little damage to the structure of the ship but laying up some urgent work for the sailmaker and boatswain and bringing to an abrupt and messy end the life of Joseph Short, ordinary seaman.

The *Sturdy*'s broadside, some three times heavier, was much more devastating. Splinters blossomed from the side of the brig and her rail, her gun-ports were driven in and bloody swathes cut through the men crouched at the guns and in the waist. The *Swiftsure* was also firing, pouring roundshot into the brig from a distance of no more than two cables and the *Martin*, coming up fast astern, was hitting her with her bow-chasers. The privateer, cornered like a rat, fought as desperately as one, firing from both sides at once. Her fourteen nine-pounders crashed out again and again, overturning one of Kennedy's guns, killing two of his men and beheading the Marine sentry at the aft companionway. The *Swiftsure*'s mainyard was cut in two, leaving the mainsail sagging to leeward. A midshipman was killed on her quarterdeck by the same shot which removed the arm of the quartermaster and Captain Beamish's gig was reduced to splinters, an event that caused him considerably more grief than had the death of his midshipman.

The privateer fought bravely but the outcome was inevitable. One by one her guns fell silent as her deck was repeatedly swept with canister and roundshot and the dead, the dying and the wounded were sprawled over her blood-soaked planks. Her foremast lay across her starboard bow and her other canvas was in shreds. But, in spite of the wreckage and the carnage, her few remaining guns still roared defiance; the raw courage displayed by her crew and their absolute refusal to admit defeat stirred Lamb to grudging admiration.

'For God's sake strike,' he muttered as Kennedy's guns crashed out yet again and a hail of iron smashed into the brig's shattered bulwarks.

Tyler, his face black with smoke, caught Lamb's eye and grinned.

Lamb shook his head angrily. 'This is butchery,' he yelled, across the deck.

Tyler looked surprised. 'They are vermin,' he answered shortly. 'They deserve all they get.' He turned back to his guns.

'Stand fast the guns!' The order came from Maxwell in response to a shout from the quarterdeck. The sweating gunners straightened their backs and stood beside their hot, smoking guns, looking silently out over the narrow stretch of water at the drifting, haze-covered wreckage of the privateer. The *Swiftsure* was still firing, close enough now to bring her powerful carronades into play. They were aimed low and in quick succession a dozen of their thirty-two-pound roundshot smashed into the side of the brig, opening her up to the sea. Satisfied with this final, devastating blow, the *Swiftsure*'s guns also fell silent and for several moments the men of both frigates stared across the water, seemingly awe-struck at the death and damage they had wreaked.

The brig was settling rapidly as the sea poured into her. A number of men were still moving about her deck, heaving timber and a hatch-cover into the water. Aft, several men were huddled around a figure on the deck and as the brig settled deeper the man was lifted up, carried to the side and handed down to the men squatting on the hatch-cover.

Bright flags fluttered from the *Swiftsure*'s signal halyard: 'Send boats'.

Within a few moments Lamb was seated in the stern of the launch, being pulled vigorously across the flat water in the direction of the sinking brig. Her deck was now very close to the level of the sea and her survivors had taken to the water, clinging to pieces of wreckage and the sides of the hatch-cover.

'Back oars!'

The launch came alongside the hatch-cover and Stone thrust out his boat-hook to keep it close. There were two men kneeling precariously on top of it, with one hand for themselves and the other for the body of the man sprawled on his back in the red-

144

stained water washing over the timber. Lamb gestured to the four men in the water, hanging on to the side of the hatch-cover.

'Get those in first.'

The men were dragged over the gunwale and into the bottom of the launch, where they slumped, weary and bedraggled, under the cutlasses of the seamen.

Lamb beckoned to the two men kneeling on the hatch-cover. 'Come on. *Ici, vite, vite.*'

The men shuffled awkwardly to the edge of the cover, pulling the body of the man with them. It was plain that they intended to put the body in the boat. Lamb could see at a glance that he was very much a corpse; part of his jaw had been shot away and a gaping wound in his side exposed his ribs. Lamb put up his hand in a gesture of refusal.

'*Non, non, il est mort.*'

The two men broke in a torrent of rapid and angry French. Lamb understood only one word in three but he gathered that the dead man was the captain of the brig and the father of the two men. They would not give him to the sharks without a Christian burial.

Lamb was firm. '*Non.*'

'*Oui, oui!*' they cried and hauled the body forward, draping it over the side of the launch so that its head hung down between the thwarts.

'Marsh, Steptoe, put that thing over the side,' snapped Lamb.

The two seamen grabbed the corpse by the shoulders and heaved it into the water. It fell with a dull splash, rocking the hatch-cover and bobbing away on its back, its staring, lifeless eyes raised to the sky. A howl of outraged fury came from one of the brothers and snatching his knife from his belt he launched himself at Lamb. A back-handed slash from the coxwain's cutlass struck the side of his neck with a horrible sound and he dropped from the gunwale with a sharp cry and fell back into the sea beside the body of his father. For a moment there was silence; the man left on the hatch-cover fixed his glittering eyes on Lamb with a terrible look of absolute menace. Lamb took a deep breath.

'Thank you, cox'n,' he said shakily.

'My pleasure, sir,' said Stone cheerfully.

Lamb pointed a finger at the Frenchman and then at the launch. '*Vous – venez – maintenant,*' he said loudly and firmly.

The man glanced down at the bodies of his father and brother floating side by side, linked by tendrils of blood. He turned his gaze back to Lamb, folded his arms across his chest and shook his head slowly from side to side. The two stared silently at one another for a few seconds, the one nonplussed, the other with a look of implacable hatred on his dark face.

'Let's leave the bugger, sir, if that's what he wants,' suggested Stone.

'Right. Pull for the stern, cox'n. There are several men there.'

The launch pulled away from the hatch-cover, leaving the man staring darkly after it.

They dragged another five men from the water, too exhausted to help themselves in any way and one so badly mangled in the legs that Lamb doubted if he would survive the day. The cutter from the *Swiftsure* was working her way along the other side and from what Lamb could see her haul would be no greater than that of the launch. A gurgling, bubbling noise came from the brig; she was sinking below the surface, still on an even keel.

'Shove off!' Give way together!' shouted Lamb, anxious not to be caught in her suction as she went down. The boat pulled away and bodies by the score floated off her as she went under, her mainmast sinking down through the litter on the surface until its tip vanished beneath the water. A large, red stain clouded the sea and a few air bubbles rocked the corpses and the wreckage. Lamb glanced at the hatch-cover. It was empty.

Four days later the squadron skirted the south-eastern corner of Ceylon and entered the Bay of Bengal, confident that its pickings would be richer here. For a week the frigates prowled the shipping lane between Madras and Calcutta and were finally rewarded with the capture of the privateer *La Belle Femme* of fourteen guns. She was in company with another privateer but such was the speed and manoeuvrability of this Frenchman that it escaped the squadron's clutches and made off before the wind, leaving her companion trapped under the threatening guns of the men-of-war. The master of the *La Belle Femme* was not made of the stern stuff of the captain of the black and yellow brig and he immediately backed his topsails and hove-to when the first, ranging shot of the *Swiftsure* raised a plume of water beside her bow. The frigates edged closer, their guns trained menacingly from both sides. A boat pulled from the *Swiftsure* and shortly afterwards returned, taking with her the privateer's captain. Orders came from the *Swiftsure* – each frigate was to send twenty hands and ten Marines to the privateer. The officer from the *Swiftsure* would command and she would travel in company with the squadron to Madras.

Cutler smiled; Captain Beamish was clearly not a man to turn his back on a few guineas and Admiral Shillington's orders notwithstanding, he was not about to burn a stout, well-built prize such as this. He passed the word for Mr Lamb.

The boats from the *Swiftsure* and the *Martin* arrived at the privateer a few minutes before that from the *Sturdy* and when Lamb climbed over the side he found that her new commander had lost no time in getting matters organized. The brig's crew was crowded together in the bows under the muskets of the Marines and British seamen were at the wheel and filing down through the open hatch to search below decks for hideaways.

The officer from the *Swiftsure* advanced on Lamb with a wide smile and an outstretched hand.

'How d'you do? I am William Bell, second officer, *Swiftsure*. I like my friends to call me Billy.'

'Matthew Lamb – I like my friends to call me Matthew,' said Lamb, holding his smile with some difficulty as his hand was crushed in Bell's grip.

The officer chuckled. 'Fair enough, Matthew – if I call you Matt, you retaliate by calling me William.'

He had the build of a young prize-fighter and energy, strength and humour radiated from his square, handsome face as he grinned up at Lamb.

'Perhaps you would be good enough to take your Marines and collect the weapons of those villains for'ard and then see them made safe and comfortable below – the bilge would be a suitable place, I think!'

Suitable as Bell considered the bilge to be, it was not nearly commodious enough to accommodate one hundred and sixty men and Lamb settled for the hold instead. He stationed Marines at intervals from the hold up to the deck and the corsairs were sent down one man at a time, leaving a growing heap of pistols, knives, axes and short swords on the deck as they went. They were a surly, hard-looking lot of men and Lamb felt a great deal happier when they were safely beneath battened hatches with armed Marines standing by and two of the ship's nine-pounders loaded with grapeshot trained forward from either side of the wheel.

Two hours later the brig was slipping quietly through the calm, black silk of the sea with the dark shapes of the *Sturdy* and the *Swiftsure* off to larboard and starboard and the *Martin* out of sight somewhere astern. The night was warm and hushed; ten thousand stars, their light undimmed by the smallest slice of a moon, shone brilliantly from a clear sky, almost close enough, it seemed, to be brushed by the masthead. The men had been fed and were now curled up in odd corners of the deck. Lamb was amused to see how they had segregated themselves – *Sturdy* to larboard, *Swiftsure* to starboard and *Martin* in the bows. The separation was not imposed or deliberate but instinctive – the air of faint contempt which each group displayed for the other and their own fierce clannishness were sufficient to draw clear territorial lines.

Lamb leaned against the taffrail with his two fellow officers. Bell was smoking a captured cheroot and holding forth on the navy's system of promotion.

'Prospects are not so bad now, of course, as they were a year or two ago,' he was saying, in his easy, fluent way. 'With the war nicely settled in as it is and no end to it in sight – thank God! – and the yards turning out ships as fast as they can knock 'em together, experienced officers are at a premium, and long may it remain so. And of course, with hundreds of young gallants gaining a glorious death every year, the prospects for those of us remaining are even brighter. The trouble is, so far as we ambitious young lieutenants are concerned, the trouble is, not enough senior men are getting killed. I always think of the navy as a pyramid, you know – ten thousand midshipmen at the base, thousands of lieutenants above them, then hundreds of post-captains, then a few dozen admirals and right at the peak, the First Sea Lord himself. Now, if by some stroke of good fortune a score or two of captains were to depart this earth at one foul swoop, so to speak, what a shuffling and a scrambling would take place then, in the pyramid! And what joy for a lucky few, eh?'

He drew deeply on his cheroot and then flicked it high into the air where it traced a brief red line in the darkness before vanishing into the wake.

'They call me Ambitious Billy, you know. I'm not ashamed of it; we are all ambitious in our own ways and if we are not, then we should not be wearing these uniforms. I have my heart set on being made post before I am twenty-five and when I achieve that I shall be the happiest man alive.'

Maybe, thought Lamb, but your ambition will not end there – there will always be the next step to hanker for – the admiral's flag, the blue, the white, the red. Lamb yearned for promotion as much as the next man but Bell's openly-confessed hunger for it made him uneasy; such thoughts, he considered, should be part of a man's secrets, like his lust for women or boys or money. He strongly suspected that Bell would be utterly ruthless where necessary – he was not the type to hesitate if a few fingers needed to be crushed on his way up the ladder.

'Won't we all?' he responded.

'Amen to that,' said Sexton, raising his glass.

He was the *Martin*'s fourth officer; dough-faced and stout, he had a nervous habit of sniffing every few seconds, a sound which Lamb found intensely irritating. He did not envy Sexton's fellow officers in the *Martin*'s gunroom.

'Of course, it may well be –' began Bell. He stopped short and peered into the darkness of the deck. A seaman had emerged from the aft companionway and was walking quietly and quickly forward.

'Hold hard, there!' snapped Bell, striding forward. Lamb and Sexton followed him. The seaman turned, his arms behind his back.

'What is your name?' Bell demanded.

The man gave him a sullen look. 'Addison, sir.'

'He's a *Martin*'s man,' said Sexton. 'I know him – he's always in trouble for one thing or another.'

'What are you hiding behind your back?' asked Bell.

Addison brought his hands forward and spread them. 'Nothing, sir.'

Bell reached out a muscular arm and spun the man round.

Tucked into his belt at the small of his back was a bottle. Bell plucked it out and peered at the label.

'Nothing, eh? A funny sort of nothing, this. You have a taste for fine brandy, have you, Addison?'

The man's temper visibly flared and he thrust his face forward. 'I can see you ain't doing without,' he snapped, nodding at the glass in Sexton's hand.

'You are not being civil, Addison,' said Bell pleasantly. He took a quick half-pace forward and drove his fist into the man's stomach. Addison doubled up in agony and his knees buckled. Bell gripped him by the shoulder and hauled him upright.

'That was for thieving,' he said. He slammed his fist into the same place. This time the man did go down, landing on his knees and falling forward on to his hands. He struggled for air, wheezing and gasping.

Bell tapped him on the shoulder. 'That was for insolence, Addison.' He gripped the man's shirt and pulled him to his feet. 'If I were not in a genial mood you would get another for lying. Now get for'ard and be thankful you got off so lightly.'

He gave the man a push and Addison, still wheezing, stumbled off clutching his stomach.

Lamb had been aghast at all this. He had never before witnessed such summary and quite illegal punishment.

'My God!' he muttered, shaken. 'Do you make a habit of that sort of thing?'

Bell tossed the bottle into the air and caught it. He smiled. 'Only when the occasion demands.'

'But you are taking an awful risk. Supposing the man had fought back? An officer brawling with a seaman? It could be the finish of your career.'

Bell laughed, as if the idea was nonsense. 'When I hit them, they are in no state to fight back – I make sure of that. Hit first and hit hard, that's always been my way. Don't look so shocked, Matthew. That man was lucky just now. What he did would have earned him a dozen lashes at least, if he had been charged, and he knows it.' He bunched his fist beneath Lamb's nose. 'That fist has saved the backs of a good many men on my ships. They know me and they know what to expect if they misbehave themselves. It's quick and it's just and it saves a good deal of formality. Our punishment lists are never very long.'

'And does Captain Beamish know of your – um – little ways?'

Bell shrugged. 'I'd be surprised if he did not but he has never mentioned it.' He stretched and yawned. 'Well, it is your watch, Matthew. I am off to the captain's cot for my beauty sleep. Call me if you need me – and don't let go of mama's hand,' he added, nodding in the direction of the *Swiftsure*, dimly visible to starboard. He strode off to the aft companionway, leaving his farewell chuckle hanging in the air behind him.

Sexton sniffed. 'Mama's hand!' he sniggered and sniffed again.

God! Does the fellow not possess a handkerchief? thought Lamb.

'Are you not going to get some sleep?' he enquired hopefully. 'You will be on watch yourself in a few hours.'

Sexton noisily drained his glass. The privateer's captain had enjoyed a very fine claret and Bell had considered it his bounden duty to sample it in order to ascertain its fitness for British palates. The first bottle had passed the test and Sexton was busily working his way through the second.

'Oh,' he said, with a sniff, 'I am not really tired, you know. I thought I might stay on deck for an hour or so,' – sniff – 'and keep you company. Have a chat, perhaps. It does make a change to have a new face to talk to.' Sniff.

No, spare me that, thought Lamb in alarm. 'Yes, that would be pleasant,' he agreed, 'but much as I would enjoy it, I am afraid I must decline. I have long made it a habit of mine, the day before the Sabbath, to spend my evening hours in silent contemplation of my inner self; I find that it prepares my soul for the blessed day to follow. Perhaps you would care to join me in silent prayer for an hour?'

'No, I think not, thank you,' said Sexton with a stiff smile, backing away from the lunatic. 'I find that I am more sleepy than I thought. I shall leave you to your devotions. Goodnight to you.' Sniff.

'Goodnight,' said Lamb in a saintly voice.

Chapter 8

Lamb tucked in his chin and peered down the length of his body with a critical eye. He sighed and shook his head. His shoes were presentable enough, as were the glittering buttons on his coat, but the rest of his attire made him cluck his tongue in near despair. His best coat had obstinately refused to give up its wrinkles and creases, in spite of enthusiastic brushing and sponging; somehow, a streak of irremovable tar had appeared on one of the legs of his white breeches and his best silk stockings, carefully preserved for an occasion such as tonight, had revealed the need for urgent darning when removed from his sea-chest. His stitches were neat enough, he supposed, and not too blatant, but even so – darned stockings! He would be aware of the damned things all evening. His eye picked out a speck on one of his shoe buckles and he bent to give the pair of them a final polish with his handkerchief. Surely silver should not tarnish like that? He had been assured they were of the purest silver – the price he had paid for them was still painful in his memory. He straightened, jerked at the hem of his coat and leaned forward to peer into his tiny shaving mirror as he adjusted the set of his stock. Well, damn it, I can make myself no better, he thought; if people do not care for my appearance it is just too bad. He took his dress hat from its box and brushed it with loving fingers; this, rarely worn and protected from shipboard knocks in its leather case, was the one piece of his uniform he could wear tonight without shame. At least no-one can fault that, he thought proudly, holding the hat on the fingers of one hand and spinning it with the other in front of his appreciative eye. But even so, he mused a little sourly as he placed it carefully fore and aft on his head, it will probably make the rest of me look even shabbier by contrast. He stepped back half a pace in order to bring the set of his hat into his shaving mirror and cursed as a deck beam brushed it from his head.

'Matthew!'

Kennedy's impatient bellow sounded again from the bottom of the aft companionway.

Lamb snatched up his hat and rubbed at it with his sleeve.

'I am on my way,' he called and with a last, anxious glance at his shaving mirror he ducked his head and left his cabin.

The sun was setting in huge, glorious majesty behind the low hills to the west of the town as the *Sturdy*'s boats pulled across the Madras roadstead, giving a bloody tinge to the water and the faces of the officers as they sat facing forward. The four lieutenants shared the cutter and astern, in the *Sturdy*'s gig, sat the three captains of the squadron. There were other boats, too, from the *Swiftsure* and the *Martin*, carrying their lieutenants to the town. From one of the boats came a loud hail and the wave of an arm. Lamb, recognizing Bell's voice, raised an arm in return.

Tonight the frigates would be left in the care of their warrant officers – all the commissioned officers were required ashore. The arrival of a privateer-hunting squadron, together with a captured brig and the news of the destruction of another, had delighted the Madras merchants and shippers and the officers of the Honourable Company. Within a few hours a reception had been planned and organized and the invitations delivered and accepted by Captain Beamish on behalf of the officers of his squadron. The commodore did not plan to stay in the Madras roads for long – his time was limited and the two privateers accounted for to date would not satisfy the expectations of Admiral Shillington – but he had no intention of forgoing the pleasure of being the focus of the town's adulation for a few hours and he had graciously postponed the departure of his squadron until the following day.

The cutter pulled across the bows of the *La Belle Femme* and Lamb glanced up at her. She was dark and silent, almost empty of life. The head of one of the three seamen put on board as watchmen appeared over the rail.

'What ho, mates,' he called down, somewhat wistfully, ill at ease on his lonely duty and missing the crowded companionship of his mess.

'Watch your back, George, that's a 'aunted ship you're on,' said a voice in a sepulchral tone from the cutter's bows.

'Oh, don't say that, mates!' cried the watchman desolately and a low, gleeful titter rose from the oarsmen.

'Hold your damned noise,' growled Maxwell but he, too, was grinning broadly and his tone lacked its usual menace.

The enormous reception room in the governor's residence was brilliantly lit and stiflingly hot, even with all the huge windows and its several doors wide open to the night air and the insects. The room was crowded and the portly little man engaging Lamb's attention had to raise his voice in order to be heard over the loud buzz of excited chatter and laughter. The man had buttonholed Lamb and Kennedy within minutes of their arrival but Kennedy had slyly slipped away after a few moments, leaving Lamb to listen with apparent fascination to the complexities of the transfer of capital from one money market to another. Lamb's knowledge of the subject was probably on a par with that of the *Sturdy*'s cook but he politely struggled to maintain a look of interest on his face, inwardly cursing Kennedy for deserting him. He could feel the sweat trickling down his spine to collect in a small puddle at his waistband.

Bell suddenly appeared at his elbow, a grave look on his face. He gave a brief bow to the civilian.

'Your pardon, sir.' He turned to Lamb. 'Your presence is required by the captain, sir, immediately, if you please.' He turned again to the merchant. 'Important naval matters, sir, you understand. If you will excuse us?'

'Of course, of course.' The little man bowed to Lamb. 'I must not keep you, sir. I am delighted to have made your acquaintance.'

Lamb bowed in return, his mind turning over a dozen reasons why Cutler should need him so urgently. 'And I yours, sir.'

He followed Bell through the crush of people to where, at the side of the room, stood Kennedy, grinning widely and with a glass of wine in each hand.

'I must apologize for the little deception there, Matthew,' said Bell, his grin as wide as Kennedy's. 'You looked as though you needed rescuing.'

Kennedy thrust a glass of wine into Lamb's hand. 'Here, get outside of that. You are giving the service a bad name, standing there without a glass in your hand. You look disgustingly sober, don't he, Billy?'

'He does indeed,' said Bell. 'Here's me and Tom three parts awash, and you looking like a bishop at a tea-party. What were you talking about with that civilian, anyway – women?'

'No, something much more closer to my heart – money markets. I was able to give the man a little advice on one or two matters. Did you know that if you bought forward in Hong Kong dollars and sold in sterling, you could double your profit – or was it the other way around?'

Bell dived into the crowd and returned holding three fresh glasses. 'Here,' he said, sharing them out. 'Your turn next, Matthew.'

They stood and sipped their wine, slyly eyeing the ladies.

'You know, these affairs are all very well,' said Bell thoughtfully, 'but I think, on balance, I would rather spend an evening in a London tavern. There at least you could sprawl, shout, sing, drink what you want and have the chance of an honest fumble beneath a girl's skirts. No such chance of that for us tonight – I have never seen such a collection of tight-faced wives and virtuous daughters.'

'I shall get some more wine,' said Lamb.

Captain Beamish strolled by in the company of several elderly gentlemen and flicked his eyes coldly in their direction. The three lieutenants assumed expressions of grave sobriety. From the advantage of his height Lamb could see a slow trickle of people disappearing into the supper room and he instantly became ravenously hungry.

'The supper room is open,' he announced. 'Are you two hungry?'

The others moved off as one before Lamb had finished speaking and he followed them as they sidled their way through the crowd in the direction of the supper room. Plates in hand they filed along the laden tables, spearing slices of beef, legs of chicken, filled pastries, duck in aspic, fresh bread and pickles. Clutching their overloaded plates they made for a quiet corner and busied themselves with their forks.

'Ha, the best part of the evening, this!' grunted Bell through a mouthful of chicken.

Two young men, both in civilian dress and similar enough in

looks to be taken for brothers, brought their plates to the same corner and the officers politely edged to one side to make room.

'May we make your acquaintance, gentlemen?' asked one of the men after a while, a little shyly.

'Yes, of course, delighted,' said Bell. 'My name is Billy Bell and this is Tom Kennedy and Matthew Lamb.'

The young men were delighted, absolutely delighted to make their acquaintance. Their names were John Wilkie and Tom Brown, they were both employed by the Honourable Company and had arrived on the same ship more than a year ago. They were very anxious to hear the details of the recent exploits of the squadron at first hand and between them, gilding the lily more than somewhat, Bell and Kennedy gave such an imaginative account of the *Sturdy*'s desperate struggles with hordes of privateers that Lamb silently squirmed in embarrassment. Brown and Wilkie listened enthralled, drinking in every word with total belief and when the pack of lies was at an end they insisted on shaking hands all over again.

Wilkie shot out a hand and stopped a passing servant, resplendent in full beard, white gloves and red sash and carrying a tray of brimming glasses. He went on his way with a much reduced load and the five young men downed their wine and looked around for more. The talk grew lively and animated as the wine added to the effect of the previous intake and laughter rang out with increasing frequency.

'You see the large, bald man there, talking to one of your captains?' said Brown. Heads swivelled and turned back and nodded. 'He is Sir George Frisk, a past Member of Parliament and the owner of one of the largest shipping concerns in India. Looks respectable enough, does he not?' The heads nodded again, eyes fixed on Brown, waiting for the piece of scandal that the question had promised. 'He owns a large house ten or twelve miles out of town. His wife died a couple of years ago and she was scarcely cold before he had dismissed all his male servants from the house and replaced them with female servants – young, pretty, female servants. It has never been my good fortune to visit there but the story goes that while he is at home he does not allow them to wear any clothes.'

'What, they go about stark naked?' queried Kennedy, his eyes round.

'So I understand. Then, whenever he feels the need, there they are, just for the taking.'

Bell groaned as if in deep pain. 'My God, what a prospect! No, I cannot think of it – it is sheer torture. I have been too long at sea.'

Lamb eyed Brown a little sceptically. Perhaps he was not so green as he had appeared when listening to the colourful lies of Kennedy and Bell and was now playing them at their own game.

Wilkie spoke up. 'It sounds as if you fellows are in need of a little close female contact. What say we introduce them to Mrs McCalden, Tom?'

Bell pricked up his ears. 'Mrs McCalden – who is she?'

'She runs a high-class establishment not far from here – for gentlemen only. Hand-picked girls, all very clean. Tom and I have paid a visit from time to time and have always been well satisfied. If it were not for fear of shocking the tender susceptibilities of innocent young naval officers we would be happy to take you there, would we not, Tom?'

'Just point us in the right direction and we will show you how tender our bloody susceptibilities are,' countered Bell, grinning.

'My God, yes!' said Kennedy.

'Fair enough, but it must be our treat. The navy must not put its hands in its pockets tonight.' Wilkie pulled his watch from his pocket. 'It is a little early yet. We have time for another glass or two before we leave. What say we try the punchbowl for a change?'

Lamb had been listening to these arrangements with some unease. As a midshipman, barely fifteen years old, he had been taken by a couple of more worldly colleagues to a brothel in Plymouth. For him the experience had not been a happy one. The coarse, drunken harridan who ran the place had jeered at his youth and nervousness and put him in the care of her oldest and most worn girl, a fat slut with about as much tender finesse and patient consideration for a green young boy as the foot-scraper outside the front door. Lamb had stared in fascinated revulsion at the spread thighs, coarse hair and flabby, bug-bitten stomach and the last traces of his faint, nervous desire and curiosity died on the spot. He had thrown his coins on to

157

the bed without a word and fled from the room and the house, the slut's scornful laughter hastening him on his way. It was a long time before his companions allowed him to forget his shameful reluctance and longer still before he put the memory at the back of his mind. He had never visited such a place since and today he was as virginal as when he entered the world.

The glass or two of punch was followed by another glass or two and Lamb was feeling cheerfully awash when Wilkie gave a firm rat-tat-tat on the heavy teak door of the large, square bungalow not five minutes walk from the governor's mansion. The door was opened by a silent Indian woman who stepped aside and bowed her grey head to each of the men in turn as they stepped over the threshold. A stout, pretty-faced woman bustled from a doorway adjoining the brightly-lit hall and advanced on them with a wide smile of welcome and out-stretched hands.

'Mr Brown! Mr Wilkie! How very pleasant to see you both again. I quite thought you had forsaken me.'

The two men each took a plump hand and bent over it.

'Forsake you, dearest Kate?' said Brown in a voice of the deepest sincerity. 'How could we, when your beauty is etched so deeply on our hearts and minds?'

'La, you flatterer! If only I could believe you. Will you introduce me to your friends?'

Mrs McCalden's drawing room was large and well lit and furnished with enough chairs and sofas to seat a score of guests without crowding them. The lady busied herself at the sideboard.

'I shall give you a glass of hock apiece. It only arrived last week but then hock always travels well, does it not? I cannot abide red wines. I was told many years ago – well, not too many – that constant drinking of red wines will give you an evil complexion. So be warned, gentlemen! Shun that nasty claret you always have on board your ships or you will look old before your time. Now just sit there and enjoy your wine and I shall go and fetch my girls.'

There was silence in the room following the lady's departure. Lamb sipped his hock and wondered if the others felt as guilty as he. He felt no passion, no desire, no stirrings of tumescence in spite of the many thousands of times he had looked forward to this moment. He gave a wry inward smile; put him in the solitude of his cabin at night and he was as horny as a ram; now, damn it, when it was needed, nothing.

Bell raised his glass. 'Well, this is all very jolly, ain't it? Cheer up, Matthew – if you are careful it won't hurt you a bit.'

'Don't concern yourself over him,' said Kennedy. 'He's a bit of a dark horse. Did you know that when we were at Gibraltar he was the only one of us to – ?'

'Here come the girls,' said Wilkie.

They swished into the room, arch and coquettish in their colourful saris, smiling, twirling, long lashes fluttering, lining up in front of the seated men. Mrs McCalden walked along the line, giving their names one by one. They were all Indian or Eurasian but their names were surprisingly European – donated, Lamb guessed, by Mrs McCalden. One girl, introduced as Letitia, caught Lamb's interest, a small, slight Eurasian in a yellow sari, with large violet eyes set in a neat, grave face.

Mrs McCalden stood to one side as the girls flounced enticingly and flashed their eyes while the men sat and gazed, the officers wide-eyed and entranced, the civilians with the quiet smiles of old campaigners.

'Come, gentlemen, make your choices, if you please,' cried Mrs McCalden, a trifle tartly.

'The navy has first choice tonight,' said Brown, waving his hand at his guests.

The three looked at one another, each reluctant to make the first move. Bell solved the problem neatly.

'You are the junior, Matthew, you must be first into the boat. Choose your lady.'

Lamb put a brave face on things and rose from his chair with an air of nonchalance. 'Very well. The one in – the lady in yellow, I think.'

'Ah, Letitia!' cried Mrs McCalden. 'You could not have made a better choice. One of my very best girls – and so ardent!'

On hearing her name Letitia stepped close to Lamb and gripped his arm, pressing herself against him and looking up at his face with her wide, violet eyes.

'Come,' she whispered, tugging him gently in the direction of the door. Lamb allowed himself to be led away but paused at the door as Bell gave a shout.

'If you need any assistance, Matthew, just give a call. I won't be too far away.'

The others chuckled. Lamb struggled to find a suitable stinging rejoinder but could think of nothing. He managed a brave grin and turned to follow the girl down the hall.

Letitia closed the door to her room and smiled up at Lamb's face. 'Undress, please. Me give bath.'

Lamb raised his eyebrows at this but made no protest and modestly turning his back he removed his clothes and piled them neatly on a nearby chair. Cupping his hands over his groin he faced the girl, feeling more than a little foolish. She had removed her sari and was waiting, naked, beside the bed. As she saw Lamb's attempt to protect his modesty she giggled and pointed to the bed.

'Come.'

Lamb stretched out on the bed, hands still clasped firmly over his manhood. Letitia smiled and shook her head.

'No, no,' she said and taking his hands she placed them beside his hips. Lamb felt his face flush crimson. She shook her head sorrowfully at the sight of Lamb's limp unreadiness and gave another little giggle as she flicked at him with her finger. Lamb, mortified, clenched his lips and lay still.

The girl squeezed a sponge into a bowl on the small table beside the bed and leaning over Lamb began to sponge his chest. The water was cool and strongly scented. He fixed his eyes on the dark-nippled breasts swinging gently above his face and felt the first faint stirrings of tumescence. Taking a nervous breath he put a tentative fingertip on one proud nipple, half-expecting an indignant rebuff. Letitia smiled and nodded.

'Nice, nice,' she whispered.

Encouraged, Lamb reached up with both hands and squeezed and pressed and stroked, fascinated by the warm, smooth, yielding touch of them. They were the first breasts he had touched since he was a suckling and now, as if to make up for all those breastless years, he could not touch them enough. He stroked the nipples, rolling the hard little points between finger and thumb, traced the faint, blue ridges of her veins and cupped a breast in each hand to feel the weight of them. The sponge moved down to his stomach and then to his groin.

Letitia murmured appreciatively and tossing the sponge into the bowl she placed her hands beside Lamb's shoulders and in one quick movement, swung her legs across his body and straddled him. She fixed her wide eyes on his face as she felt beneath her and wriggled slightly to position herself more accurately. Her buttocks pressed downwards and her eyes closed momentarily as she gave a sharp hiss of indrawn breath. Lamb's stomach muscles tensed as he instinctively pushed up to meet her and her fingers dug deep into his shoulders as her body slowly rose and fell. He reached forward and clasped her hips as she began to emit deep little grunting moans that coincided with the increasingly urgent downward thrust of her buttocks. As Lamb felt his moment nearing she threw back her head and closed her eyes, as if in deep concentration on her own approaching instant. Lamb gripped her hips and pulled her tightly on to him as he spurted, groaning. She gave a sharp cry, shuddered and fell forward, her breasts crushed against his hammering chest.

Lamb stared up at the ceiling, his heart thudding savagely in his chest. He felt a sense of triumph, of near exultation. At last, at last he knew and it was more wonderful than he had ever dreamed it would be. He closed his eyes for a few seconds to savour and enjoy the feeling of the moment to the full. He felt the girl sit up and remove herself from his body and opened his eyes to see her standing beside him with her sari wrapped around her.

'Go now, please,' she said. 'All finish now.'

The abrupt demand took the edge off Lamb's euphoria somewhat and as he struggled damply into his uniform the thought crossed his mind that the girl's ardent performance was perhaps no more than professional artistry. He gave a mental shrug. So what? The joy had been in the moment and to quibble now was pointless. The girl was crouched over a basin in a corner of the room with her back to him, knees splayed, washing herself. He hesitated at the door, unsure of the conventions of departure. After such intimacy, it seemed churlish in the extreme to leave without a word. The realization suddenly struck him that so far he had not uttered a single syllable to her. What a bore he must seem!

He dived his hand into his pocket and brought out a fistful of coins. The light was dim and he peered closely, looking for the gleam of gold. Damn, there was none. He removed the silver from the copper and placed it in a little pile on the chair. He gave a preliminary little cough.

'Goodbye.'

Letitia turned her head and gave him a flash of small, white teeth in a brilliant smile.

'Goodbye. You nice!'

Kennedy was chatting to Mrs McCalden in the drawing room when Lamb entered and within the minute Bell joined them, a huge grin on his square face. Mrs McCalden showed them to the door; Mr Wilkie and Mr Brown would be staying the night, she informed them, a piece of information which caused Bell to give a low whistle of envy.

They walked back to the reception through the dark, hot night, Bell and Kennedy loudly and gleefully exchanging notes on the performances of their girls. Lamb walked beside them in silence, listening to their coarse chatter but determined to take no part in it. Tonight would be a memory to savour in the long night watches at sea and he had no wish to throw mud at such a milestone in his life. The lights from the open windows of the governor's residence made cheerful yellow rectangles in the darkness and the noise of talk and laughter from within carried clearly to the road. They made their way past the sentries at the open gate and through the gardens to the open doors at the side of the building where their return to the reception would, hopefully, go unnoticed.

'God, I'm thirsty,' said Bell as they mounted the wide stone steps.

Chapter 9

At four bells in the forenoon watch the squadron weighed anchor and sailed out of the Madras roadstead to continue its sweep of the trade route to Calcutta. The hands were surly and slow-moving, the officers unusually sombre and much given to wincing. The immediate effect of their common pains was an uncommonly large number of defaulters' names on the first lieutenant's punishment list; however, twenty-four hours in the sparkling air and clean winds of the bay were sufficient to cure the sourest of stomachs and the keenest of headpains and within the day the *Sturdy* was back to its normal level of efficiency.

Beamish was anxious to add to his short list of successes – too short by far to satisfy Admiral Shillington – and the squadron took up its customary widespread, line-abreast position of sail. The amount of time the commodore had left to him before he was due to report back to Simon's Town was limited and when the squadron reached the outer limits of the shallow waters and sandbanks that extended many miles from the estuary of Calcutta the frigates turned south and continued their search in the open waters of the vast bay. Within hours they had trapped a small privateer schooner and left it sinking, the survivors scrambling into what boats remained to them. That same afternoon, towards evening, they cornered another, a sizeable brig and a likely prize. It put up a stiff resistance, however, and was so knocked about that it was not worth the taking in. The *Swiftsure* opened it up with her carronades and left her, allowing her survivors to make their own arrangements.

From this moment on, the squadron's luck changed. It may have been that news of the squadron's presence in the bay had reached the ears of the French marauders or, like unlucky anglers, their lines were in one place and the fish in another but, for whatever reason, the days spread into weeks with the lookouts squatting dumbly at the mastheads. Beamish took the squadron south to the limits of the Bay of Bengal, east to the entrance to the Straits of Malacca, north-west to Calcutta again and then south once more and never once was a gun fired in anger. The winds were invariably light and the days constantly hot; the unvarying routine of the ships continued day after day, a time-filling process that gave little scope for the hands to become bored and discontented. Lamb revelled in the weather and climate of these latitudes; the heat and colour of the day as he paced his watch on the quarterdeck, keeping an eye on the leisurely activities about the ship, were a joy to him after his long years in the grey, cold waters of the English Channel; the warm, soft nights with their myriad brilliant stars and the huge, low-hung moon were times for quiet thought and contemplation. Lamb, ever introspective, was never weary of his own company and was often surprised at how swiftly the ship's bell sounded the passing half-hours.

As the squadron scoured the waters of the bay and one fruitless day followed another Cutler, isolated from the mainstream of life on the frigate by rank and quarters, became increasingly morose. He spent less and less time on the quarterdeck and overwatching the exercising of the guns and when he did he was noticeably irritable and snappy. Occasionally he would make an appearance smelling strongly of drink and at these times his mood was much more agreeable. At one period he never stirred from his quarters for over twenty-four hours and when Maxwell, in the course of his duties, knocked and entered he was driven out with a volley of abuse that was heard the length of the ship.

The wardroom grew increasingly concerned and daily Maxwell's face grew grimmer and his expression more preoccupied. Drunkenness among captains was not unknown but it was outside the officers' experience; the ability to drink hard and show little sign of it was more common, although Lamb's last captain had been an avowed abstainer. Lamb suspected he might have been a much sweeter individual had he been otherwise. Among the seamen the problem was a perpetual one; with a gallon of beer, or wine in lieu, and two quarter-pints of rum diluted with water served daily to each man it was small wonder that the most common crime on board ship was drunkenness. Diluted rum did not keep and the beer was weak but the *Sturdy*, like most ships, had its quota of men who were resourceful enough to be able to spend their days in varying degrees of stupor. But providing they did their work reasonably well and kept a civil tongue authority showed a tactful unawareness. It was the man who stepped over the mark, who was let down by a loose tongue or was too obviously less than capable who found himself on the first lieutenant's list of defaulters. One such man was Simon Yates, ordinary seaman, afterguard, charged with insolence to a superior officer and drunkenness on duty. .

When Yates appeared before the captain in front of the assembled hands one hot forenoon it was clear that he had gone to considerable effort to present a neat, clean and eminently sober appearance. His face was shaved to a tender closeness, his pigtail was stiff and freshly braided and his shirt and trousers as clean as salt water and sun could make them. On his face was fixed a look of pious sobriety. Cutler stood at the break of the quarterdeck, swaying rather more than anyone else on the near-steady deck; his eyes were rimmed with red and his face was puffy. He frowned and blinked in the strong morning light as the master-at-arms read the charge and the gunner gave his evidence.

'Yates was employed in greasing the gun-tackle blocks, sir, and in the course of my duties I passed the man at his work and noticed that a quantity of grease was improperly on the deck. I reprimanded the man, sir, and ordered him to clean the grease from the deck as it was a hazard. He stood up and immediately fell against me, sir, leaving grease on my uniform. I remonstrated with him, sir,' – Yes, I can imagine! thought Lamb – 'and enquired if he was drunk. Whereupon he replied: "That's none of your business, you fat Welsh fart." I immediately reported him to the officer of the watch who had him removed below by the master-at-arms, sir.'

Cutler nodded slowly, his eyes half-closed against the sun's glare. There was a long silence during which every man on the ship stared at the captain and the captain stared at the deck. The silence dragged on and still Cutler said nothing. The officers glanced furtively at one another, increasingly uncomfortable and yet not daring to break the silence. It was the captain's place to speak and he, seeming oblivious of the

165

awkward, stretched hush, continued to gaze down at the deck seams. The watching men, delighted with the novelty of the situation and keenly aware of the officers' embarrassment, began to smile and hide broad grins behind their hands. The calculated expression of piety on Yates's face had now slipped and been replaced by a look of frowning concern. Maxwell decided to take the intitiative and took a pace forward to glare at the assembled hands.

'Silence on deck!' he thundered at the silent, startled men. 'The next man to speak will find his name on my list!'

The outburst, not a yard from the captain's ear, brought his head up at last and he stared in apparent bewilderment at the group of men standing before him. He ran his tongue around his lips.

'Yes, Mr Bryce?'

The gunner looked nonplussed. He shot a quick glance at Maxwell. 'That's all, sir,' he said. 'I've finished, sir.'

Cutler nodded. 'I see.' He turned his attention to Yates. 'It's Yates, is it not?'

'Yes, sir.'

'What have you to say, Yates?'

Yates launched into his carefully prepared lies. He was very sorry, sir, it had been a temporary lapse, no more, quite unlike him, sir, ask anyone. He was very sorry if he had caused offence to Mr Bryce, an officer for whom he had always had the greatest respect, sir.

Cutler's head had dropped again while Yates was speaking but this time he brought his gaze up when the man had finished. Lamb, standing to one side, caught sight of the captain's face and he was shocked at its appearance. It was startlingly white, quite bloodless, like that of a corpse. Cutler's voice was little more than a whisper.

'Loss of hammock for a month. Dismiss the hands, Mr Maxwell.'

He turned away, staggered wildly and clutched at Lamb for support. Lamb smelled the awful, stale reek of the man, on his breath and oozing from every pore. As Cutler pulled himself upright Lamb instinctively put out his hand to steady him. Cutler impatiently struck it aside and walked unsteadily to his quarters. Maxwell stepped over to the surgeon and whispered urgently in his ear. Meadows nodded and hurried across to Cutler's quarters. The door closed behind him and Lamb cocked an ear, expecting an outburst, but none came.

Maxwell dismissed the hands to their duties and in the same breath ordered Yates to wipe the smug smile from his face. Mr Bryce stalked off as rapidly as his short legs could manage, his round face scarlet with indignation at the humiliatingly light sentence Yates had been awarded while that surprised and delighted individual scampered forward to join his mates – a month without benefit of hammock was no hardship in these latitudes.

The surgeon made no comment on Cutler's condition when he later put in an appearance in the gunroom and although the junior lieutenants burned with curiosity they were wise enough to ask no questions. Later, while Lamb was on watch in the dusk of the last dog-watch, he saw Maxwell and Meadows strolling the quiet maindeck together, the first lieutenant nodding his head as the surgeon talked. During the next two days Meadows made frequent visits to the captain's cabin but remained as tight-lipped as ever. At the end of those two days, as Lamb was making his way to the quarterdeck to relieve Kennedy, he almost fell over Watson making his way aft with a bucket of steaming water in each hand. He seized the opportunity to put some sly questions.

'Hallo, Watson! What's the need for all the water, then?'

The little man carefully placed the buckets on the deck and brought a knuckle to his forehead.

'Just going to give the capting a quick scrub down, sir,' he said and added bitterly: 'Two buckets of warm water, sir, and you'd think I was asking the cook for his other leg! I had to practically go down on my knees for this, sir.'

Lamb laughed. The wooden-legged cook was renowned for his irascibility and was treated with fawning servility by the hands. It was an unfortunate man who fell out of favour with the cook, particularly if he liked his pipe; the galley was the only place in the ship where he could legally smoke it.

'And how is the captain progressing?' he asked carefully.

Watson smiled happily. 'Oh, he's doing wery well, thank you, sir. He's been eating today – I made him some nice broth and perhaps tonight I might make him some toasted cheese.

He's wery partial to that, sir.'

'Splendid, splendid,' said Lamb. 'You, um, you think he is over his trouble now, then?'

Watson's smile vanished. 'Trouble, sir, what trouble? The capting ain't got no trouble, sir, what I know of.' He nodded at his buckets. 'The capting's water'll be getting cold, sir, you keep me standing here.'

Lamb took the pointed comment. 'Of course, Watson, you carry on.'

He stood aside and the steward picked up his buckets and walked on, leaving Lamb with the feeling that he had put his nose in where it was far from welcome.

The wind freshened considerably in the afternoon and before the end of the first dog-watch Lamb sent the duty midshipman down to the first lieutenant to request leave to shorten sail. Maxwell followed the midshipman back on deck and after a glance at the sails and the sea and feeling the tension of the mainmast backstay he had ordered the customary evening reduction of the sails to be brought forward. By four o'clock in the morning, however, when Lamb took over the morning watch, the wind had noticeably decreased and the sea, though still high, was less broken and confused.

The ship awoke and began its daily routine, the sounds and sights of the morning activities so familiar to Lamb after months on the morning watch that while his outward, duty eye remained observant to his responsibilities, his inner gaze was able to dwell without distraction on the ramblings of his secret thoughts and hopes and memories as he paced back and forth, moving without conscious volition to the scrubbed weather side of the quarterdeck the moment the men were ready to bring their heavy bibles to bear on the lee side.

The watch was nearly over and Lamb's thoughts were turning with growing urgency to the delights of coffee and breakfast when the captain appeared from his quarters and bade his sentry a good morning. He glanced about the ship and sniffed the air in his old, familiar way before mounting the wide ladder to the quarterdeck. He looked pale and drawn but his smile was bright.

'Good morning, Mr Lamb.'

'Good morning, sir,' said Lamb, touching his hat.

'A little cooler today, perhaps?'

'I think it is, sir.'

Cutler peered in at the binnacle, glanced at the course chalked on the board, and walked around the quarterdeck running his eye over the lashings of the guns and carronades. He descended to the maindeck and made his way forward along the weather side, casting quick glances at gun lashings, the netted hammocks along the rail and the racks of roundshot along the side and beside the hatch coamings. He returned by way of the lee side and stopped at the break of the quarterdeck.

He raised a finger in the air. 'Mr Lamb!'

Lamb hurried down the ladder and saluted.

'Sir?'

'Number fourteen hammock under the starboard fore-rigging is badly lashed. See to it, if you please.'

'Aye aye, sir.'

Cutler vanished into his cabin and Lamb bellowed for the master's mate who had overseen the stowing of the hammocks that morning. Together they inspected the offending hammock. It was neatly rolled beneath the regulation seven turns of its cord but one of its clews had escaped from beneath the lashing and was hanging loose through the netting. It was a mere trifle, the smallest peccadillo; Lamb knew at once that Cutler had pointed out this tiny imperfection in order to demonstrate the complete and absolute return of his authority and faculties; a more obvious breach of order – a rope hanging judas or rusting roundshot – would not have needed the same alertness of eye. Lamb smiled; the owner of hammock number fourteen had done the captain an unwitting service by his slipshod haste.

'Shall I take the man's name, sir?' enquired the master's mate, anxious to pass on the responsibility for this slovenliness to other shoulders.

'No,' said Lamb. 'Just jump up and tuck it in.'

The uneasy atmosphere which had been prevalent in the gunroom vanished that day with the re-emergence of Cutler into shipboard life as his familiar, authoritative self. Maxwell in particular was looking more cheerful. The awful thought of Cutler sliding into alcoholic derangement with the moment looming daily closer when, after consulation with the surgeon, he must signal the commodore that the captain was no longer fit to command must have been a burden for the first lieutenant that Lamb was happy not to have shared. Maxwell was not an easy man to serve under; his cold, dour manner and his bitter tongue kept him at a distance from the junior officers but Lamb's opinion of him had gone up a notch of late. He had kept his worries to himself, with little increase in the irascibility that he habitually displayed.

The squadron swept south the length of the bay and turned west to skirt the southern shores of Ceylon. It had come across several ships since turning south off Calcutta; a few harmless merchantmen had been sighted, closed and cleared; one or two distant sightings had shown every reluctance to be closed and had withdrawn at high speed, their eventual disappearance aided by Beamish's refusal to allow independent chasing by his frigates. Time was now running short for the commodore; the demand for frigates in theatres elsewhere was urgent and the date for the squadron's return to Simon's Bay was firm. South-west of Ceylon Beamish summoned his captains to the *Swiftsure* for a conference.

Captain Beamish had no intention of seeking advice from his juniors. He was a man of firmly held opinions, a post-captain of some years and in line for an appointment to a ship of the line, but he was prepared to note and listen to suggestions and objections, if only for the sake of courtesy. The problem he had been turning over in his mind was one of choice between two courses of action: to retain the unity of his command and thereby limit its area of search or to separate it, with the resultant risks to lone ships from prowling French frigates. With the limited amount of time left to him and the lamentably short list of successes to present to Admiral Shillington he was drawn to the conclusion that he must choose the latter course, and having made his decision and laid it before his captains he sat back and awaited their comments. They were brief; both men were delighted at the prospect of independent cruising and Beamish would have been surprised if they had been otherwise.

The three men got down to details. The relative sailing qualities of the three frigates were discussed and after a little heat had been raised from Blake who considered one adverse comment to be grossly unfair, their respective courses were settled, exactly as Beamish had already planned. The heavier-gunned *Swiftsure* would take the more southern route and pass east of Mauritius, the French-held lair of privateers and frigates, before turning west for the Cape. The *Sturdy* would head for Madagascar and sail midway between its thousand miles of coastline and the island of Bourbon, also in French hands. The lighter-armed, smaller *Martin*, although under-manned, was probably the speediest of the frigates and certainly the better performer close-hauled. She would head west across the Indian Ocean and then follow the trade-route south along the coast of Africa and through the Mozambique Channel.

'Bear in mind, gentlemen,' said Beamish, tapping the chart with a massive forefinger, 'that time is of the essence. If you are late arriving at Simon's Town without very good reason, searching questions will be asked. I want no enthusiastic dashing-off on long, fruitless chases. Keep your noses pointed along your respective courses and if a Frenchman happens to venture near, well, good luck to you. One last thing. I take the reports of French heavy frigates and frigate squadrons cruising these waters with a pinch of salt but if you do happen to sight one, do not allow yourselves to be tempted – an immediate withdrawal will be called for. That is an order. None of us is cast in the mould of Grenville, I think.'

The squadron dispersed immediately on the return of the captains to their commands, the *Swiftsure*, in fact, getting under way before Cutler had reached the side of the *Sturdy*. The sight of the broad blue pendant being hauled down brought a buzz of comment from the deck of the *Sturdy*, denoting as it did the break-up of the squadron into independent ships, causing considerable excitement among the officers and none at all among the hands. The *Martin* was the first to fade from sight as she headed west; the *Swiftsure* and the *Sturdy*, on southerly but diverging courses, kept within sight of each other for several hours but as the violet dusk crept over the sea the *Swiftsure* flagship was also lost to view.

Cutler seemed now to be completely back to his old self again and as the frigate began the long haul across the vastness of the Indian Ocean he spent a good deal of the burning days on the quarterdeck and maindeck. He no longer considered it necessary to carry out gun practice every day and in its place substituted sail- and spar-handling. Competitions were initiated between the three divisions of sail-handlers, marks were carefully totted up and at the end of each week the winning division was awarded extra tots of rum all round. Officers stood beneath the masts with watches in hand, timing the lowering and raising of the royals, setting the staysails, striking the topgallant masts to the deck and raising them again, bending on new topsails, reefing and shaking out. The men's favourite was the relay race, up to the masthead and down again over each mast in turn, with no cheating by sliding down the stays. This was a truly exhausting event, a young man's sport; Lamb had taken part in similar races as a midshipman and he vividly remembered the agony of leaden arms, aching legs and madly-pumping heart and lungs. He was more than content now in his role of benevolently smiling onlooker. The hands entered into the competitiveness of the thing with a will – the intense rivalry that already existed between divisions was spur enough without the added edge given by the chance of extra rum – and loud cheers, boos and shouts of laughter rang out from the deck as they followed the progress over the masts.

On the evening of their third day of independent sailing the captain entertained his officers to supper. Cutler's stores were almost as depleted as those of the wardroom but the cook made a valiant effort and slices of salt beef and pork, cut thin and well-fried with onions and served with pickles, with figgy-dowdy and jam to follow, were sufficient to make the officers' eyes gleam with appreciation. The captain's wines, however, were much superior to the stuff the gunroom had been drinking of late; their stock of white was long gone, they had finished the vile navy claret and were now reduced to supping Black Strap, the very roughest of rough reds warranted to take the skin off the tongue of the most hardened toper. Cutler was able to offer them madeira, port and a superior claret but it was noticeable that he took no wine himself, confining his drinking to his water glass from which he sipped every few minutes as if in constant thirst.

The evening was extremely warm. The ship was very close to the equator and in spite of open doors and skylight the sweat ran freely.

'I think, gentlemen, that I shall throw formality to the winds and remove my coat,' said Cutler. 'I shall drown in my own sweat otherwise. Please feel free to do the same, if you wish.'

The officers needed no second bidding and sweat-damp jackets were removed to reveal sweat-soaked shirts. A loud peal of laughter rang round the table when Tyler's elbow was seen protruding through a large hole in his sleeve. He had the grace to blush.

'I do apologize, sir,' he said, reaching for his coat again. 'I never imagined that we would sit in our shirtsleeves.'

'That is only too apparent, Mr Tyler,' said Cutler with a broad smile. 'No, no, leave your coat be. A naked elbow is not so very shocking – I doubt that any of us will become inflamed!'

The informality of dress brought an early relaxation of the stiff awkwardness induced by the captain's presence and light banter and easy laughter crossed the table before the soup was finished. Cutler was a man of sharp wit and he entertained his guests with a dry account of an escapade from his midshipman days. It involved a hungry ship, an unpopular, grasping purser and a raid on his stores by starving midshipmen which proved only half-successful. They got away with a solitary cheese but Cutler, the smallest and youngest, had been collared as the others made their escape.

'Luckily for me the cheese was not missed and so I was not charged with theft, as I deserved, but beaten soundly and sent to the masthead for a few hours. The freezing Channel winds soon cooled my smarting backside but the thought of my share of the cheese kept me warm enough. Imagine my rage when I returned to the cockpit to find that my greedy mess-mates had not left me a single crumb. So much for honour among thieves!'

The sound of laughter rang round the table and through the open skylight to the ears of the quartermaster, who had been listening to the clink of bottle on glass and the gurgle of pouring refreshment with deep envy and a growing thirst. He rolled his dry tongue around his lips and allowed his thoughts to concoct an improbable chain of events which ended with the captain pressing him to take a seat and make his choice from the wines on the table. His wild imaginings left him thirstier than ever and he vented his spleen by snarling at the indignant helmsman.

'Steer small, blast your eyes!'

Beneath the quartermaster's feet, in the captain's cabin, the evening was drawing to a close. The officers had been given a blunt warning by Maxwell beforehand, without explanation, to be moderate in their drinking and Lamb felt the first lieutenant's cold eye was upon him every time he raised his glass. Nevertheless, in spite of their enforced sobriety, the evening had been a merry one and as Lamb proposed the health of the King and looked at the damp, shining, smiling faces around the table he felt proud and happy to be amongst their number.

The *Sturdy* continued her slow crawl across the vast, empty ocean, heading south-west by south, crossing the equator into the southern latitudes of the same ocean. They were very close to the track that French privateers would take on their journey from Mauritius to the Bay of Bengal but the sea remained obstinately empty. Eventually, eight days and fifteen hundred miles after the squadron had dispersed the lookout earned himself one of Cutler's guineas for being the first to report a sail, far to the east, just after sunrise. Cutler took to the shrouds himself, a measure of his eagerness. He studied the distant ship for some minutes before returning to the quarterdeck.

'She is just too far off for us to chase,' he said to Maxwell. 'Heading as she is, Captain Beamish might come across her. I was unable to see much detail, looking into the sun, but she is certainly a Frenchman, in these waters.'

Within the hour the sail was lost to the lookout and the *Sturdy* sailed on with the sea to herself again.

The following day the frigate ran into heavy weather which persisted for several days. At first they were able to run before the wind with shortened sail but as the storm progressed the wind changed, veering to the north-west and increasing in strength. With everything battened down or double-lashed, courses furled and topsails fully reefed, the *Sturdy* rode out the storm with her head to the wind. The order to put the other reef in the topsails resulted in the death of Jonas Spencer, a prime young topman whose eagerness to be first to the yard cost him his life. As he raced up the shrouds the studdingsail boom tore free from the rigging and swinging down from its ring at the end of the yard it caught Spencer a massive blow to the head. He fell past his horrified mates without a sound and bounced from the mainmast chains into the sea. There was nothing that could be done; he was almost certainly dead before he hit the water, in any case.

The sea was still very lumpy beneath a cloudy sky allowing intermittent shafts of sunlight when the lookout next reported a sail. The *Sturdy* was labouring to make her westing, close-hauled with the wind on her starboard beam. Kennedy had the watch; he cupped his hands to his mouth and bellowed upwards.

'Say again!'

The lookout's arm was pointing almost dead ahead; his voice was faint, overlaid by the noise of the wind and the buffeting canvas.

'One point off the starboard bow, sir.'

Cutler emerged from his quarters with his napkin in hand, chewing the last of his midday cheese.

'Call the hands, Mr Kennedy,' he snapped as soon as his feet touched the quarterdeck. 'We'll turn into the wind.'

Maxwell and Lamb, disturbed from their meal by the noise and commotion on deck and guessing the reason, appeared at the aft companionway.

'Mr Lamb!' called Cutler, beckoning with his napkinned hand.

Lamb raced up the quarterdeck ladder and touched his hat.

'Away aloft with you, Mr Lamb. Take your glass and report back on deck.'

Lamb tossed his hat to Midshipman Blissenden, snatched a telescope from its rack and ran to the mainmast shrouds. He scrambled up the ratlines, swung out and over the maintop with its multitude of ropes and up on to the topgallant yard. Breathing heavily he hooked an arm around the back-stay and levelled his glass at the tiny patch of sail, now off the larboard bow. The roll of the ship, although moderate enough on deck, was at this height exaggerated into a wide, lurching swing which, coupled with the rise and plunge of the bows, gave Lamb a giddy, swooping, circular ride through the air. The image of the distant ship slipped in and out of his vision as he struggled to keep his telescope fixed on it. He muttered the details aloud to himself as he picked them out. Three masts – square-rigged fore and main – raised quarterdeck – one row of guns – narrow, French yards – no colours. So, a French frigate, a heavy one, too, by the look of her, probably a forty-four. He scoured the sea around her. Well, at least she seemed to be alone. He returned quickly to the deck and reported to the captain.

'Heavy frigate, sir, a forty-four, I think. Mizzen course clewed up, no t'gallants set, no colours, French-cut yards, sir, wind on her larboard beam.'

'Thank you, Mr Lamb.'

Cutler considered the situation as he paced slowly back and forth along his side of the quarterdeck. A forty-four gun frigate would be no mean opponent. She could throw a weight of metal with each broadside almost half as heavy again as his own and he had been given clear orders not to engage such ships. An opportunity for a ship-to-ship action came but rarely for a frigate captain, however, and here was a splendid chance for him to test the mettle of his men and his guns and, more importantly, perhaps, his own. If they came to grips it would be a bloody affair, he had no doubt about that. For a tiny moment the urge to cut and run, sheltering behind Beamish's orders, hovered in his mind but it lasted no more than an instant and he pushed it aside with a grimace of disgust. He turned to order Kennedy to clear for action but checked himself as a hail came from the lookout.

'She's luffing, sir!'

Cutler gave a thin smile. Now both ships were heading into the wind, competing for the weather gauge, both heading for a distant point as yet undetermined and probably never reached, the apex of a triangle which had the line of sight between them as an ever-shrinking base. Well, there would be a good few miles and much tacking and wearing before that point drew near, he thought grimly as he turned to give his order to Kennedy.

As the afternoon wore on and the two ships beat into the wind it gradually became apparent that the Frenchman was winning the battle to gain the advantage of the weather gauge. It showed a slight but distinct ability to sail closer to the wind and with a small added assistance from the wind's direction she was inching ahead with every tack. By the start of the first dog-watch the two vessels had approached to within two miles of each other and Cutler maintained a wary eye on the heavy frigate. With the wind now firmly in his favour, her captain could at any time decide to truncate the peak of the shrinking triangle and bear down fast on the *Sturdy*.

The ship's cook and his mates made their way along the deck, giving out the men's suppers at their stations, ship's biscuit and cheese, the cheese no longer hard and giving off a sharp, rancid smell but the men were hungry and they wolfed it down eagerly. The evening grog was served from the maindeck, the men lining up one gun-crew at a time, the purser's mate standing by with his book of names to ensure that no man, even on the eve of battle, obtained a tot to which he was not entitled.

The sun was low in the sky. The ship was suddenly very quiet, the men standing silently at their guns, the only noises those of the sea and wind, the creak of masts and the rattling mutter of blocks. The lieutenants waited by their batteries, staring out over the untidy water at the Frenchman, glancing occasionally at the quarterdeck and the still figure of Cutler, dressed now in his best coat and hat, his sword at his side. Maxwell prowled restlessly up and down the rows of guns, his pale eyes flitting critically from crew to crew.

The captain's voice sounded from the quarterdeck, pitched deliberately loudly enough for his order to be heard the length of the ship.

'Run up the colours, quartermaster!'

The order, the old blood-stirring challenge, brought a little growl of excitement from the men at the guns. Lamb glanced at their faces as he paced slowly beside his battery. They knew as well as he that this was no easy fight they faced. The Frenchman was not a privateer, vicious and dangerous when cornered but no match for a frigate; now they were about to square up to a ship larger and heavier-gunned than their own, manned by disciplined, practised men. If his men felt awed or concerned at the prospect they showed no signs of it; most of them had broad, eager grins on their faces, as if they could not get to grips quickly enough and even the older men, those who had experienced this sort of battle before and knew of the horrors of it, gave Lamb a quiet smile as his glance fell on them.

A murmur came from the gun-crews and Lamb turned to see the blue, white and red colours of the Frenchman streaming from his mizzenmast. So, he had declared himself!

Cutler called quietly from the quarterdeck. 'When you are ready, Mr Maxwell.'

'Aye aye, sir,' bellowed Maxwell, saluting, and in a roar that rang throughout the ship, 'Open ports! Run out your guns!'

The thunder and squeal of the wooden trucks on the deck came hard on his order and the guns were run up tight to the ship's sides, their black snouts questing out over the water as if sniffing for the enemy, ready to let fly with their double loads of canister and roundshot. The gun-captains crouched beside their charges, blowing gently on their slow-matches to keep them brightly glowing, the men standing by with their handspikes, worms and rope-handled sponges. They would have to wait a few minutes yet, thought Lamb, glancing over the bow at the other frigate. She was about a mile and a half off, still well outside the long-guns' maximum range. As he watched her, he saw her gun-ports swing up and her guns appeared, the wide muzzles grinning wickedly along her side. Doubleday's voice sounded from beside the wheel and the *Sturdy*'s head swung, pointing her bowsprit at the Frenchman. On the instant, as if she had been waiting for this move, the other frigate tacked towards the *Sturdy*.

'Stand by, my lads,' shouted Lamb, excitement welling up within him. 'It will not be long now. Remember your drill and keep your eyes inboard.'

Less than a mile separated the two ships, a distance that would be covered in about three minutes.

'See what your bow-chasers can do, Mr Tyler!' roared Maxwell.

The forecastle guns had been waiting anxiously for this very order and the flat, double bang sounded within seconds, the familiar, acrid tang of gunsmoke washing back over the deck. As the sound faded in Lamb's ears he heard the answering bark of the Frenchman's chasers and an instant later the deck shook to the thud of iron somewhere below the gun-muzzles of his battery. He kept his eyes fixed on the approaching ship, anxious to see on which side of the *Sturdy* she would pass. Her bows swung slightly, her starboard guns came fully into view. She would come under his guns first!

'Stand by the starboard guns!'

Maxwell's bellow brought those men assigned to the guns on both sides running across the deck to take their places at the starboard guns. The forecastle guns fired again and Lamb saw the hammock nettings along the Frenchman's bulwark jump and sag. A hit! The chasers would not be able to bear much longer, he thought; they must be trained hard round already. It will be my guns next. He swallowed, feeling the familiar, tight, faint nausea in his stomach that always came upon him before action started; it would vanish, he knew, with the first firing of his guns.

Suddenly the bowsprit of the Frenchman was visible over the *Sturdy*'s starboard bow, no more than a cable distant. Lamb stood well back from his guns where he could keep an eye on Maxwell. A stillness seemed to settle over the deck. It was so quiet that he could hear the pounding of the blood in his ears.

A flash and a bang came from the enemy's foremost gun, followed by the next in line and then the next, each gun firing as it bore on the *Sturdy*. Lamb gritted his teeth as the shot tore through the courses and topsails, tearing great gaps in the canvas and bringing blocks and severed ropes into the netting rigged above the deck. Hammocks and shredded netting flew into the air and tumbled down among the guns, knocking some men sideways and raising curses from the crouching gun-captains. Lamb kept his eyes fixed on Maxwell, standing just abaft the mainmast, his sword raised high in the air. The first lieutenant's mouth gaped wide and his sword flashed down, his bellow going unheard in the din.

'Fire!'

Lamb and Kennedy yelled together and their respective batteries fired simultaneously, the enormous, ear-singing, multiple crash of the explosions sending the gun-carriages hurtling savagely back to the limits of their breechings. The crews threw themselves at their charges, worming, swabbing, reloading, gun smoke swirling thickly about the deck, not daring to waste an instant to peep over the side at the results of their broadside. Lamb was not bound by this restriction and with the advantage of his height he could see clearly as the roundshot and canister, fired low in the usual British fashion, hit the Frenchman's bulwarks and gun-ports, splinters and iron whistling murderously over her deck. The French guns continued to fire one by one as they were reloaded, the shot aimed high on the uproll of the ship but one or two, fired in haste, coming low over the *Sturdy*'s deck. A crash, a heavy jolt and screams came from behind Lamb's back as one of the larboard guns was knocked from its carriage. A heavy block bounced as it hit the deck beside his foot and he jumped in alarm as a length of severed rigging fell with a startling thump across his shoulder. As the starboard guns were reloaded and hauled back to the side the deck heeled sharply. The ships had passed each other and Cutler, intent on sticking close, was swinging the *Sturdy* across the wind in an attempt to cut across the Frenchman's stern.

The French captain was no fool; as the *Sturdy* tacked to starboard so he swung to larboard to shield his stern and both ships headed in the same direction, with the wind on their larboard beam. The turn had put the ships some six hundred yards apart, with the Frenchman in the lead. Cutler instantly seized his chance and the *Sturdy* heeled viciously as he swung her like a cutter, putting her before the wind. She raced down at the Frenchman's stern.

'Now we've got her!' yelled Tyler as he caught Lamb's eye, his voice cracking with excitement.

Lamb grinned back across the width of the deck. He had seen immediately, as had Tyler, the dilemma facing the French captain. He could do one of three things – luff, to bring his ship bows-on to the *Sturdy* (too late, she would never get round in time), keep her as she was or, like the *Sturdy*, come before the wind. The last two would leave her stern vulnerable.

Lamb chuckled aloud as he saw the frigate's stern begin to swing away from them. He had reacted too late – the *Sturdy* was tearing through the water with the wind astern and would be across the Frenchman's stern before she had half-completed her manoeuvre. He could see her name clearly now – *Trompeur*.

'Stand by the larboard guns!' roared Maxwell. 'Fire as you bear! Fire as you bear!'

It was Tyler and Maxwell's turn now. Tyler, short, cocky and strutting like a young tiger behind his battery, grinned at Lamb and gave him a huge, confident wink. No more than fifty yards separated the ships as the foremost gun fired, blasting canister and roundshot through the *Trompeur*'s wide stern-windows. As the other guns went off in succession, Cutler brought the *Sturdy*'s head round to come along the forty-four's starboard side. Her captain was desperately trying to remedy his error and his yards were already swinging to reverse his turn as Maxwell's guns began their thunder. Suddenly both vessels were parallel, larboard to starboard, and the *Trompeur*'s broadside erupted with a tremendous smash of sound. Chain-shot and bar-shot screamed through the tops and topsails, shredding already torn canvas, severing more rigging, gouging lumps of timber from the masts and yards and killing a dozen Marines at their swivel guns. Tyler and Maxwell were in a high state of excitement, roaring, swearing, running from gun to gun as the men worked frantically to reload. Tyler raised his arm — his guns were ready. Maxwell waited until the ship rolled to larboard and then screamed the order. The broadside struck with devastating force at the *Trompeur*'s side, hitting her above and below the waterline as she rolled away, and at her chains and gun-ports. The huge thunder of the quarterdeck carron-ades sounded, the shot blasting a great section of the *Trompeur*'s tumblehome into ragged shards of timber that whirred and thrummed across the deck, wreaking bloody havoc.

The Frenchman's broadside crashed out again, more ragged this time, and thinner, but the heavy weight of metal hit the *Sturdy* desperately hard. By accident or design, the guns were fired earlier on the uproll and the ironwork came low over the *Sturdy*'s deck. On the quarterdeck Midshipman Cowan was killed, hurled into the mizzenmast shrouds gouting blood from a torn throat; Bennet, the quartermaster, lost both legs below the knees and Cutler was sent staggering by a flying splinter that ripped his arm from elbow to shoulder. On the maindeck men to larboard and starboard were hit and in an instant the deck became a bloody, untidy mess of sprawled bodies and slewed and overturned guns. Something slammed into Lamb's legs, sending him crashing on to his back; the missile was Tyler, the top of his head sliced off revealing his bloodied brain. He lay on his back staring with wide, blind eyes at Lamb, his mouth a red-toothed snarl. Lamb threw a scrap of torn sail over the ruined head and crossed the deck to take Tyler's place at his battery.

The quarter-gunners and gun-captains, hard, experienced

men, were already striving to bring order to the chaos. Their first thought was for the guns – the dead and wounded were not their responsibility and were ruthlessly pulled away and kicked aside as the survivors struggled to lever displaced guns back into position. Several of the remaining guns, in the process of being reloaded, were short of men and Lamb hastily directed men from the crews of the damaged guns to make up the numbers.

'Mr Lamb!'

He turned to find Maxwell's dark face glaring up at him, his fists bunched on his hips, his legs spread wide. His breeches were spattered with blood and his pale eyes were slitted in anger.

'What in hell is taking you so long with these guns? Where's Tyler?'

Lamb gestured at the body sprawled beneath the scrap of canvas. 'Dead, sir.'

'Well, get these bloody men moving and get these guns back in action. Christ, man, I shouldn't have to tell you your duty!'

The first lieutenant turned and strode aft, leaving Lamb staring after him, bubbling with impotent fury at the unfairness of his remarks. Callous bastard! He couldn't even spare a word for poor Tyler. He turned back to the guns and within moments Maxwell was forgotten in the sweat and struggle into which he plunged.

The two frigates were still running side by side, with less than a cable between them. The light was fading fast and tiny, yellow flashes sparked from the *Trompeur*'s tops as muskets added their lethal, little bits of lead to the massive weight of iron from her guns. Smoke and flames burst from the forty-four's gun-ports at precisely the same instant that the *Sturdy*'s guns erupted and both ships shuddered from the recoil of their own guns and the impact of their opponent's shot. Time appeared to have stretched for Lamb; as the green evening light gave way to violet dusk and then to darkness, and the battle-lanterns were lit and the broadsides gave way to firing by batteries and then to individual guns, slower now as the men tired, the noise and smoke and screams and stench seemed to him to have lasted for many hours. The horrors around him became commonplace; as he moved from gun to gun, slipping in the thick blood on the deck, helping to drag wounded men clear of the guns, heaving bodies and parts of bodies over the side, assisting a wounded gun-captain here and throwing his weight on a tackle elsewhere, his main concern was with his raging thirst. The heat, his exertions and the gritty, bitter gunsmoke had made him parched; he had grabbed a passing powder-boy, white-faced and wide-eyed at the sights around him, and sent him off to the scuttle-butt – and cursed his luck when the boy returned with the news that the butt was smashed. The men at the guns had their own buckets of drinking water and Lamb was tempted to take a gulp from one of these but a glance at the filthy liquid remaining in it persuaded him to suffer his thirst.

The *Sturdy*'s topsails, spars and rigging were showing the effects of the high aim of the French guns, fired on the uproll with the intention of crippling her opponent. The safety nets rigged over the deck bulged with the weight of rope, blocks, shards of timber and the bodies of men fallen from the tops. The foretopgallantmast leaned back drunkenly against the mainmast stays and in the foretop itself there was not a man left whole. It was fortunate for the *Sturdy* that the *Trompeur* carried no carronades but even so, the grapeshot that periodically swept her deck was taking its bloody toll. The effects of the *Sturdy*'s guns on the *Trompeur* were not so apparent – aimed low, the shot had left her upper canvas and rigging relatively undamaged but the constant sweep of roundshot and canister across her deck, aided by the smashing, splintering blows from the carronades, had wreaked far greater havoc amongst her men.

The firing from the Frenchman, although persistent, was now very ragged; great holes had been torn in her bulwarks and a number of her guns had been silenced – those remaining were firing individually, slower now but still damaging.

'Sir! Sir!'

It was a powder-boy, tugging nervously and unlawfully at Lamb's sleeve, his thin voice scarcely audible over the din. Lamb glanced round and followed the boy's pointing finger. He saw Maxwell, squatting beside the main hatch, head bowed and hands clutching his groin. Lamb ran aft and bent over him, noting the dark growing pool of blood in which the first lieutenant was sitting. He touched Maxwell on the shoulder.

'Are you all right, sir?' he asked, realizing with the words the idiocy of his question.

Maxwell slowly lifted his head. The pale eyes rested on Lamb's anxious face and a wry half-smile touched the corners of his mouth. He struggled to speak.

'That's a – bloody – stupid –' he whispered faintly. His head fell forward and he toppled on to his side, revealing the awful cavity where his lower abdomen and manhood had been shot away.

'He's gone, has he?'

Lamb looked up to see Kennedy standing over him. He nodded.

'And poor Tyler, too. Well –'

Kennedy was interrupted by a rending crack of breaking timber from the quarterdeck and both men whirled round to see the mizzenmast falling. It crashed down across the larboard quarter, broken off below the crossjack yard; its upper length, still tethered to the ship by the remnants of the standing rigging, splashed into the sea. Doubleday's powerful voice could be heard, bawling for the boatswain and the carpenter, as the *Sturdy* slewed to larboard, the drag of canvas and spar in the water acting like a brake. As if in joyful response to the damage, several of the *Trompeur*'s guns roared out, almost together. Iron shot thrummed through the air above the two lieutenants' heads and a crash and a scream came from the maintop.

'You had best get back to your guns, Matthew,' said Kennedy. 'This cannot –' He paused as the *Sturdy*'s guns fired, a long, rolling, ragged fire. 'This cannot go on much longer. If she does not try to board soon, then we must, while we still have some men left to do it.'

'Unless she strikes first!' threw Lamb over his shoulder as he walked forward.

He had barely reached his battery when young Blissenden came trotting up to him, a handkerchief bound roughly round his forehead and a patch of blood showing over his ear.

'The captain sends his compliments, sir,' he panted, 'and could you spare him a moment on the quarterdeck?'

'Very good, Mr Blissenden.'

The carpenter and boatswain and his mates had cut through the mess of rigging around the broken mizzenmast and were in

184

the act of heaving the broken butt off the side as Lamb mounted the quarterdeck. The mast hit the water with a sullen splash and the quarterdeck lifted as the weight was taken off its quarter.

'I intend to board very shortly, Mr Lamb,' said Cutler. His face was white and grim; a deep scratch ran across one cheek and the back of his left hand showed small rivulets of blood from the injury on his upper arm. 'Get every man fit enough to hold a weapon, including the men from the guns. Split them into two groups; Mr Kennedy will command the aft party and you the forward. Tell Mr Kennedy to blast her with grape and canister just before we touch. Have you got that?'

'Yes, sir.'

'Good. I will join one or other parties as I see fit. Jump to it, Mr Lamb, whilst we still have a tops'l.'

Lamb passed the captain's instructions on to Kennedy and received a huge, smoke-lined grin in response. The Marine sergeant, now in charge of his men since Potter had lost an arm early in the battle, nodded gravely as Lamb gave him his orders.

'Very good, sir,' he said in his unseamanlike way and strode off to round up his men, scattered at their stations throughout the ship.

Cutler stared across the short stretch of water at the *Trompeur*. For several minutes her guns had been silent and then, as he watched, a red flame stabbed the darkness as a gun thundered from a forward position, followed immediately by the roar of a gun aft, and then silence and darkness again. Her deck must be in a bad way, he thought. He licked his lips; suddenly the need for alcohol was very urgent, clamouring at his throat and stomach.

'Edge her over, Mr Doubleday,' he called over his shoulder. 'Not too sharply – I don't want her to sheer off before we have a chance to close.'

'Aye aye, sir,' said the master. 'I shall take the helm myself, sir.'

Cutler turned from the side and nodded. 'I must fetch my pistols,' he said and made his way down to his quarters.

The carronades continued their slow fire as the *Sturdy* slanted towards the *Trompeur*. The long-guns had been stripped of their crews; in the waist two solitary gun-captains crouched over their breeches, breathing softly on to their slow-matches, their guns, hot from long use, triple-shotted with grapeshot and canister. Lamb stood at the side beneath the forecastle, a pistol thrust through his belt and his sword, yet to be swung in anger and still unfamiliar in his grip, clutched sweatily in his hand. He eyed the narrowing gap between the two ships.

'Stand by the grapples!' he shouted.

The two seamen assigned to the task sprang up on to the side, their hooked grappling irons swinging from their hands by the stout ropes which had their other ends attached to the ring-bolts of the gun places. One of the men immediately gave a coughing grunt and fell backwards on to the press of men behind him, the victim of a stray or lucky shot from a French musket. Lamb opened his mouth to order another man to take his place but there was no need; a young seaman had grabbed the hook and jumped up into the shrouds almost as the man fell.

'Well done, Crooke!' called Lamb. The seaman responded with a wide grin.

The *Trompeur* was now very close, close enough for Lamb to make out the dark shapes of men standing at her side, staring at the approaching *Sturdy*. The French vessel made no move to keep her distance, although the intentions of her opponent must have been plain. Perhaps they welcome the thought, mused Lamb – the final bitter struggle between weary, bloodied men. One way or another, it would soon be over. Suddenly, he was wet with sweat, as if the pores of his skin had gaped wide, drenching him; even his hair and scalp prickled with sweat. He tucked his sword beneath his arm and wiped his palms surreptitiously down his breeches and his sleeve over his forehead. Was this fear? The image of Kennedy's face came into his mind, his confident smile wide as he wished Lamb good luck and strode off to join his boarding party. Does he feel as wretchedly nervous as I do, wondered Lamb? He glanced at the faces of the men around him. Few were smiling, true, but none of them looked less than grim and determined. Did he look grim and determined to them? The thought brought an involuntary wry smile to his face but the familiar play of muscles in his cheeks did little to dispel the horror he felt at the prospect of cold steel he was about to face.

Captain Cutler rested his haunches against the edge of his table and stared broodingly at the bottle in his hand, fighting his own private battle – to pull, or not to pull, the cork. The urge was great, his need desperate and yet he hesitated, a tiny part of him struggling not to yield. Suddenly, like little animals with minds of their own, his fingers were twisting and pulling at the cork while he observed them with something close to disgust on his face. The cork came out with a squeal; he stood, raised the bottle high and hurled it into the corner. He swore softly, snatched up his sword and strode from his cabin. The bottle, unbroken, rolled to and fro in the corner, brandy gurgling from its mouth and filling the cabin with its sharp, enticing odour.

The mainyards of the two ships were now almost touching. Just a few yards separated them and the men with the grapnels drew back their arms ready to throw.

'Stand by, lads!' yelled Lamb, his voice husky in his dry throat. 'Let us hear you give a cheer as you go over!'

'We'll do more than cheer, sir!' shouted a voice, a boarding axe brandished high in the air.

A loud growl of agreement came from the waiting men.

'Make way, my lads. Let me through. Would you deny your captain a crack at them first?'

It was Cutler, pushing his way through the press of men, his sword held high, his coat discarded and his left sleeve red with blood. He forced his way through to Lamb at the side and grinned at him like an excited boy. 'Let us go over together, you and I, shall we?'

'I would consider it an honour, sir,' said Lamb, smiling back, suddenly eager to get amongst the Frenchmen.

They clambered up on to the side together and stood clutching the foremast shrouds. From here Lamb could see clearly the deck of the *Trompeur* and the press of waiting men at her side. He caught his breath; the horror of the deaths and woundings he had witnessed on the *Sturdy*'s deck was multiplied several times over on the *Trompeur*. Her bulwarks and gun-ports were holed and splintered and through the gaping wounds he could see several slewed and overturned guns. Bodies, dragged from the guns, were heaped untidily along the midline of the deck – he wondered that she still had guns to fire. As if in denial of this thought, two of her guns belched flame and smoke, the shot passing harmlessly over the *Sturdy*'s near-deserted waist. Kennedy's voice sang out from the other end of the deck and the two long-guns immediately thundered, sending their deadly loads of little shot scything wickedly through the armed men crowded in the *Trompeur*'s waist. Lamb could see men falling, crumpling forward, flying backward.

The yards of the two frigates came together with a crunching, splintering noise and there was a shuddering crash as the two hulls collided. The *Sturdy* bounced away a yard or two and then closed again as Doubleday held the wheel hard over. The grapnels flew across the gap and the ropes were pulled taut.

'Come on, my brave lads!' shouted Cutler and launched himself across the gap. Lamb found himself at his side, unaware of making the leap, clutching desperately at the *Trompeur*'s shrouds with one hand and striking out with his sword with the other. A mass of men stared up at him, mouths wide, shouting unintelligibly, pikes and cutlasses thrusting upwards, the cheers and curses of his own men roaring in his ears. Beside him, Cutler screamed. For a time-frozen instant Lamb saw his captain falling backwards, his mouth and eyes wide, his hands clutched at the handle of the pike driven into his stomach. A pike thrust up at Lamb – he twisted sideways and deflected the weapon with his free hand, teetering danger-ously, slashing down with his sword, feeling the jar of the strike in his teeth. Somehow he landed on the *Trompeur*'s deck, not knowing whether he had jumped or had been pushed from behind, striking left and right at the press of men about him, shouting and cursing as loudly as the men pouring across the gap between the ships. One tiny part of his mind remained remote, detached, noting with amused surprise the stream of filth pouring from his mouth. For a few wild, desperate, hard-pressed moments the Frenchmen held firm but as more men leaped across, some of them hurling themselves with slashing axes and cutlasses on to the very heads of their opponents, they began to fall back. Suddenly Lamb was moving forward, stumbling over bodies beneath his feet, glimpsing Stone beside him lunging upwards with his cutlass at a striped shirt. A pike stabbed at him from the crowd of retreating men and he struck at it too late, feeling a tearing pain in his side as the pike-head glanced off his ribs. The blow knocked the breath from his lungs and he almost fell, clutching at Stone's shoulder for support.

'Got yer, you bastard!' grunted the coxswain happily as he slashed his cutlass back-handed across the pike-man's throat.

Lamb drew a painful breath into his lungs and pressed forward again with raised sword. The Frenchmen were still falling back but slowly, fighting stubbornly every inch of the way and Lamb's arm was beginning to tire as he slashed and hacked at the faces and bodies of the men before him. A huge Frenchman was suddenly in his way, swinging an axe in a vicious sweep that kept the area around him clear of Englishmen. He caught sight of Lamb's sword and uniform and with an animal-like roar he sprang towards him, swinging his wicked, long-handled weapon with both hands. Without conscious thought, Lamb transferred his sword to his left hand, plucked the pistol from his belt, thumbed back the hammer, levelled at the man's chest and pulled the trigger. The man continued his rush and for one brief, blood-chilling instant Lamb was certain he had missed. The axe came down on his pistol, knocking it from his nerveless fingers as the man crumpled to the deck.

Suddenly, above the uproar around him, Lamb heard thunderous cheers from the afterpart of the ship – British cheers! His heart leaped – Kennedy had secured the quarterdeck! For a moment or so the Frenchmen to Lamb's front were pushed forward by the pell-mell scramble of their retreating comrades at their rear but then suddenly, infected by the panic, they, too, broke and ran, fleeing to the forecastle, the far side of the deck and into the rigging. A tremendous roar of triumph erupted from Lamb's party and the men surged forward at a run, hacking and jabbing at the backs of the retreating men. Lamb watched them go, leaning on his sword, his ribs in agony from the pike-thrust, exhausted beyond belief. He pressed his hand to his side, the blood wet and sticky beneath his fingers. Another ringing cheer sounded from the quarterdeck and he looked up to see the French colours jerking their way down the halyard.

Good Lord! he thought dully, we have done it. He felt no joy, no sense of triumph, only a strange sense of loss and an overwhelming weariness. His wound seemed to be making a good deal of blood; he took his hand from his side and stared at it in sudden, shocked revulsion. His little finger was gone, severed near the palm, leaving only a tiny stump from which the blood was still strongly welling. With the sight of it came the pain, pulsing and throbbing. He fumbled awkwardly for his handkerchief and bound it roughly around his hand, pulling the knot tight with his teeth.

He made his painful way forward, skirting the overturned guns, sprawled corpses, groaning wounded and torn, splintered deck planks. The blue jacket of a British midshipman caught his eye, huddled beneath the corpse of a French seaman. He rolled the corpse to one side and knelt on the bloodied deck beside the small body. It was Blissenden. He was curled on his side, his dirk clenched in his hand, his fair hair matted to the side of his face with blood. He was quite dead – his head had been laid open from temple to crown. Lamb sighed, closed the blue, staring eyes and patted the still shoulder before rising to his feet.

The French officers stood in a small group on one side of the quarterdeck, guarded by a solitary Marine. Two of the *Sturdy*'s seamen were at the wheel and as Lamb climbed the wide ladder from the maindeck he passed a beaming quartermaster descending with several French swords tucked beneath his arm. Kennedy was talking to the Marine sergeant, his outstretched arm pointing along the maindeck. He broke off as Lamb approached and advanced to meet him. His broad smile changed to one of concern as he saw the blood on Lamb's shirt.

'My dear fellow, you are wounded.'

'It is no more than a scratch, I believe,' said Lamb. 'The captain is dead; did you know?'

'Yes, Stone told me. Sad, very sad.'

'Blissenden has been killed, too. I just saw his body.'

'Yes, I saw him go down, poor little fellow. I shall have to write to his people. They live very close to mine, you know.'

'Oh, yes?' said Lamb.

He looked back along the maindeck. The Marines had collected the Frenchmen by the forecastle and were now shepherding them below. The *Sturdy*'s men were prowling the moonlit deck, turning over bodies, separating the British corpses from the French. He glanced at the *Sturdy*; she looked a sorry sight with her truncated mizzenmast and her crazily-leaning foretopgallantmast. He caught sight of Doubleday beside the wheel, waving triumphant arms madly in the air and he lifted his sword in reply. The thought came to him that he and Kennedy were the only two commissioned officers left alive and the realization of the work that lay ahead of them and the pain of his wounds made him give an involuntary groan.

Kennedy clapped him on the shoulder. 'Never say die, Matthew! You became a hero today – we both did. It will be the making of us. A thirty-six taking on a forty-four – and what a bloody butcher's bill! We shall be the envy of the entire fleet. Is it not a marvellous feeling?'

Lamb swayed with pain and increasing nausea. 'No,' he said. 'I think I'm going to be sick.'